THE CURSE OF OPHIDIA

VICTORIA BLACK

First paperback edition 2024

ISBN: 979-8-9899130-2-2 (trade paperback); 979-8-9899130-1-5 (ebook)

Imprint: Victoria Black Books, LLC.

Visit www.victoriablackbooks.com

For anyone who knows what it's like to be spoken over.

I hope you reclaim your power.

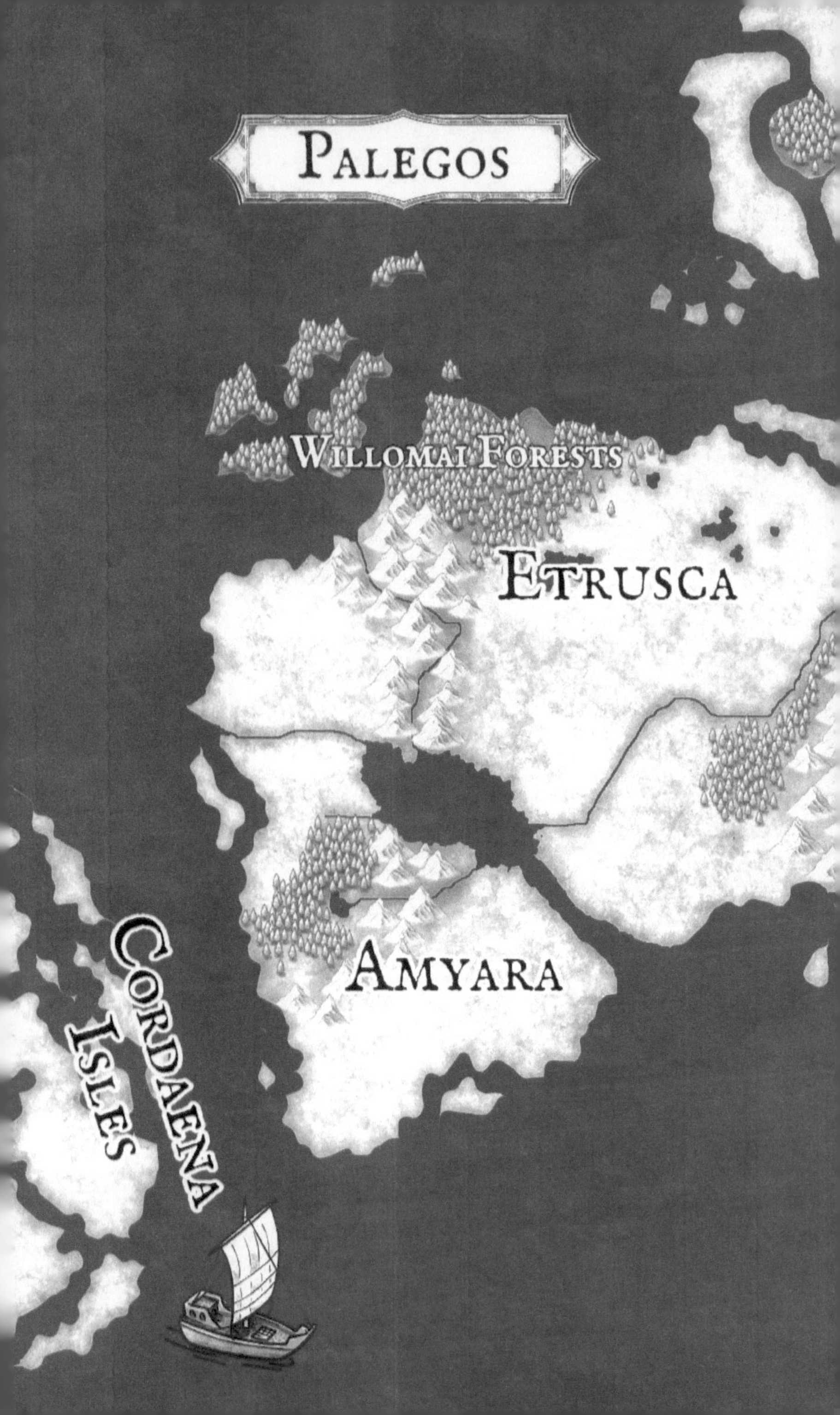

PALEGOS
WILLOMAI FORESTS
ETRUSCA
AMYARA
CORDAENA ISLES

DRAZURC
POR
FYNGR MERES
GALESTON
BORGONA MOUNTAINS
NAQAD
MALNOVA
EGRYT
TENCANYA WASTE

PRONUNCIATION GUIDE

Naqadian Court

- King Alaric Amunet

  - *ah-LAR-ic am-YEW-net*

- Queen Helvettica Amunet

  - *hel-vet-ih-cah am-YEW-net*

- Queen Tamariya Amunet

  - *tah-MAIR-ee-yah am-YEW-net*

- Lord Doric Venrylst

  - *DOOR-ic ven-RILLST*

- General Brom Balenek

  - *brahm BAH-len-ek*

- Lord Terrin Speelstling

  - *TAIR-rin SPEEL-stling*

- Lord Frydrik Moscar

  - *FREE-drik MOS-car*

- Lord Henry Lopaegra

  - *HEN-ree Loh-PAY-grah*

Etruscan Court

- King Dalm Cazaar

  - *dallm cah-SAR*

- Prince Caryk Cazaar

  - *cair-IK cah-SAR*

Others

- Aya Jesper

  - *EYE-yah JES-per*

- Calliope Torino

  - *cah-LYE-ah-pee tor-EE-noh*

- Ives Zemyslah

  - *EYEVS ZEH-mee-slah*

- Katzima

  - *kat-SEE-mah*

- Marcus Enora

  - *MAR-cus EE-nohr-ah*

- Rohesia Zemyslah

  - *roh-HEE-zhah ZEH-mee-slah*

Places

- Amyara

  - *ahm-YAR-uh*

- Cordaena Isles

  - *cohr-DAY-nuh EYELS*

- Drazurc

  - *dra-ZERK*

- Egryt

  - *EE-grit*

- Etrusca

  - *eh-TROO-scuh*

- Fyngr Meres

  - *FING-ger MEERS*

- Galeston

  - *GAIL-stun*

- Malnova

  - *mal-NOH-vuh*

- Naqad

  - *nuh-KAHD*

- Palegos

  - *PAIL-eh-gohs*

- Por

  - *POHR*

- Tencanya Waste

  - *ten-KAHN-yuh WAYST*

AUTHOR'S NOTE

This work contains topics that may be difficult for some readers including violence, blood, death, animal cruelty, characters dealing with PTSD and grief, torture, and explicit sexual content.

ONE

I blamed my magic. It was a pathetic spark that had reduced me to nothing more than a puppet queen. If I had my power, no one in the realm would dare touch a mage. I would be lounging in the palace, basking in the glory of being the most powerful soul in Palegos. Instead, I was doing the work of a foot soldier, unable to trust that my order would be obeyed.

But would I ever trust another when it came to *her* life? The wound of my missing gift had long since scabbed over, but my fear for Katzima was fresh. There was but one thought I clung to as I raced north through the Naqadian countryside.

Not her.

I had the fastest mare in the Egrecian herd and still she was not fast enough. I squeezed tighter on the stirrups, willing her onward.

Each plot of farmland I passed seemed to stretch forever. But there, in the distance, I could make out the speck that was Malnova's keep. It had to be.

Not her.

Katzima didn't deserve to die. She was a Healer. She was good. She was kind. But she was a mage. Lord Doric Venrylst, my chief advisor, would say that the lords had a right to execute justice as they saw fit in their territories. He would have told me not to leave the palace in Egryt.

Not her.

I inhaled against the hard wall of air that had been assaulting my cheeks since the moment I began this race. Doric Venrylst was not here. And he had not been at the palace to stop me from leaving. The Lord of Malnova had crossed a line. Screw Doric — Gerome would answer for his crimes.

Teeth clenched tightly against the wind, I leaned forward in the saddle. The black speck of the keep was growing into a dot. I would arrive in time. I had to.

The uneven farmland underneath me was transforming into a worn path, giving sure footing to my mare. I urged her faster.

Gerome Gendran, Lord of Malnova, had been hunting down mages. I had known it. And I had done nothing to stop it. Puppet queen indeed.

It is not your mess to deal with.

Let us handle the wayward lords.

You need not involve yourself in such matters.

My council's advice echoed in my mind. What had seemed like sage advice a fortnight ago, now soured against my tongue.

The keep was a looming fortress upon the horizon. No sound of chiming bells or shouting drifted to my ears. I was still outside the village walls, but I prayed that it boded well for Katzima's fate. It had to. She was the closest thing I had to family, and her death could not be due to my inaction, my foolishness, my ineffectiveness as leader of Naqad.

Shaking my head, I urged my horse to keep her pace. Later, I could reflect on my many pitfalls as ruler, but now there was only one thought I could allow into my mind.

Not her.

The guards came into view, lounging at their posts before the gaping walls. Malnova was a small farming territory in the valleys; they had little reason to be on alert since the war. Large burn marks scoured the stone, entire sections of the wall crumbled, yet to be repaired. I paid them no heed, catapulting through the gates. They had the sense to shout, pushing up from their comfortable positions and stumbling over to their horses. Hooves clattered behind me, but I was already navigating my way through the city.

Good, let them follow. The more witnesses, the better.

My mare navigated the streets with an expert's precision. Under different circumstances, I would have beamed at the evidence of her rigorous training. The guards were still floundering their way through the streets behind us when we approached the keep's inner wall.

I paused, assessing the guards stationed here. Unlike those positioned at the gates, these men stood upright, their eyes keenly monitoring my approach.

"Open the gates," I commanded.

The man on the left narrowed his eyes. "Who makes such a demand?"

I raised my chin high, pinning him with my gaze. "Your queen."

The guards snickered. "And we're the Royal Guard."

My eyes blazed as I fought the burn threatening to bloom up my cheeks. "You dare question your queen?"

The one who spoke stepped forward. "Look, we're not dumb, ma'am. The queen does not charge into keeps — she *parades* with her court." He smiled smugly, clearly proud of himself for the clever distinction.

I did not have time to waste conversing with small men. My teeth snapped together, and I clicked my tongue at my mare.

She responded as if we were one, galloping to the wooden gates. At the last moment she jumped, thrusting her front hooves into the wood. It gave. We burst through, and she continued past the meager gardens to the keep.

The Lord of Malnova had done us the courtesy of leaving the door open.

To flaunt his great victory over the mages?

My horse raced up the steps, coming face to face with the guards positioned at the door to the great hall. I did not hesitate this time.

The doors would not be bolted, so with a flick of the reins, my mare burst through these doors as easily as the last.

We landed in a hall illuminated by the sun's rays. The Hall itself bore little decoration, save for the hanging banners bearing the red hammer of House Gendran's sigil. A breeze rippled through the room, stirring the fabric behind the hammer, transforming the crest into a bloody reminder of all that the Gendrans were capable of. My teeth ground together.

At the front of the hall, bright white light danced off a raised sword. The man holding the weapon looked out of place with his smooth round face and wide eyes. He used those soft brown eyes to glare down at the older woman who knelt shackled on the floor. Defiant tears leaked from her eyes. A rage glimmered there that I understood far too well. My nostrils flared.

Lesser nobility, wealthy townspeople, and soldiers alike lined the aisle that we now occupied. Every eye in the hall was upon us. Except for the lord and his captive. Katzima.

Lord Gerome Gendran flicked his gaze toward us, pausing for only a moment before returning his attention to the woman to whom I owed my crown.

I snarled.

"Guards," the lord drawled over his shoulder, as if I were no more worrisome than a curious mouse. "Dispose of these intruders."

Head cocked sideways, I assessed the assembled crowd, waiting for his guards to move on me. Relief rolled through my chest as I spied a familiar blonde braid among the spectators. A splash of anger followed. I should have been able to trust the captain of my guard to intervene on my behalf. I shook my head. I would never again trust anyone when it came to Katzima's life.

Gerome's soldiers rushed me, right as Katzima cried out.

"Monster!" Her eyes were obsidian daggers. "You would let your people die for spite," she spat, despite the sword he held over her head.

My gaze was yanked from the dais as the guards reached me. *Anytime now, Calliope.* I parried their attacks easily with my long knives, their country training no match for me still astride my mare.

"Katzima, you are sentenced to die in the name of the Crown for practicing witchcraft and aiding the Ophidians." Gerome's words dripped with cruel anticipation.

I urged my mare to the dais. Swishes of metal reverberated around me. The Royal Guard had finally come to my aid. *Took them long enough.*

"Witchcraft — you mean healing the sick. The Crown would not stand for this," Katzima hissed. I could practically see her jaw clenching, eyes alight with fury as I forced my way closer.

The hall seemed to stretch forever, and the lord did not pause for the battle brewing in his Great Hall. His faith in his guard was almost admirable, if foolish. I broke free of the melee, careening toward them.

"Pity the Crown isn't here to pass judgment. That would leave it up to the ruling lord to decide then, wouldn't it?" He examined the glittering blade, appearing almost bored.

I drew a knife from its sheath, but I was still so far away. This blasted hall.

"Your death will be a great victory for this kingdom," he proclaimed, raising the sword again, madness overtaking his features.

Enough. I flung my knife, praying to Cieri that the throw was strong enough.

Katzima's screech reverberated through my bones as Gerome's sword sliced the air, approaching her neck. Too fast.

The knife toppled end over end as it approached the Healer. It wasn't going to make it in time. But then a ring echoed around the great hall as my weapon found its mark. The sword flew from Gerome's grip. Relief coursed through my veins so strongly I almost fell from my horse.

I had hit the hilt of his blade, where his hand had gripped it a moment ago.

He whirled to face me at last, fury sputtering in his gaze, red trickling from his hand.

My lips twitched as I beheld the zealot.

"In the name of the Crown, you say? The queen wants this woman dead?" I dismounted swiftly, as if this were a casual meeting, my mouth open innocently. The battle behind us died down as the soldiers watched. Despite my tone, my eyes were glittering emeralds as I leveled my piercing gaze at Lord Gerome Gendran. My eyes did not leave his as I drew another knife from my belt.

He took in my auburn hair pulled away from my pale face in intricate braids and fighting leathers of fine make. His lip curled as he assessed the expertly stitched leathers, worn enough to suggest they were not merely for show, but still gleaming in the sunlight, suggesting my wealth. I wondered if he believed me to be a knight, perhaps a mercenary? Or even worse, I could be one of the fabled Ophidians, the abhorrent serpentine assassins whom no one had seen or heard from in years.

He shrugged, likely dismissing me as nothing more than a foolish girl challenging the Lord of Malnova. "It appears that two may die today." He chuckled darkly as he sauntered up to me. The motion cast his cheeks into shadow, their hollows darkening with the promise of another victim.

I laughed, loud and unfeeling. "I doubt anyone else here is foolish enough to attack their own queen."

On cue, soldiers bearing the amethyst and silver livery of the Naqadian Royal Guard stepped forward, barely a scratch upon their armor. Warmth danced across my chest.

I sent my guard the moment I heard a mage was to be publicly executed in Malnova. The news that it was Katzima had not reached me until much later. Without thinking, I had hopped on my horse to ensure my command would be obeyed. I pressed my lips together. Would they have acted without me? I filed the thought away.

The Lord of Malnova's eyes were wide, the flush in his cheeks deepening as recognition sparked. This was not our first meeting. He had been one of many suitors attempting to win my hand at one of the earlier balls, right after I had taken the throne. It hadn't taken more than a conversation for me to know that I would sooner die than marry the self-important lord.

Now, he sank into a bow before me. "Queen Tamariya Amunet, Your Majesty, if you would allow me to explain—"

"Why are you attempting to murder one of the most gifted Healers in Naqad? I would like to hear from her. Katzima, please join us."

Katzima's furious snarl had deflated into open relief. Her eyes crinkled, tears sparkling at their corners. She gestured to the chains shackling her to the dais.

"Calliope," I ordered. The commander of my guard, my reluctant third, and perhaps the most annoying member of my force, came forward and helped her up and out of the heavy cuffs. Calliope and her damn rule-following had nearly refused my plan. I was sure to get an earful about interfering in the territories later.

"Katzima is a danger to the realm. She's been turning the people against you, plotting to steal your throne," Gerome interjected, words rushing out all at once. "I was stopping her. Every word she speaks is poison, Your Majesty. She is a mage."

"As am I," I spat, fire sparking in my eyes. I allowed the flames to burn as I beheld the sniveling lord, pretending they hinted at a greater power beneath.

Gerome paled.

"The young lord lies." Katzima had recovered enough to steady her voice and wipe her tears from her olive cheeks. While smoothing her hands over her dress, she shot me a look of gratitude, but there was a sharpness to the way she tossed her curtain of jet-black hair over her shoulder.

Did she think I would not come for her?

"You are aware of the executions across Malnova. The hundreds of lives lost at their lord's hand. The people starve in the streets as he turns neighbors against each other." She spoke steadily as her fierce brown eyes met mine. "I was not the first mage to stand against him. Nor was I the first he sought to execute. Your Majesty, you need look no further than the castle doorstep for proof of the lord's guilt." Katzima's filthy white dress clung to her as she flexed her jaw.

Under other circumstances, I may have laughed at the formality in her tone. But there were hundreds of eyes upon us. My personal intervention would seem suspicious enough — we did not need to give more wings to gossip.

In truth, I had no idea the reach of Gerome's corruption, but perhaps I had turned a blind eye to the other rumors circulating about the young lord in favor of the image of a realm at peace. A realm I had gone through great personal sacrifices to ensure existed. Perhaps that was why I had allowed myself to be influenced against interfering.

I fought a sigh. Only three short years had passed since the war, since I accepted the crown, and I had little taste for entering into a new war anytime soon. Antagonizing the lords would only push them closer to rebellion.

I turned to Gerome. "Do you deny the allegations against you?" I asked the lord, my voice echoing around the hall.

He growled at me through clenched teeth. "I had to protect what is *ours*. To protect our people from the poisonous serpents you welcome into our cities." His brown eyes were manic as he was forced to the ground by two of my guards.

Someone in the hall gasped. I felt movement behind me as the whispers began. My stomach twisted. I shoved the emotion down.

I arched a brow. "You do not deny massacring the people whom you are oathbound to protect?"

The whispers stopped.

He merely glared.

I had no choice. Gerome had taken the law upon himself. I turned to the assembled crowd. "The mages are citizens of Naqad just as everyone else. We do not execute mages in Naqad."

Muttering from the crowd followed. *Bring destruction... helping Ophidians... villages burned.* It was utter nonsense. Gerome had twisted his lies throughout the village.

Turning back to the lord, I picked up my knife from where it had clattered to the ground and returned it to its sheath. Something tugged within me, warning me that this was wrong.

You are no murderer. Not anymore.

But the voice was faint, and the law required consequences for treachery. I drew in a deep breath.

You saved her; you can leave now. Let the council deal...

The voice faded. I should leave this up to a vote at the council — that was protocol for replacing a lord.

But Gerome had been about to execute Katzima. My jaw slammed shut. Doric could whine to me later about my impertinence. The law required consequences.

And I was the law.

"Lord Gerome Gendran of Malnova, I, Queen Tamariya Amunet, Ruler of Naqad, sentence you to die for ruthless persecution of the mages in Malnova."

With a sharp singing of steel, I unsheathed the blade at my waist and raised the sword high so all could see. I inhaled sharply. I had given up on power, but this, this felt like power.

Kill.

My eyes widened a fraction at the voice. I had not heard *her* speak to me in years.

I obeyed. I brought the blade down in an arch. The Hall went still. A small thud echoed on the stone floor. Lord Gerome Gendran's head rested at my feet, lifeless brown eyes staring blankly at the ceiling. I fought to keep my bread and cheese from earlier from resurfacing in the back of my throat. My thirst for bloodshed had quelled since ascending the throne, and an ache began in the back of my skull. Perhaps it had been dormant for too long.

Unable to look at the young lord's head any longer, I turned to Katzima.

"Katzima of Galeston, you are cleared of all crimes. Go home." I met her gaze steadily, the gesture both a command and a threat. I did not trust that my declaration today would keep the mages of Malnova safe. I would need to stay in the city and unravel Gerome's lies — as soon as I settled the ocean roiling in my stomach. I ground my teeth together. I was no stranger to bloodshed.

I turned on my heel, walking my mare deliberately down the hall. When we got to the doors, I handed her to one of my guards.

"Take me to my quarters," I said tiredly to Calliope.

She glared, likely offended at being treated like a servant, but I did not care. I had been forced to fight my way into a keep in my own kingdom because I couldn't trust her to act. I owed her no pleasantries.

In my borrowed quarters at last, I lay on the bed with my eyes closed, breathing deeply. The mages were being hunted. Again. Would the mages in Naqad ever know peace? I pulled a pillow in front of my face and screamed. It was my job to protect them, and I had failed. Katzima had nearly died for it.

I dug deep into my core, feeling the flicker of my fire gift, nearly spent after that show with the flames in my eyes. I pushed past it to where unbridled power used to lurk. The space was empty. Utterly empty, the same as it had been for years. I screamed again. *Cieri*, I was fucking tired of this game.

Perhaps it was unwise to evoke the goddess of fate, but Cieri had always seemed like the only god of Hel worth a damn. Kallipsis', goddess of witchcraft, followers had an odd way of disappearing, Katzima being the only witch I'd heard of to live more than a few decades. And Anu, God of the Afterlife, was simply useless. So to Cieri I prayed, casting up curses to a goddess imagined to make us feel better about the terrible things that happened to humans.

I wondered briefly if whoever stole my magic had anything to do with the mages being hunted. But I could still *feel* my gift. It was there, somewhere in my body, just not where it was supposed to be.

If I had my power, the lords of Naqad would fall in line. There would be no more foolish politics to play, no more demure queen. Certainly no more talk of my betrothal to some lesser noble. I pounded my fists against the mattress. This hel had been the entirety of my rule.

But someone was hunting the mages. Someone wanted them gone. To weaken the Ophidians? It was possible; the humans hated them enough. No, there was more to it. There had to be. Perhaps Cieri herself was rallying the other gods of Hel back to Palegos for a final triumph over the human world. I smirked at the ludicrousness. The gods of Hel weren't real. Maybe at one point they were, but not anymore. The only things left in Hel were the helmai, and we had already won that war.

TWO

Peeling myself off the dusty mattress, I hobbled over to the wardrobe. The selection before me was abysmal. I scowled, considering how the fabric would feel tearing under my hands as I ripped it to shreds. Seams would pop, and with each unraveling thread, I would imagine another of Lord Gendran's guards losing their head. My hand was already stretched out, stroking the fabric of a blue dress.

I frowned as it scraped against my palms. Gowns for visiting nobility should be made of the finest silks, imported from the Cordaena Isles. I gnawed my lip. The fabric reminded me of the many mage imitations I had sampled in Egryt. Mages could not spin silk from nothing, but the palace mages had tried growing the trees the fickle silkworms fed on in one of the many greenhouses. Despite their extensive efforts, the mages had never quite gotten it right. I pressed a hand to my temple. Gerome Gendran had been stocking his palace with mage-made silks while hunting them in the streets. What a fool.

Fake luxury would suit my purposes tonight, so I supposed it was not the greatest insult to bear. My fingers landed on the blue fabric again. The gown was simple, save for its plunging neckline that would reveal just enough of my decolletage that none would suspect a respectable noble lurked in their midst, least of all the queen. Pursing my lips, I considered the thigh sheath that laid next to the dress. I should have brought more. In Egryt, the single thigh sheath was a comforting token of my former glory, but away from the palace my fingers were constantly twitching for a blade that was not there.

Get your shit together, Tamariya. You're going to a pub, for Cieri's sake.

After moving to the small basin, I splashed some water on my face, threw on the dress, secured the knife to my thigh, and headed into the village to find the only man who had ever held my heart. I dared not risk seeking out Katzima; I prayed she had returned to Galeston without looking back. Even if she lurked in the village, it would be unwise to draw attention to our friendship. Despite being a renowned Healer, Katzima had a reputation for dabbling in the dark arts. Playing mage for the Ophidians would do that.

I walked down the cobblestone streets of Malnova, noticing the quiet, stale air and the people whispering in shadowed doorways.

This was not the bustling valley town where I had traveled at my father's side. The people in the town of my youth had round faces and smiles for strangers; they wore bright clean colors that looked like flowers in the meadows.

Now, the peasants' clothing appeared muted, as if the sun itself had ceased to shine quite as brightly in this valley, dulling the colors and people in the town. Nary a soul met my eyes as I walked, and beyond the gray wooden buildings, blackened soot had replaced the bright-green pastures.

Gritty soot slid between my fingertips, grating against my skin as if it could travel through my veins to clench my heart. I inhaled deeply and froze. A smoky tinge polluted the city's air, seeping into its pores— I never thought I would miss the pungent scent of manure. The Herbal mages. They were supposed to keep the pastures green and the crops fruitful. I knelt, pressing my fingers to the cobblestones, head bowed. I did not need Marcus' information to know the full extent of Gerome's abhorrent actions. In an agrarian village as large as Malnova, Herbals should be everywhere. I shook my head and rose, brushing the soot off the cheap gown and continuing down the street.

Lights and music radiated from a single wooden structure, eerie against the silence of the town. As I approached the pub, shouts and laughter echoed from the structure, and my shoulders loosened. The town wasn't completely abandoned.

Inside, I scanned the scattered tables where people chatted and played cards then the wooden bar where several patrons talked with the barkeep. There was no sign of Marcus' curly dark hair or warm amber eyes. While moving through the room, I received a few whistles and an invitation or two to join a game of dice. I resisted the urge to grit my teeth. There was a time I would have flayed a man alive for looking at me incorrectly. Instead, I arranged my face into a shy smile. I was no fool. I did not survive twenty-three years of court games and a coronation at twenty years old to be unaware of the effect this dress would elicit. But today, there was only one whose reaction I craved.

There he was, holding court in a corner booth, whispering into the ear of a lovely peasant. Her light-brown skin crinkled as she laughed at something he was saying, and her doe-like eyes lit up. But her hand that wasn't circling his chest rested on her thigh, clutching something... a dagger? Who had Marcus become entangled with these past months? I swallowed the sour taste in my mouth, reminding myself that I had no right to such emotions. We had never agreed to keep each other's faith — it was something I would never be able to offer him.

I returned to the bar and ordered a drink, asking the barkeep about Gerome. Marcus would join me when he was finished.

"I was just riding in as I heard what happened to the lord here. I heard the queen executed him," I whispered conspiratorially, appearing to the world as an innocent gossip.

The barkeep's mouth was set in a firm line as his gaze met mine. "Indeed" — his eyes drifted lower — "but between you and me, I say good riddance." At least I was right. It was disgusting, but the barkeep certainly wasn't trying to place why I looked vaguely familiar. Not that many villagers would recognize me. The coronation tour was years ago, and I rarely got close enough to any commoners to leave a lasting impression.

I widened my eyes and gasped. "Your own lord?" I should join a theater caravan.

"Aye." He nodded gravely. "The man's been picking off mages left and right. Everyone knows it. Any mage with any sense has fled, leaving our crops to rot."

Another gasp escaped me, ever the vapid damsel. "And with winter on the way?"

"Aye." He nodded again. "Are you in town long?" he asked, eyes drifting once more.

I fought the growl that threatened to climb its way out of my throat.

"You know, I was wondering precisely the same thing." I didn't need to turn to see who the hand tightening on my shoulder belonged to. The warmth seeped into my veins as he let it linger. I closed my eyes for just a moment before I turned around, forcing his hand to fall. My exposed collar bone chilled.

I met his molten gaze, his eyes churning like the whiskey being poured next to me. My own eyes roved over his dark curly hair pulled back to a bun at the crown of his head, committing every freckle on his brown skin to memory. I looked at him greedily, forgetting for a moment that he wasn't mine to want.

Marcus smiled. The returning grin on my face was probably unseemly for a queen. "Let's dance." His whisper caressed my ear, sending shivers down my back.

"Bored already?" Against my better judgment, I arched a brow and glanced in the direction where the doe-eyed girl had been sitting.

"About as bored as you are with the suitors that line the palace walls in Egryt." His eyes gleamed a challenge as he led me onto the small dance floor where other villagers were already dancing in tune to the music.

"The endless parade is tiresome," I admitted. "You'd think by now Doric would be bored enough to give up."

Marcus' eyes darkened to a cool amber. "He's never going to tire. The realm needs a king. You know that as well as I do." His hand tensed at my back.

Allowing him to guide me into the steps, I scowled. "A queen isn't enough for the realm?"

He smiled, eyes warming. "If it were up to me, aye, a queen would be all we need." He pulled me in close, his lips brushing my ear. "Perhaps a queen with a merchant's son for a consort."

Heat bloomed from the spot his breath caressed, and I let out a giggle as we swayed to the music. I closed my eyes for a moment, allowing myself to picture Marcus' fantasy. He would rule by my side, content to follow my lead, supporting my every move. But never taking any power for himself. And I would have him. He would be mine, and only mine. I grasped at the image, but it began to fray as the pain slicing through my heart shattered the image.

I looked up, and my own pain was reflecting back at me through the pools of whiskey in his eyes. His hand found my chin, and I leaned into the touch.

"I'm yours, Ry. Forever. No matter what." Those pools of whiskey caught fire as his gaze seared into mine.

I swallowed, heat blooming from my core. "I love you, Marcus," I whispered.

"And I, you." He smiled, lips quirking to one side, but then his smile fell. "But you did not come here for my promises."

My shoulders deflated, and I leaned into the arm he still had locked firmly around me. "No," I whispered. "I didn't."

The steps to the dance were easy, something I had memorized as a child, but the beat was picking up, granting me the mercy of delaying my next question. If only Marcus were just a merchant's son, but I had to fall in love with one of the realm's best spies. At least I could pretend our rendezvous was business related.

Thick, corded arms swallowed me as Marcus pulled me into him and lifted me off the ground for a moment. I closed my eyes. He set me back down and we continued the dance.

There was no more delaying it. "Tell me, what have you found out about Gerome Gendran?" My mouth set into a firm line, and an unpleasant emotion curled in my stomach. I hated to use Marcus this way. I had informants of my own of course, but Aya's intel had only gone so far. So when I heard rumblings of trouble in Malnova, I had sent Marcus a coded letter to investigate. It was his answer that had brought me here.

His steps slowed, bringing me to a sway as the music let up. "Nothing good." He twirled me again, my back against his chest this time. I breathed in his warm, woodsy scent. My back burned where we touched. He spun me again so we were face-to-face.

"Gerome has been at this game longer than you feared. The villagers talk," Marcus warned.

"I feared as much." The door to the pub opened, and the chilly night air breezed up my spine. "Tell me."

He sighed. "Lord Gendran never had a problem with his sister being the heir until a year ago. Then one day he locked her away in the dungeons, pretended that she was ill, and began ruling as if nothing had happened. Everyone in Egryt bought the lie: Gesibelle was ill." He shook his head, mystified that it took this long for word to reach the capital. "It took a long time for anyone to notice what was happening. He started with a simple tax increase on traded goods. Then he increased taxes further on mage goods. Villagers slowly stopped buying their trinkets. Then mage work became so expensive, few could even afford an Herbal to help their crops survive winter. The mages tried trading their services under the cover of night, so Lord Gendran implemented a curfew. Anyone caught in violation by his soldiers was killed on sight. The mages grew poorer and poorer as the people grew hungrier.

"Then Gerome started outright hunting them. Anyone accused of being a mage was put to death. There were no more trials, and he went so far as to burn down the fields, proclaiming that rations would only be given to those who turned in a mage. Villagers were turning on each other, terrified of being the next ones accused. All the real mages fled, leaving the crops and the people to suffer without any magic."

I had stopped dancing while he talked. Rage and pain were warring in my chest. I was no stranger to monsters, but the Lord of Malnova had crossed a line, nay, a trench that made me want to dig up his corpse and kill him all over again.

"And we had no idea," I whispered, my hand coming to my hair, fingers pulling through the loose strands.

Marcus' eyes were amber gemstones. "He knew what he was doing," he growled. "Those mages, the ones that tried to flee? Anyone caught leaving was killed. This town has been secluded for nearly six moons."

The blood drained from my head. And we didn't know. *Someone had to know.* My own negligence was one thing, my interest in Naqadian politics was negligible at best, but the council's? They kept close eyes on the kingdom, Marcus' role as living proof.

I shifted from foot to foot, creaking against the woodgrain. "Have you found Lord Gendran's comrades?"

"He had his inner circle, but they all fled after you beheaded him. It was quite the relief to hear you were wielding a blade again. I was worried they had feathered and painted that part out of you for good." His eyes sparkled, likely remembering some of my less than ladylike encounters as princess. A piece of me ached for who I had been. The same piece that purred at Marcus' fond memories of her.

But today I had felt like her again. The farther I got from the stuffy palace and endless council meetings, the freer I had become.

"A queen can be more than one thing, can she not?" I challenged, barely keeping the pleading out of my voice. I prayed that it was true.

"Could have fooled me with the way you've acted since taking the throne."

I wanted to take him by the shoulders and shake him, demanding to know how I was supposed to act.

I didn't used to think about these things. I simply existed, taking what I wanted. Something had changed within me, as if I had become an entirely different person the moment the crown had crested upon my brow. Or perhaps it was the day my magic left, and I realized I didn't know a thing about court politics. I opened my mouth to tell Marcus this but closed it again. I couldn't bring myself to admit that I was so weak. Instead, I picked up the steps again, not missing a beat.

"Do you think Gerome masterminded this all on his own?" I mused, changing the subject. I searched the room. The other couples and singles on the dance floor paid us no mind. Other women were dressed as I was in simple, flowing dresses in a rainbow of muted colors, and Marcus was neither the poorest nor best-dressed man in the room. It was a relief to finally talk to someone without every eye in the room on me. I leaned into his hand and relaxed.

"I think you already know who was behind this." He squeezed my waist, and I wasn't sure if my heart raced from his words or his hand. "The Viper," he said. "The slithering monster has been vying for your throne from the moment you lifted the Serpent's Crown over your head."

"If the Viper wanted someone dead, she'd do it herself. Or commission an Ophidian to do it," I pointed out, ignoring his comment about the Serpent's Crown. Few people still called it that, and I hated the name.

"No one has ever seen the Viper, or any Ophidian since the war. Who knows, maybe Malnova is their stronghold, and this city is crawling with them. Maybe this was a test." We sashayed apart as I considered his words.

What he didn't say was how we likely failed the test, whoever was testing us. We let too many die before intervening. I prayed that our enemies were not paying too close of attention.

We drew together. "The mages in Malnova were innocent. The Viper is ruthless, sure, but she doesn't kill innocents," I said carefully. Especially not mages. The Ophidians needed the mages to survive, for an Ophidian could not be born, only made from a powerful mage. It was a lesson my mother had instilled in me since I had been able to walk. Despite her death nearly a decade ago, my mother's lessons were as clear in my mind as an Allurant's command. I shivered at the thought. My mother was no Allurant, and I prayed I never encountered one of the mages capable of bending a person's will to their own.

"The Viper doesn't care about innocent lives; she steals children in the night and razes entire villages. We stole the Ophidian's kingdom out from under them by killing off low mages centuries ago. Do you honestly think it's a coincidence that it's happening the same way now?" he challenged, voice in my ear as he clutched my waist.

I rolled my eyes. He sounded just like Doric. "The Viper does *not* steal children in the night, nor do the Ophidians *raze* villages. Those are old wives' tales, Marcus."

He shook his head. "We begged them to ally with us in the war, and when they did, we didn't give them so much as a thank you. The Ophidians are angry; I can feel something stirring," he insisted, urgency in his voice as his grip tightened. He spun me.

"The Ophidians have been attempting to gain a foothold in Naqad for centuries, that much is true. But they have been quiet for *decades*. Who's to say they don't already have the foothold they want?" My face burned as I spoke, unused to being so bold. But I was right. I *knew* that the Viper wasn't behind the killings.

Marcus' brow furrowed as we centered our frame. "Where did you hear that?"

I shrugged. "Conjecture." The lie rolled easily off my tongue.

His eyes narrowed. Marcus wasn't wrong. The serpent shifters were cruel. I knew that better than most; *she* was one of them. Getting them to fight in the war had been a harder task than even I had anticipated, even when their own society would have been decimated by the helmai. But that did not mean that the Viper was ordering the destruction of her own kind.

"Rumor has it the Viper can bewitch the weak minded with her serpent eyes. People think she got Gerome alone and *changed* him," Marcus said knowingly.

"I'm not here for rumors and bedtime stories made to scare children. The Viper's gift is death, you know that as well as I. None of the legends have ever mentioned another gift," I snapped, tired of his unrelenting questions.

The mages and Ophidians reemerged four years ago to help us fight the demons, and the Viper's army made the difference that drove the demons back underground. They may be ruthless, but they were not beyond reason. They could be convinced about as easily as they could be killed. Neither was a trivial matter, but it could be done.

Finally, he acquiesced. "I'll have my people look into it."

He twirled me again, this time freeing me from the chains of our conversation, from the burden of protecting an entire kingdom, from the Viper. I was just Ry; I was weightless. I jumped, and his strong arms lifted me from the responsibilities of my position. Marcus and I had never been able to dance like this at the palace balls.

He let me fall slowly back to the ground, my entire body pressed against his as he softened my fall. My chest grazed his nose, then my chin was at his forehead, nose brushing his cheek as my feet landed on the ground again. A burn followed where his nose had touched my skin.

"Ry," he breathed onto my lips as he cupped my jaw in his warm, calloused hand and pulled me tight against him. An acute awareness bloomed each place our bodies connected. It didn't take me back to moonlit nights and easy laughter this time. I was here, his body was all there was. When his lips brushed mine, I gasped at the contact.

His hand slid across my back as we both leaned into this kiss, his mouth working in tandem with mine. His tongue probed my lips, and I gasped again as I felt him exploring my mouth, remembering, memorizing, savoring. My resolve faded completely as I lost myself in his kiss.

Whistles broke my trance. Marcus and I parted as I realized that several villagers had stopped dancing and were staring at us. I ducked my head, blushing. I didn't need anyone looking at my face too hard. Marcus grinned at the whistlers but tugged my arm and led me to the back entrance of the pub.

We stepped into a dark alley with just a sliver of light from the streetlamp visible. He placed his arms on either side of me, but the spell was broken. I ducked around them and spun to pin *him* against the wall. "That was a mistake, and we both know it," I said, even as my chest ached for him.

"Even the queen deserves to have fun, Ry," he said softly. He shifted his chin, his lips nearly touching mine.

I fought a grin. Marcus was the only person to ever speak to me like that. To imply that fun should be anywhere on the queen's agenda. I leaned in, giving him a playful peck on the lips, embarrassment forgotten. The corners of my mouth pulled upward.

"Stay here with me, just a few more days," Marcus whispered.

My face deflated. "I can't." My eyes begged him not to press further.

Of course, he didn't listen. "Why not? You're the queen. You can do whatever you want."

I wished that were so. "There's another ball tomorrow night. Apparently, some Etruscan prince that Doric wants me to meet." My eyes conveyed the apology I could not put into words. I would need to leave tomorrow at dawn to make the half day's ride back to Egryt.

"And yet here you stand, spending your only night of freedom with a commoner." He reached up and brushed a strand of hair from my face, eyes conveying a depth of emotion that both scared and delighted me.

I grabbed his hand, closing my eyes for a moment, savoring the connection. "Come back to Egryt with me," I implored him, eyelids fluttering open.

"And watch you dance and flirt with yet another arrogant foreign noble?" He scoffed. "I'd rather pluck my own eyeballs from their sockets."

I winced. A crack splintered my heart. I needed Marcus. I hated to admit it, but since he had come back into my life, I had burned for him with an insatiable addiction. "Be there to celebrate with me when I send him back to Etrusca." I forced a gleam into my eye, praying he would see the playful invitation for what it was. He knew I would never pick a husband. I had found cause enough to convince even Doric that not a single suitor had been worthy of a betrothal to the queen.

It worked. Marcus' smile returned. "Okay, Ry. How could I say no to you? I'll see you in Egryt." He pulled me in, hand sliding to my neck, the other grasping my waist, and his lips claimed mine.

The kiss said everything that we could not. He would not walk me back to the keep for fear of being discovered, but I knew he wished with every morsel of his being that he could. That he could burst through the ballroom doors tomorrow and declare that no more suitors would be seen, for I was promised to him, and him alone. But it was just a dream.

Our kiss broke, and I pulled back. A dark wash of emotion settled over me, and I willed myself to begin my retreat. "Goodnight, Marcus."

"Goodnight, Ry." His words were nearly lost to the shadows as he retreated into the pub.

Breathing deeply, I put one foot in front of the other, forcing my mind to drift to anything but the man I had just left.

THREE

The wall of the keep loomed in front of me, and I marveled at the atrocities committed by the previous occupant. Fire threatened to spark at my fingertips, replenished after that parlor trick I had done on Gerome. It was absurd to think that the Viper could be behind this. The Ophidians were a lot of things, but mage killers were not among them.

I whirled at the sound of a crash from the street to my right. Past the dim lighting, I could almost make out the village square. Then the screams started. People dashed down the street, practically running into me, some with bloodied faces and hands, sobbing. Gerome's reign of terror had not ended with his death. I unsheathed my dagger, hitched up my dress, and sprinted to the square.

When I got there, I stopped in my tracks. Almost a dozen soldiers bearing the red and black livery of House Gendran were running around, slaughtering the townspeople. I didn't see a single peasant carrying weapons. The scent of blood hit me in a wave, calling to my magic, begging that long dormant part of me to break free. But it was useless. My magic was gone. The dagger in my hand seemed to pulse, reminding me of what I could accomplish with a blade alone.

I smiled, flipped the dagger in my hand, and plunged into the melee. Before me, just out of reach, a soldier grabbed a villager by her hair, dragging her backward as she screamed.

"You know what happens to mages caught after curfew," he growled, drawing a blade as I raced closer.

"The queen said—" She was cut off by her own scream as he shoved his dagger into her side. His sword was sheathed at his waist, but he had chosen the dagger instead. It was more personal that way. Something deep within me uncoiled.

I pounced. My dagger was at his throat and across it before he realized someone had attached themselves to his back. His hold on his own blade sagged as he fell to the floor. The woman was injured, but she might have a chance.

"Go to the keep. Tell them the queen sent you; ask for Calliope." I didn't give the woman a chance to register what I said before I drew the soldier's sword from its sheath and dashed to the next soldier, who demanded penance from a baker by the looks of his colorfully stained apron.

I was quicker this time. I flung my stolen sword out in front of his as he sliced at his victim. The blade was heavier than I was used to, and his parry sent me onto my back. The red-and-black-clad soldier lunged, sword angled for my heart. I rolled, and his blade skimmed the back of my dress. I shot to my feet. He was off balance from his attack. Before he could recover, I thrust my sword through his leathers, feeling the break of bone as I plunged the blade into his heart. The light faded from his eyes as he fell. Bracing my foot on his corpse, I pulled the blade out, wiping it on my skirts.

A quick glance around the square confirmed that the other soldiers had noticed someone taking out their companions, and they started to converge. There was no doubt now: a fighter was in their midst, and it would only be a matter of time before someone realized it was the queen herself. So much for anonymity. I supposed it would serve as a reminder for the realm and any other lords with an inkling to follow in Gerome Gendran's footsteps.

"You must know that your lord is dead," I drawled. "Is it for sport, then? Perhaps some helmai linger here in Malnova." My words were a challenge as I bent to add the fallen soldier's knife to my sheath and sank into a crouch. I was no prey.

The meager light from the streetlamps danced in their eyes as they rushed me. Lips curling, I kept still until they were close. The first one reached me, swinging his sword. I rolled to the side, sweeping my legs under him as I slashed his manhood with my blade. An unearthly shriek erupted from his lungs, and he fell to the ground, body contorting.

I felt the whisper of wind at my back and spun. Steel rang as our blades collided. Reaching in quickly, I jammed my dagger into the second one's side. He stepped back, and I wasted no time shredding his leathers.

Six remained. Seven if you counted the one bleeding out from his bollocks, but he would die soon. Too soon for my taste. Each and every one of these bastards deserved a slow, painful death. The six surveyed me, reevaluating who dared challenge them. I lifted my head and gave them my most wicked grin. A precious morsel of my fire gift escaped, sending a mad flame into my eyes.

"What are you waiting for?" I crooned, batting my eyes as they blazed. I supposed it was more than a parlor trick.

Slowly, they approached, unfazed by my taunting. Tossing my knife aside, I grabbed another sword. I slid the two blades against each other, sending the last reserve of my fire magic onto them, bathing them in flame. More than a parlor trick indeed.

"She's a mage!" a soldier with long brown hair yelled, his voice strengthening with renewed purpose.

The others faltered. But it only took a moment for them to recover before they struck, two at a time, darting in and out, two more taking their place after each collision. I was breathing heavily now, trying to keep up with all six of them, clashing over and over. My magic was draining quickly. Sweat coated my brow. If I didn't make a move soon, exhaustion would set in.

As the next two came to blows with me, I lunged at the smaller of them, putting both my weapons and my full weight into him, catching his leathers ablaze. The other's blade scraped my back. I barely felt it as I knocked the soldier's sword to the side and landed my killing blow. The putrid smell of burning flesh filled the air as he went limp under me.

I spun to the one who wounded me and launched into a roundhouse, kicking his sword away, landing my flaming blade into his chest. The flames began to flicker as fatigue gnawed at me. I reached for the well of dark power but hit a foggy wall. Sweat rolled down my temples as I tried desperately to pull out my dormant power. *Anu's ass.* It would just be the weak flames today.

My arms shook, not used to the weight of these blades as I heaved the flaming sword from the man's chest. The remaining four surrounded me. I lunged at the first, attacking with both swords, and had him on the ground in seconds. A blade sliced my right arm when I was too slow to get out of its way.

Sloppy. I flipped the hilt of a blade into my palm, driving it backward into my target. Two rebels remained. They took one look at me — face bloodied, blades dripping with blazing droplets of blood — and started to back away.

"I am Queen Tamariya Amunet, ruler of Naqad." I lifted my chin, swords flickering, and met their shocked expressions with a snarl. "Allow me to clarify. When I removed Lord Gendran's head from his body, his reign of terror ended. Tell your comrades that pillaging innocents will not be tolerated in this kingdom."

They obeyed, any thoughts of testing their strength vanishing as they disappeared quickly into the crowd. I scanned the square. We had gathered quite the audience of villagers, many of whom had fresh blood leaking from various wounds, several on the brink of passing out. I would soon, too, if I didn't extinguish these blades.

"If you are injured, come with me to the keep; we have a Healer," I pronounced, rather unceremoniously. Turning, I gestured for them to follow as I, at last, extinguished the flames. Only a few hesitantly walked behind me, the rest hanging back, unsure. As I continued to the gates, the uncertain peasants trickled into our ranks, daring to believe that I may be who I claimed. Some hobbled along on their own, but others leaned on their kin, barely able to travel the few streets to the meager keep.

The keep staff took in the injured graciously. Calliope was waiting for us at the gate, expression icy, with the single remaining Healer, whom my guards had found chained in the dungeons along with Gesibelle Gendran. The Healer jumped into action the moment she saw us approaching. I nearly growled at Gerome Gendran's hypocrisy. She scanned the group the way I had the rogue soldiers, moving to where she was needed the most. A bloom of admiration spread across my chest for the woman.

"How many were there?" Calliope was looking at me now, arms crossed.

"Just under a dozen." She started to open her mouth and I held up a hand. "Save it."

She sighed. "Are you at least going to tell me what you were doing in the city?" Her stormy gray eyes were turning with anger. I was in no mood for a debate on the morality of ditching one's guard. I was the Queen; I had a right to my own damn privacy.

You should have allowed your guard to deal... a faint voice began.

Fuck the voice. My anger flicked its sharp tongue at the mental fog that had become my constant companion, weighing in on every Cieri-cursed decision I made these days.

But I'd had enough of the voice and of Calliope's overbearing protectiveness. Years ago, I had made my peace with this new-found conscience of mine, but today it had only been a nuisance.

Pushing the thoughts away, I answered my third. "I was meeting with an old friend. He had some information I required." I tried to sound casual as the memory of my body sliding against Marcus' on the dance floor pressed into my mind. I welcomed the image in place of my more troubling thoughts.

She narrowed her eyes. "A *friend*?" She looked pointedly at the deep V and what was left of my torn dress. When her gaze reached my arms, her stormy eyes turned. "You're injured."

"Let the Healer attend to the villagers. I am fine." Glittering green met tumultuous gray, and I silently dared her to make a move.

"Carrie, could you come over here?" she called across the court-yard.

The Healer rushed over and set to work on my minor cuts. "You are lucky these are not deep; the one on your back would have been impossible to heal," Carrie commented.

I narrowed my eyes at Calliope, letting her know that this was officially her problem.

"You don't get to be my age in this line of work without exercising appropriate caution," Calliope said vaguely. At least she had the decency not to gloat.

I rolled my eyes, but the graying strands of her thick blonde hair only proved her point. With four decades of life behind her, she was the most senior member of my guard. Also the most opinionated.

"One of us needs to make sure we both stay alive, and you seem hell-bent on making that an impossible task, even in peacetime. What's with the swords?" She nodded to what I still clutched at my sides.

"Look," I murmured, gesturing to the hilt. A finely crafted serpent lay coiled as the pommel, the neck extending into the handle.

Calliope stiffened and dropped her voice to a low whisper. "Are you going to tell them?"

I sighed. "They need to know."

FOUR

The dress was positively ridiculous. When Aya had held it up in the mirror, I had nearly growled at her, my blood still roaring from the race back to Egryt. Deep-emerald silk and billowing sleeves cascaded to the floor, the dress's color its only redeeming quality. Perhaps I could stomach the silver embroidery, teasing the severed serpent's head of Naqad's crest. But the skirts were far too expansive and the corset too restrictive to be practical for anything more than an ornament. And the queen was no ornament.

Doric had sent in the crown's stylists the moment I'd reached my quarters, leaving Aya and I no time to discuss my escapade to Malnova. My second gave me a subtle nod, her jet-black hair bobbing, as I entered the room — the only indication that her spies had gotten into the city at last, and she knew of my small victory. My hair had been piled high onto my head, graceful strands of auburn curling into my face, my cheeks softened with pink rouge; even my lips bore a sickly shade of pink. I had scowled as they applied it, and I fought my scowl still as I sat upon the grand ballroom's dais, Lord Doric Venrylst standing at my side. Were it up to me, I would have lined my eyes with kohl and painted my lips with the deepest red the crown could find. Only my fingertips clawing into the wood of my throne, concealed by my ample sleeves, gave away my discomfort as I plastered a glowing smile on my lips.

It was all a charade, of course. I would play the part of benevolent queen seeking consort, and Doric would leave me alone for a few months, or until he found another nobleman to thrust in my face. I had met nearly every eligible lord in Naqad, most either far too elderly or youthful to merit an appropriate match. Many of the kingdom's of-age lords had died in the war, and those who had not were needed at home to rule their own lands. I was grateful to the helmai for this small mercy. So Doric had begun searching for a foreign prince for me.

Unluckily for me, Lord Venrylst was one of the most well-connected people in Palegos. There had been an endless parade of dignitaries and princes, second sons, and random nobles from Drazurc to the Cordaena Isles. They had all been vapid, self-important pricks, and I had told Doric as much. I expected no less of the Etruscan prince. A few hours of pleasantries would pass, and I would finally be able to collapse into Marcus' arms. I smiled grimly, resigned to my fate for the evening.

Bright colors swirled as the courtiers navigated the dance floor. A light breeze fluttered in from the sea, invigorating the revelers with the cool promise of autumn. The trade ships that flowed constantly through the port carried goods from around Palegos to be distributed throughout Naqad. Nearly every room in the castle boasted a stunning view of the port, and the grand ballroom was no exception with its massive arched windows. The veranda beyond opened to the side of the crashing waterfall that fell from the castle's rivers down into the bay, the palace's architecture acting as a dam for the river that flowed from the north. The palace was, objectively, stunning. A gemstone upon a glistening cove — the airiest cage a girl could hope for.

Precisely half of an hour had passed since the commencement of the ball when the doors to the ballroom burst open. His lateness was absurd, considering I had overheard the maids whispering that the visiting noble had arrived two nights ago. Trumpets blared, announcing the presence of His Royal Highness, Prince Caryk Cazaar, second son of the Etruscan King, Dahlm Cazaar. I did my best not to roll my eyes.

The prince entered, flanked by Etruscan courtiers. I noted their king was not among the convoy. I wondered mildly if I should be insulted. The Prince of Por had brought his mother, the queen. Even the Amyaran nobleman had traveled with several members of the royal family. But they were not Etrusca. Our fathers had been friends, and yet Dahlm Cazaar did not feel obligated to grace me with his presence.

The jewels dripping from the bodies of each member of the convoy rivaled the decadent necklace at my own throat, even the crown atop my head. I had not seen an Etruscan noble since the war, when opulence was discarded for bloodstained leathers. My brows rose a fraction. I smiled, arranging my face into a flattered expression.

Prince Caryk Cazaar prowled across the room. His dark-brown hair fell past his ears, nearly brushing his shoulders, playing perfectly off his light-brown skin. He wore an ornate sword for the occasion, yet he walked like his athletic frame was used to carrying much more than a single broadsword. He was smiling, but even from a distance, I could tell the gesture didn't quite reach his eyes.

"Your Majesty." He reached the dais and bowed.

He lifted his head, and I was pinned by burning sapphires lined lightly with kohl. My perfect posture cracked as I jolted back on the throne, caught off guard by the unbridled fury upon the prince's face. My jaw slackened, about to demand what I had done to warrant such disrespect, when the prince blinked, turned to Lord Venrylst, and inclined his head.

"It is my honor to meet you, my lord, Your Majesty," he said smoothly. The bastard didn't even look at me, his smile directed toward my advisor.

The rest of his face was just as striking as his eyes, from his high cheekbones to the playful set of his mouth, framed by his close-cropped beard. A feeling of familiarity itched in the back of my mind, but I was certain I had never met the Prince of Etrusca.

I smiled. "Your Highness, it is a pleasure to meet you as well." For once I almost meant it. He may hate me, but his hatred was a refreshing difference from the ass kissing I had become accustomed to. Something about the way the Prince of Etrusca surveyed the room behind glowing eyes told me he was anything but boring.

"The pleasure is mine, Your Majesty," he purred, shoulders stiff as he turned to me. He extended a hand and asked for a dance. Several large silver rings glistened on his fingers. His eyes held me in place as he awaited my response.

"Of course, Prince Cazaar." I gave him a tight smile and took his hand delicately with my gloved one. Heat rushed into my palm despite the silk layer between us. My cheeks flushed. I stole a sideways glance at the prince.

He smiled a courtier's smile as he led me off the dais, spinning me perfectly into the dance pattern. The flowing emerald gown was not thin, yet his hand seared through the smooth fabric at my back. His other hand secured my gloved one as he guided me around the dance floor.

Perhaps he was a fire mage, like me, and he was one word away from exploding into flames. Now *that* would make this ball interesting.

It had taken practice for me to learn to allow a man to lead, but I was finally getting the hang of it. For once, it appeared I may have a dance partner who actually knew the steps. He twirled me in perfect time to the music, and I allowed myself to relax as we completed one of the more difficult steps flawlessly. The angry prince had my attention.

The dance ended, and we bowed to each other, my head barely dipping. My heart thrummed with the anticipation of another number, my cheeks flush as I extended my hand, palm facedown. He smiled, sky-blue eyes bright, and I returned the gesture, my grin light with an anticipatory kind of joy, my head clear for once. I was dying to know why this adept dancer hated me so much. He pulled me close as the slow dance began.

"People are beginning to stare." I nearly giggled in his ear. *Who am I?* For a moment, I let myself pretend that I was the kind of girl who could get whisked off her feet by a handsome prince. Like I was someone who would be able to choose who she shared her life with. Like I wasn't just high on the thrill of manipulating yet another suitor.

He pulled back to look at me. "Your people need a distraction."

"Would you like to know a secret?" I whispered conspiratorially in his ear, resting my hand on his shoulder. He nodded, giving me an equally sly look. "I don't usually dance with princes who hate me."

His face remained unchanged, but his eyes sparked. "What made you accept my invitation?" He spun me around into a graceful twirl.

"I'm dying to know what I've done to earn such ardent hatred," I whispered breathlessly, answering honestly.

He chuckled, dipping me backward, and a lock of dark hair fell into his face. "I'm not sure you could handle the truth if I told you, love." His deep voice rumbled as his eyes bore into mine.

His words jolted me, and I fought the urge to stiffen. I supposed it would only prove his point if I lost my composure now. I forced my body to stay pliable as I let him lead me around the ballroom. "Oh?" I kept the word as light as I could, willing the threat to leave it.

His smirk only grew. "I have no love for Naqad, it's true."

I snorted. "*No love* is one way to put it." He spun me in a quick circle. I considered. "What *do* you have love for, then?" I quirked a brow at him playfully.

The prince scowled. "I do not seek your hand for a love match, if that's what you're getting at." He continued the steps, body growing stiffer.

My grin grew. I had gotten under his skin. Of course, I knew I would never end up betrothed to this prick, but he didn't. "You think me unlovable?" I prodded, a mockery of a pout on my lips.

"Perhaps," he said through his teeth. His back was straight as a battering ram, not a bend to his entire form.

Ouch. Anger began to burn in my chest. This arrogant prince did not know a damn thing about me. "Then it may shock you to know that there are those who would love me without question." I did not mean for the words to come out so fiercely, but I thought of Marcus and the things he would do to this noble if he were present.

The prince's posture loosened with a smirk. "I'm well aware of a certain childhood *companion.*" My blood chilled. This was no casual courtship. The prince had to have gone to great lengths to learn that particular piece of information. Marcus and I were careful, and very few knew about our childhood connection.

"If you hate us so much, why would you want to be the king consort of Naqad?" I hissed. This game was no longer amusing, and the prince knew far too much for me to allow him to live.

He is the Prince of Etrusca. You better not be thinking of murdering him.

I clenched and unclenched my jaw. I could not kill Caryk Cazaar.

"My father needs allies, and you need gold." He sounded almost bored as he sent me into another twirl.

"And you do everything your father tells you?" I demanded, with a bit too much intensity for it to have the goading effect I wanted.

"Perhaps I believe I can help your *people*," he purred. His eyes were glittering jewels, as if there was some double meaning I was missing.

"My people are quite fine without a king consort," I spat.

We stepped in a slow circle, his gaze pinning me. "Your people starve. Naqad has not been rebuilt since the war. Your country is poor, and you need Etrusca's money. Your mages are fleeing. Don't be a fool."

Thankfully, the dance was over. I stopped, a snarl upon my lips. "Naqad is rebuilding just fine. The mage problem has been *handled*."

His eyes widened a fraction when I realized my mistake. I had allowed the bastard to bait me into revealing more than I intended. He may not have known that Gerome Gendran was in open rebellion, or worse, I had just confirmed crown intervention in a matter that took place only a day prior.

I took a step back. There was no way I would ever share my throne with this prince. He knew far too much and was far too adept at riling my nerves.

But he was right: Naqad was hurting, and Etrusca was the wealthiest nation in Palegos.

I would have to accept a suit at some point, despite my proclamation to Marcus. There was only so long that a twenty-three-year-old queen could remain unmarried.

I gave the prince a nod. "It has been a pleasure to meet you, Your Highness, but I'm afraid I would be remiss if I did not dance with my other guests this evening," I said in a clipped tone as we parted. *Cieri*, I should win an award for courtly behavior after that performance.

"The pleasure was all mine, love," he said smoothly, eyes sparkling. His blue eyes, which I found striking earlier, had now turned predatory. A chill ran down my spine. Caryk was after something in Naqad, and he would do whatever it took to get it. I turned away from the prince and made my way to the array of appetizers and sparkling wines; a drink was much needed. After downing a flute of sparkling wine, I snagged another and prayed Lord Venrylst hadn't seen the unladylike moment.

My dress was getting heavy, my tolerance for court antics waning as I maneuvered through the courtiers, welcoming them and thanking them for joining us this evening. Everyone wanted to know how I had found the prince. *Will he finally be the one to catch our queen's favor?* I answered as evenly as I could, leaning into the drink to dredge up enthusiasm over the insolent prince.

My third glass of sparkling wine was nearly gone when I saw *him.* His curly dark hair was pulled into a tight bun at the back of his skull. He smiled at a courtier, and it was so dazzling I almost believed that he was one of them. Marcus' kind amber eyes put the partygoers at ease, and they returned his smile, exchanging pleasant words before departing.

I caught his eye and glided out of the ballroom and down the hall that led to the palace gardens. Once in the balmy air, I walked down one of the less frequented paths, feigning interest in a particularly gorgeous rose bush. The fresh scent of its petals mingled with water droplets spraying from the falls, dispelling my nerves in a way the alcohol never could. This late in the season, the air was uncharacteristically damp. I prayed a storm would save us from this horrendous humidity.

A warm body joined mine. Fighting the stupid grin that threatened my face, I allowed myself a small smile. He looked at me out of the corner of his eye. His mouth quirked into a half grin.

"You're drunk." He chuckled, his cheeks flushed as well.

"Maybe." I shrugged and smiled playfully. He turned to face me, starlight dancing in his eyes. *I could stay here forever*, I thought.

"How was the prince?" I could tell he was trying to keep his voice light, but his eyes gave him away. The light in them dulled and his gaze roved over my face as he waited for an answer.

"Prince Caryk Cazaar of Etrusca," I said dryly, rolling my eyes. I took another sip of wine.

"Another bust?" The relief in his voice was too obvious.

"He's not only arrogant, he's positively impossible. Cryptic, rude, utterly *infuriating*," I snapped, finally able to voice my true thoughts of the brute.

Marcus grunted, shifting uncomfortably.

"Marcus..." I trailed off, the buzz from the wine quickly fading.

He cocked his head to the side. "That's the most emphatic response you've given yet. You claim most of them are just a bore." His mouth had an odd set to it, one I could not quite read.

"Better to be bored than under siege," I replied flatly, pressing a palm to my brow. Marcus slipped behind me, and I leaned back into his shoulder, savoring the connection.

"You seem to thrive under siege." His voice was light, but the undercurrent of truth struck deep. I turned around, placing my palms on Marcus' chest, feeling the corded fabric of his tunic with my fingertips.

"I will not marry the Etruscan," I swore, imploring the man I loved to believe me. "I will have to marry eventually, but I could not stomach a lifetime with that ass, especially not with a marriage vow in place."

He considered, a quiet sort of calculation in his eyes. "What if it wasn't the worst thing to marry the Etruscan?"

My eyebrows rose. "Marcus Inora, are you implying that I accept a suit?" I took a step back, looking up into his face. "You cannot be serious."

He shrugged. "He seems like an ass, of course. But at least he's not kissing your ass. You know what you're getting with him. He told you he won't romance you? Great. That's one less thing we have to worry about."

My cheeks burned. "What are you saying, Marcus?"

"Don't make me spell it out, Ry. Please." His eyes pleaded with me, and there it was. Everything we never dared tell each other. The love and desperation to have me as his own.

"You want me to enter a loveless marriage so that our relationship never changes," I whispered.

He shook his head, confusion clouding his gaze. "Come on, Ry. Isn't that what you want, too? You don't want a partner, you want a figurehead to get Doric off your back. I'm your partner. I always will be. I swear it."

My heart swelled and sank at Marcus' declaration. I bit my lower lip, tasting the pink rouge with a flick of my tongue.

Marcus' eyes were pools of molten metal. He reached out a hand and brushed my collarbone lightly with his knuckles. My stomach fluttered as my body responded. I closed my eyes and felt him brush against me. I wanted nothing more than to forget this conversation and lose myself in him. That was what this was supposed to be: an escape.

"You look beautiful tonight, Ry," he whispered, breath skimming my ear. My heart ached. "Look at me, please." His voice cracked on the last word. He tucked a strand of hair behind my ear.

I opened my eyes. What I saw in his almost broke me. He was right, after all. I was doomed to a loveless marriage either way. Would it really be so bad to marry someone apathetic? Better to have apathy than false flattery.

"Ry." He grabbed my wrist and entwined our fingers as he searched my gaze, his own shattered. The cracks in my heart splintered. "I love you." He nodded, squeezing my hand one last time, then walked away.

"Where have you been?" Doric snapped as I took my seat on the dais.

I avoided his eyes and cast my gaze on the ballroom instead. "Welcoming my guests," I said mildly.

Doric made a noise of disapproval in the back of his throat. "Some more than others."

"I danced with the prince. I managed to be cordial," I said dully. The dancers still spun in swirling colors. Shame pierced my gut at the memory of dancing with Caryk. My excitement at the thrill of his hatred seemed childish now. I sank deeper into the throne. I was tired. Tired of playing these court games. Tired of pretending to care about the doting courtiers. Tired of pretending like I wanted to marry an entitled prince. I pressed my hand to my forehead. This wasn't who I was supposed to be. I wanted to be *her* again. But she had been buried alongside my magic, in some dark corner of my mind that I would never find. So here I was, stuck in this weak form, a good student of the court. It was better this way. At least that's what I told myself.

"You know precisely what I'm talking about," Doric hedged, an edge growing in his voice.

Honestly, I didn't. I was hardly paying attention to him. But I couldn't let Lord Venrylst know that or he would explode here on the dais. *Cieri*, he was unrelenting. Always with some opinion or other about court, the politics of the realm, or lately, which suitor would make the best match. The problem was, Doric was usually right. He knew this realm and the people in it in a way I sometimes envied. But what had he asked me? The guests... oh. *Bollocks.*

"If you keep sneaking off with that spy, people are going to start talking." I could hear him gritting his teeth. Let him explode. The ball was practically over, and I didn't care much to enjoy the party. Not like this. I used to love balls as a girl but being constantly scrutinized will do that to you.

"Let them talk," I said, waving a hand.

"Tamariya," he hissed.

"Isn't the whole point of being queen having the ability to do whatever to whomever I want?" I kept my voice bland, knowing it would only aggravate him further.

"You're being petulant. It doesn't suit you. Look at me," he ordered.

I sighed and turned my head to him. "What?"

"If you don't agree to a suit, I'll be left to assume your *spy* has something to do with it," Doric said through his teeth, leaning forward in his seat.

I straightened. "The prince's lack of desirability has nothing to do with whatever you think you know," I said cautiously.

"I'll remain unconvinced until you find a match. Terrin's spies have been known to go rogue and wind up in the dungeons."

"You wouldn't." Fire ignited in my gaze as I looked up at the lord. My nostrils flared. He would not dare. I wished my gift were ample enough to light the lord's thin frame ablaze.

"Don't test me." He picked a thread off his tunic, throwing it onto the floor.

I swallowed, my gust twisting. Marcus... in the dungeons. He was a spy. He had put Cieri-knew-how-many traitors there. Wine threatened to reemerge in the back of my throat.

"The prince would be a good match," he continued. "Don't you think so?"

I scowled, fighting to calm my rolling stomach. "He's a prick." The truth tumbled out, despite my rising pulse. My stubbornness would not cause Marcus harm. If I had to choose a blasted husband to save him, I would.

"He's rich. Etrusca is the wealthiest nation in Palegos. We need their money, Tamariya, *think*," Doric implored. He ran a hand through his receding reddish-blonde hairline. Threat made, he was back to reason. I tried to relax.

"Surely there is someone less... angry that I could spend my days with?" I lifted my brows. I hated to beg.

"You have found cause to hate nearly every suitor who walked through these doors. I am running out of princes, Tamariya. You've already gone through every eligible noble in Naqad." My advisor was gritting his teeth now, frustration evident.

I closed my eyes, clawing at the throne. Perhaps if I dug long enough, I could disappear into the wood. Deep down, I knew I had to pick one, Doric's threat aside. The royal line had to continue, and the longer I put it off, the weaker and weaker Naqad would look.

"Did he offer you anything interesting?" I met my advisor's gaze. I was not usually so direct, but I knew that Doric was negotiating the terms of my engagement with each suitor. It had to be something good for the councilman to choose today to become so insistent.

He surveyed me, giving nothing away. "Perhaps."

"Tell me."

He sighed. "More aid than you would think. Look, Tamariya, I truly am running out of options." I looked up into his pale blue eyes, so light they were almost white. They swirled, and I saw the truth there: Naqad needed the money. I needed to make a decision. There would be no more chasing suitors away.

I thought through the other suitors. The Prince of Por had been so gracious he could hardly be trustworthy. The Drazurcan noble had found himself far too important. Compared to them, the Etruscan's hatred did not seem so bad. Hatred, I understood. I could work with that. While he had learned far more from me than I cared to admit, I had also succeeded in needling the prince.

Better to be under siege than bored.

I smirked. *Cieri*, I *was* intolerable. Perhaps I could stomach a lifetime chained to this ass. Or I could very carefully craft loopholes to our marriage vow. And we needed the money. Malnova was not the only territory struggling. I knew the other farming villages had struggled to rebuild. Even where mages were welcome, they were hard to come by, a meager offering not enough to entice them from their strongholds—it would be even harder to entice them after what had transpired in Malnova. Etrusca had been hurt the least in the war. This offer of aid would be better than any other nation could offer. My people needed the alliance.

"I'll marry the prince," I conceded. I held up a hand. "This promised aid had better be good. I want it immediately after we make the betrothal bond."

Doric smiled. "As you wish, Your Majesty."

FIVE

THREE YEARS AGO: THE WAR ON HEL

I ran my hand over my brow. It came back caked in dirt and blood. My gloves had been shed hours ago when the grime became too thick to grip my blade. Cursing whoever summoned these demons, I tried to wipe my hand off on my fighting leathers. It was futile. My body had been coated in a layer of filth for days, and we were no closer to identifying the summoner.

The night had been rough, but it was no exception these days. I was awakened three times by swirling dreams of piles of helmai, followed by the dismembered heads of my loved ones—Aya, my father, and my mother. Every time my eyes opened, I had to repeat the same mantra: *Aya is alive. My father is alive. My mother died seven years ago. It was not your fault.*

At least this time I had awakened as myself. Too often, when I slept unaccompanied, *she* woke up instead. There was something about the beating heart of a stranger and lingering regret of last night's drunken mistakes that felt so utterly human that *she* could never manage to penetrate.

But there was no time to brood on the twisted charade my life had become. I stood back-to-back with my cabal, swords outstretched as we prepared for the next wave of demons. The helmai were almost humanoid with their leathery arms ending in black claws and their oblong heads that housed their fang-filled mouths—fangs that were not only sharp enough to tear a man to shreds but possessed a paralyzing venom that could bring a wild boar to its knees. I was sure that their glistening black eyes would haunt my dreams until the day I finally died. They stood just tall enough to be formidable adversaries but short enough that my back ached from the endless days of fighting with a slight hunch.

The stench hit us first— rotting flesh mixed with slick oil: a fitting harbinger for the foul demons. Black claws struck out at me, and I ran my blade through flesh. The helmai shrieked as it fell to the earth. Even that had lost its thrill. Despite my exhaustion, my gift twitched restlessly around me. The helmai weren't technically alive, so there wasn't much my magic could do. At least the mist provided some cover.

Sharp claws pierced my back. I swallowed a scream and threw a fireball over my shoulder. The others must have been drawn away. At least fire worked on them. The demon shrieked and released me.

Whirling around, I hacked my blade across its dark leathery body before it could realize that the fire was merely a tickle. My fire gift was a parlor trick on a good day, nothing compared to my father's wildfire. Perhaps my mother's blood had silenced the fire with its darkness.

More claws, more black bodies. More corpses.

It was like looking out into a churning ocean but with a more deadly undercurrent. I'd seen too many warriors swallowed up by its mass, never to resurface again.

Bright emerald scales glistened next to me as an Ophidian summoned roots from the earth to trap the approaching demons. Our eyes met, sage green against my emerald, and we exchanged a nod. Rohesia was one of the strongest Herbals among the Ophidians, one of the few magics that worked against the demons. Thus, the Ophidian had been rising through the ranks quickly, earning her a spot in my personal battalion.

Next to her, another Ophidian with matching scales put up walls of wind, halting the helmai in their tracks, but even the Elemental's considerable gifts were weakened. Whatever god created the helmai had a sick sense of humor. Not that I cared much for what the gods thought these days, especially the gods of Hel.

Aya and Calliope were at my side again, guts splattering both of their faces. Hooves pounded the ground behind us.

"Cover me," I muttered as I turned my back on the clawing beasts to approach whatever messenger the king had sent this time.

A beast of a man stared down at me. General Brom Balenek. "Get your asses back to camp," he snarled, slicing his blade downward to decapitate a surging helmai.

"So we can miss all the fun down here?" I taunted half-heartedly, glancing at Brom out of the corner of my eye.

"The king will have your heads."

I laughed weakly. "My father isn't going to kill anyone capable of wielding a blade." I lunged, striking down another demon.

"Wish I could say the same of his daughter," Brom challenged.

I looked up in time to see his hazel eyes flashing. *Shit.* "We'll return after this wave of demons," I conceded, flicking my gaze in annoyance. I supposed it would have been foolish to believe that last night's antics would not reach my father.

The king and his twisted morals were insufferable. He seemed to think that a leader's place was behind a barricade, surrounded by guards, yet he was sent into a blind rage at what he claimed was 'needless loss of life.' I rolled my eyes. Commanding the respect of your army wasn't needless. Besides, where was the appeal in commanding an army if you couldn't kill anyone?

Brom gave me a look that told me exactly how much he believed my declaration, but he sighed and rode off back to the camp, navigating the sea of demons and humans with the grace of an expert horseman.

I reclaimed my place between Aya and Calliope. Aya shot me a sideways look, her obsidian eyes hiding a thousand questions.

"Better get all the killing out of your system now, ladies—orders to return to camp after this wave," I said in my best, bright, mocking tone.

"Cali, don't," Aya muttered, arranging her blades in a fighting stance as she surveyed the growing wave of helmai converging on us. "You'll only feed her ego."

Calliope's mouth clamped shut, and she settled for crinkling her nose at me before bringing her long broadsword into position.

I smiled, feeling the mania glimmer in my irises as I drew my twin knives. Most of the warriors believed I was mad for letting the venomous demons get close enough to reach my short blades. A kill wasn't a kill unless you could feel the tear of flesh, regardless of whether your quarry was technically alive or not. Besides, I had been pierced by venom far worse and survived.

The wave hit us, and immediately there were sharp claws and teeth everywhere. One of the demons had grabbed a sword from a fallen Naqadian and was swinging it around. I lunged to cut it down. The helmai dodged me. I hesitated. These demons weren't supposed to be smart. It swung the sword at me, but I caught it on my knives, the impact reverberating into my forearms. I grit my teeth together. It lunged again. I dodged the blade this time and struck with my knives, and it parried. I glanced over to my second and third, finding them engaged in similar duels with the demons. Something was very wrong. They should not be able to wield blades like this.

Another helmai came at me from the side, and I blocked its swing with a single knife. My knife went flying. I drew a shorter dagger from my belt, zeroing in on the two demons circling me. I smiled.

"Thank you for the challenge. Killing your kind was getting dull," I taunted as my blood sang.

I swore the first helmai smiled through its mutilated jaw. I struck, lunging in with my blade, slicing upward, feeling the jagged tear of the creature's tough flesh. The demon jumped back but didn't fall. I sensed movement at my back and whirled to face the other one, barely spinning in time to catch its sword with my knives. The shock tore at my muscles. Gods, they were strong.

A blinding pain seared against my ribcage, and I instinctively struck out with my elbow, hitting leathery skin. On my left, the helmai swiped at me again, and I staggered back, taking the force of the blow. Another shooting pain ravaged my right thigh. The dagger fell from my hand as a gash ripped across my left arm. I took another step back. Hand trembling, I reached to my belt to draw another throwing knife. My arm shook as I struggled to lift it into position. Gods, did that brainless demon sever a tendon?

Weakly, I threw the blade, and the helmai barely flinched. They were circling me now. I was not healing nearly as quickly as I should have been. With my good arm, I hurled a knife at the relentless creatures, but they blocked it easily. I gave up trying to grip a weapon with my left hand and drew another in my right.

I gripped the blade, shifting my gaze back and forth between the two demons. They shot forward, and I attacked with my knife, catching a blade. The other helmai's blade pierced my thigh, and I fell to the ground, nothing but a measly throwing knife between me and certain death. A claw raised high in the air, jowls open and ready to pounce as black gore spurted out of its mouth, drenching the ground between us. And just as I raised my knife, the tip of a blade pierced the back of its neck and thrusted through its mouth before ripping the helmai in two.

I exhaled. I really needed to stop being so irreverent. Perhaps the goddess of fate was watching over me after all. The other demon was on the ground in a matter of seconds.

I tried to push myself off my knees with my good arm, but instead, a strong hand gripped my underarm, pulling me up. Piercing blue eyes met mine.

"Didn't know they could do that," I huffed, the world tilting around me.

The stranger steadied me. "It appears this wave has mutated," he said darkly.

"Oh," I breathed, wondering why the man before me had two heads, when the ground gave out under me.

I opened my eyes, and I was floating through the air. No, it was far too bumpy for that. I was being carried. By the stranger. I turned my head and noticed his shaggy dark hair matted with gore from the battle. His head turned, and those piercing eyes were on mine again.

"Where..." I wheezed, struggling to find the words.

"Back to the camp. There are Healers there, although they might be busy. I heard some of the more arrogant nobles thought they'd try their hand at fighting today." His voice made it perfectly clear how he felt about said arrogant nobility.

Shit. He might drop me here to rot if I told him who I was. The rage bubbling inside me at being carried quelled.

"Shit indeed. You put a blade in a royal's hand and suddenly they think they're invincible," he said, the undercurrent of a growl in his tone.

I hadn't realized I had spoken aloud. *Prick.*

"I-I'm... Prin..." I couldn't get the words out. I could barely keep my eyes open. Was the ground getting closer? Why was the sky black? He needed to know who I was. I didn't want to die, not yet. And if the Healers were too busy... I knew how bad my injuries were.

"Don't worry. I know who you are, love." I thought I heard a smirk in his voice, but before I could think on it any further, the world around me faded to black.

SIX

PRESENT

I sat in a parlor off the great hall, fingernails digging into my skin. Doric had insisted I receive the prince in this room rather than the throne room. It would be a symbol of our partnership. I felt like a goat being offered for slaughter. But I had agreed to this; Doric understood court games in a way that I would never have the patience for.

So there I sat, on a plush sofa, with a winning smile plastered over my face, wearing a frivolous gown meant for nothing other than sitting on a throne. Even walking the halls was a chore in this monstrosity. I was positioned so the sunlight would radiate my face, the light breeze would tickle my hair, and the bouquet of lavender and jasmine arranged perfectly on the windowsill would waft floral notes upon my bosom: the picture of serene beauty. As if I would ever be described as such. What the sunlight really did was blind me so I couldn't see who entered the room. I fought to keep my lip from curling.

Finally, footsteps sounded outside the door, then several tall figures strode in. I did not rise. I had at least maintained that shred of dignity in my argument with Lord Venrylst. Someone stepped in front of the window, so I could at last see the party.

Doric Venrylst was striding over to stand beside me, and behind him walked a statuesque man. This time, I wasn't blinded by his dazzling smile or chiseled jawline. I could see the cruel glint behind his brilliant eyes.

The prince stood before me, holding out his hand. His silver rings glistened, and I blinked at the twisting serpent carved into the face. It couldn't be. His hand turned in the light, accentuating the wings extending from the serpent's back. The crest of Etrusca was a dragon. *Of course.*

I extended a silk glove. He bowed, pressing his lips to my hand. Even through the silk, his kiss burned my skin. I looked to the ground, then up at him through lowered lashes, a soft smile on my face. At least, I hoped it was a smile. There was a chance that I looked like one of the helmai's given human form. Aya was much better at this kind of thing than me, but I was grateful that my friend wasn't here to witness the subjugation of my power.

Caryk Cazaar's gaze heated, dark intent glittering. Something within my stomach turned. "Your Highness, welcome to Egryt," I said in as measured a tone as I could manage.

"The pleasure is entirely mine," his voice rumbled.

"I think we should leave Prince Cazaar and Her Majesty to get acquainted, don't you think?" Doric spoke now, addressing the other man in the room, the prince's manservant. The two men left.

The door had barely swung shut when the prince turned to me, smirking. "Quite the performance, love." His eyes danced.

I dropped the smile from my face. "I could say the same to you."

"Who said I was pretending?" Caryk's eyes darkened again. He leaned in, bracing his hand on the side of the couch.

I rolled my eyes, even as something deep in my stomach turned again.

"I must admit, I was surprised to receive Lord Venrylst's terms of engagement after the way you stormed off last night." The prince's eyes roved my face as he spoke.

I stood, forcing him upright. "If it were up to me alone, you would not have received a letter." The ridiculous dress threatened to pull me back down, and I immediately regretted standing.

"Oh? And who else is it up to? Isn't a queen supposed to be able to do whatever she wants?" he challenged.

My skin reddened as the prince echoed the same words I had spoken to Doric on this very topic. I crossed my arms, trying to hide my discomfort. "You read the terms. Naqad needs this alliance."

"And did Doric pick out that ridiculous dress too? Tell me, love, do you have any power here at all?" the prince asked, feigning surprise.

My cheeks burned. "More than you," I spat. My soft exterior was broken. I felt my power rumbling within me, straining to be unleashed on the would-be usurper. *Strange.*

"Oh, I wouldn't be so sure of that," he said with a twisted smile. There was something in his eyes that didn't quite match his smile. What did the prince know?

My vision went hazy as I fought to control the rage boiling my insides. This was not how a queen behaved. Not a Naqadian one anyway.

Plastering another fake smile on my face, I tugged off my glove. "Shall we?"

"Only if you are sure," the prince said carefully, the usual rage abating from his gaze. "This isn't something that we can take back."

I pulled the ancient iron circles from a pouch hidden within my skirts. My heart began to race as I felt their power against my skin. I attempted a smile. "It's only a link, right? I'm sure if our arrangement becomes truly intolerable, we can find a mage powerful enough to break it." The words came out a little breathless, less confident than I had intended. But Naqad needed Etrusca's money. I needed a consort. And the Etruscan prince may very well be the last eligible suitor in Palegos that I had not offended. Well, I had offended the prince plenty, but it appeared not to faze him as it had the others.

Caryk grabbed my hand between his and searched my gaze, as if he actually cared. "Truly, Tamariya, do you want this? To be linked to me forever? To feel what I feel?"

I swallowed, unnerved by his sudden intensity. "It is the engagement tradition of the royals. How else do you think any marriage lasts?" It was certainly the only reason my father hadn't killed my mother the moment she had revealed herself to him. Their marriage vows had explicit clauses against murdering the other. Or plotting the other's demise. It was perhaps the only reason I had believed my father when he claimed he had nothing to do with her death.

"The betrothal bond is supposed to encourage our affection as we witness the other's every emotion, so that the marriage vows are only a failsafe," he insisted, a deep sadness echoing in his eyes.

You couldn't break a marriage vow—it was part of the binding magic. It was old magic and yet so simple. If you broke the vows, you died. Some of the more clever rulers had found loopholes in the words, but a well-crafted vow was nearly impossible to circumvent. Today was only the betrothal bond. I had time until our marriage ceremony to find a way to craft our vows and give myself an out from this ridiculous concept of forever.

"I have a feeling our marriage vows will be of the more intricate nature," I said dryly.

He laughed, eyes widening, as if surprised the noise had come from him. For a moment, I allowed myself to smile back.

"On with the betrothal bond, then," he whispered, smile fading. "You first."

I cleared my throat as I held the larger ring between my fingers. My other hand held his, and I hovered the ring over his fourth finger on his left hand. "Prince Caryk Cazaar of Etrusca, do you accept this proposition of marriage and agree to receive the betrothal bond bestowed upon you by this ring?"

He swallowed. "I accept the proposition and open my senses to receive the bond." My hand shook slightly as I slid the ring onto his finger.

"Now you," I whispered. My heart raced as he picked up the remaining circle. Why had I agreed to this? I didn't want to feel this scheming sycophant's every emotion, let alone even be in a room alone with him. He held my left hand gently in his, hovering the ring the same way I had. An image of Marcus' molten gaze flashed before my eyes, searing through my chest. This was only a bonding. Nothing in our betrothal would prevent me from continuing to love Marcus. Naqad needed this union. I could still be happy. My people would finally be able to rebuild. Etrusca was the best nation to ally myself to.

His bright eyes rested steadily on mine. "Your Majesty, Queen Tamariya Amunet of Naqad, do you accept this proposition of marriage and agree to receive the betrothal bond bestowed upon you by this ring?"

No. My hands began to shake. I couldn't stop them. "I accept the proposition and open my senses to receive the bond," I whispered. He slid the ring onto my finger, and we clasped hands, rings touching. I fought back a sob as two amber eyes pierced my soul.

"A promise, a bond, a joining. Let two flames become one." We chanted the ancient words in unison, the same words we had been reciting in our studies since youth. The rings warmed and then burned. I looked down to see our hands engulfed in a flame. I wanted to yank my hand away, to stop the pain, but I couldn't, it was stuck there. As soon as the flame had erupted, it was gone.

A single tear tracked its way down my cheek as I watched my freedom disappear before my eyes.

We relaxed our hands. Bringing mine to my face, I examined the iron circlet, touching it gingerly. It was cold once more. Slowly, I peeled it from my finger, throwing it in the pouch. I felt sick. The prince dropped his ring in too.

"Interesting," he murmured, examining his hand. A pale band now sat where the ring had been. Raising my own hand to my face, I saw a matching mark on my own ring finger. Our eyes met again, a million questions passing between us. I wondered if he was as devastated as I was.

And then I felt it. Searing, white-hot pain erupted along my finger, reaching down to my very core. *Caryk's rage.* I gasped. "Could you cool it?" I hissed.

He cocked his head to the side, and the burn subsided momentarily. Blazing sapphires met my gaze, and the pain returned.

"I get that you hate me but please do your best to control it, you ass!" I had made a mistake. A grave, grave mistake in binding myself to someone who could not stand the sight of me.

He must have felt my ripe anger reflect back at him because he stepped back, eyes wide, grabbing his hand as well. "Back at you," he spat.

"Get. Out." My breathing was labored, and I could barely get the words out.

He hesitated. I drew a knife from a sheath hidden within my gown.

"OUT!" I screeched, brandishing the blade. My core was on fire as his anger only intensified. "Get a fucking grip on yourself, you prick." I flipped the knife, preparing to throw it. Even his pain would be better than this blistering anger.

He opened his mouth as if to say something. That was it. I pulled my elbow back and released the blade. It tumbled end over end, embedding in the wall a fingernail's length away from the prince's ear. Red stained his cheeks, and finally I felt a splash of fear down the bond.

"Next time I won't miss," I growled.

Nodding, he backed up, keeping his eyes on me as he fled the room. The prince must have taken off sprinting because the fierce burn was beginning to ebb, even a small distance helping.

I sagged, as much as this ridiculous corset would allow, and took a deep breath. Something had broken free in this room when I threw my dagger at the prince's head. A chill ran through my spine. I wasn't sure if I should celebrate its release or run for the hills.

SEVEN

I stared at the crown in front of me, watching the light streaming in from the windows play off the facets of glittering amethysts arranged around the base. The crown was beautiful in a kind of menacing way. I raised a finger to trace the jewels set in delicate iron, that snaked around the foundation, following the shape to trace the four deadly spikes protruding from the crown like metal fangs. Cold metal glid under my fingertips, consuming my body heat until my hands were stiff and freezing. If you tilted your head to a certain angle, you could imagine the jewels coming to life as a great serpent. I hated it.

The blood of monsters and innocents alike practically oozed from its dark base. It had originally belonged to the first Viper Queen, Ophidia of Galeston, bestowed upon her by her people after a great victory over the Naqadians. She had defended them fiercely with a magic the world had never seen before: the Gift of Ophidia, the Death Gift. When she died, her gift, along with the crown, passed to her offspring. Thus, the Ophidians were born. With the Viper's magic, the Ophidians rose to become an unstoppable force, pillaging human towns, and stealing their children away for their cultish rituals. Or so the Naqadians claimed.

For centuries, Ophidia's descendants ruled the Ophidians, and consequently the mages, until my ancestors rallied the most powerful mages to their side, decimating the Viper's forces. They slaughtered Ophidia's entire bloodline and stole the crown, hoping to put an end to their might. But the Gift of Ophidia passed on to another mage, a child no older than thirteen, yet to even become a member of the Ophidic Order. No one knew why the child inherited the gift. It was said that Ophidia's spirit sought out the cruelest soul it could find to bestow the gift upon. Considering the child was of Porish nobility, I thought it far more likely that the gift coveted power. And so the Naqadian manhunt began. Blood coated the Serpent's Crown once more.

Countless Vipers and Naqadian rulers were killed as the crown passed between realms, forever a symbol of one realm's victory over the other. It seemed more like a symbol of death to me. The Naqadians refused to believe the Ophidian proverb about cutting off the head of the snake, and the Ophidians would not cease in their quest for vengeance. Every time a Viper was killed, another child was found among the mages bearing the Gift of Ophidia. Each time the Naqadians won, suspicion of the mages only grew.

The tentative peace between our kingdoms was only several decades old—new enough for the crown to feel like a cage upon my brow, threatening to bathe the realm in blood once more. If my mother were here, she would have known what to do. She would have known if this marriage to the Etruscan would truly save Naqad. My parents' marriage was not one without love, but my mother knew what it was to marry in order to save her people.

The grating flow of emotions from the prince had ebbed a little in the hours since the bonding ritual, but his anger still prickled under my skin. No one had prepared me for the intensity of the betrothal bond. Flames lit within my stomach, my own anger rising, followed quickly by a wave of grief. Try hard as he may, Doric was no parental figure. My mother would have prepared me for this. She wouldn't have left me in a room with a man I barely knew to perform a ritual that would forever alter my very being. She would have sat there with me, coaching me through this tidal wave of emotions.

Head hanging in my hands, I gazed upon the crown again. I would need to don it soon if I was to be on time for the council meeting. *Inhale. Exhale. You can do this.*

I reached for the crown, then placed it upon my brow, studying my reflection in the mirror. I still wore the horrendous gown Doric had selected for the bonding ceremony. The long, flowing amethyst dress's floor-length sleeves were embroidered with silver tongues of flame that seemed to lick the ground. I did not mind the sleeves, they were quite elegant, but how I was to command a room in this costume was beyond me. However, this was tradition, and the nobles responded to nothing if not tradition.

I am the Naqadian crest. Instead of filling me with the inspiration I needed, the mantra fell flat. On my athletic frame, the dress was a costume, a vagabond playing at royal. *Making my mother prouder and prouder each day*, I thought dryly.

Slowly, I rose from the dressing table and floated out into the hallway. Aya smirked at me, her slim frame lifting as she stifled a laugh. I frowned. I supposed twirling my way into the court meeting wouldn't exactly give me the authority I was hoping to win back. I straightened my gait a bit, and Aya rolled her eyes.

"Meet me in the training yard after this," I muttered to my second as I breezed into the council chamber.

The men rose when I walked in. I looked each of the five surrounding the table in the eye before saying, "You may sit." The monster within me purred in satisfaction. I shut her up with a mental elbow, even though I was secretly pleased that she had risen for the occasion.

"Congratulations, Your Majesty. I hear the bonding ceremony went well." Doric Venrylst bowed, a smile upon his lips. The other councilmen were nodding enthusiastically, words of encouragement on their lips.

Someone would have heard the prince and I screaming at each other. Word would have reached the gathered lords. Their condolences were nothing but a performance. My lips lifted in the beginning of a snarl. *Not here.* This was the place for polite smiles and pointed questions. Tradition ruled in these chambers—the arched ceilings and gossamer curtains before me that had not changed since my grandfather's rule were evidence. As was the massive council table, with a severed serpent's head engraved in its center. A gruesome interpretation of Naqad's crest. Gaudy, if you asked me.

Instead of growling at Lord Venrylst, I inclined my head. "My late father must have never told you how abhorrent the bonding ceremony truly is. Although I must admit, I am grateful to have gained such a powerful ally." My words oozed as the corners of my mouth tugged upward.

Doric's eyes flashed. "The realm is lucky to have Prince Caryk Cazaar," he agreed through gritted teeth.

I fought a smile. My small victory was short-lived as I remembered why I had truly called this meeting. I placed my hands on the table before me, spreading my fingers wide, showing off the glittering crown jewels upon my fingers.

"On to the matter at hand: Malnova. Who would like to explain to me why we were so poorly informed on the true nature of Gerome Gendran's abuse of power?" I arched a brow, waiting for one of them to break.

"Your Majesty, we were surprised ourselves to hear that Lady Gesibelle now rules Malnova. Do you think it wise for a girl so young to rule such a large territory?" Lord Venrylst mused as he looked down his rather long nose at me. His sneer made it clear what he thought of my escapade to the farming territory. I fought the urge to roll my eyes at the old canker. Doric and I had been bickering since my coronation day. And he usually won.

Not today.

I opened my mouth to redirect my question, but Lord Terrin Speelstling cut in. "Come now, Doric, my spies have reported that Lady Gesibelle is quite well-liked. And she *is* the rightful heir, after all."

I shot Terrin a grateful look, and he winked at me with his kind hazel eyes. He was my favorite of all the councilmen. Well into his fifth decade, he still had a full head of wavy dark hair, touched by wisps of gray that framed his warm olive skin, a striking contrast to Doric Venrylst's receding reddish-blonde hair and cool sandy skin.

"Well-liked or not, the council did not decide to behead the sitting lord in front of all his supporters," General Brom Balenek's rumbling voice cut in. "For what? To save the life of a witch?" He directed his narrowed gaze at me.

I opened my mouth to correct him, but I was cut off again by Lord Speelstling. "Where did you get your information on Malnova, Your Majesty?" He leaned forward in his chair, eyes sparkling.

I leveled my gaze at Terrin. "Why weren't your people in Malnova? We had heard rumblings. Surely it is protocol to look after such matters?" He cast a pointed look around the table. "I am asking my spymaster, Lord Speelstling, not the Master of Coin, nor the general of my armies," I continued, in as even a tone as possible. The second I lost my temper, I would lose this battle. It had already happened far too many times in this very chamber.

He deserves to hear how useless he's been.

Oh, it was tempting. But I was better than this. Well, perhaps not better, but stronger maybe. I waited for the lord to answer.

"We cannot possibly have spies in all the villages, Your Majesty," Terrin answered, waving his hand in dismissal.

"We heard rumblings in *Malnova* of a lord taking the law upon himself. Why didn't your people look into it?" I refused to let it rest.

Terrin Speelstling narrowed his eyes. "They tried," he grit out.

"*Tried?* I imagine you have their heads now." My fingertips clawed at the table, emphasizing my point.

"Malnova was impenetrable, Your Majesty. I do not punish my people for not being able to do the impossible." Terrin pulled his fist back at the last minute so it only tapped lightly upon the table. Several seabirds flew in through the open window and onto the table. One squawked and looked directly at Lord Speelstling.

Victory. The spymaster had lost his composure.

"Terrin, control your birds," Doric snapped.

Terrin unclenched his fist, and the birds flew off. The lord was a Wild mage, capable of speaking to and controlling animals. It was what made him such an excellent spymaster. And what made his lack of knowledge on Malnova all the more suspicious.

I quirked a brow, giving a meaningful nod out the window.

Terrin glared back at me.

My eyes narrowed. Malnova was a farming village, not a fortress. There was something I was missing here, something the spymaster would not say.

"Tamariya, you clearly knew about the attacks and failed to inform the council. Instead, you took matters into your own hands and galloped away in the middle of the night." Doric Venrylst leaned back in his chair, arms crossed. His pale eyes peered into my soul.

"It was too late, and you weren't here," I shot back. "Someone needed to do something. And I saved a life, didn't I?"

"A witch," Brom muttered.

"A Healer." I leveled my icy emeralds at the general.

"Regardless, you were reckless, Tamariya. We hear there was an uprising in the village afterward. Of which *you* were front and center." Doric had not budged from his cross position. "You could have been hurt. You could have *died*."

"They were slaughtering innocents." My voice wavered, on the verge of screaming at these bull-headed councilmen.

Doric sighed. "What did you find out, Tamariya?"

The way he used my given name set my teeth on edge. Flexing my jaw, I replied, "Lord Gendran made it impossible for mages to exist in his territory. He had them under curfew and was killing violators on sight. All the farmers suffered. There wasn't a viable crop within miles of town."

The council chamber itself appeared to pause, even the curtains stilled, as if the wind were taken aback. Even the councilmen were silent for once.

As good an invitation as I would ever get. "And the *uprising* in the village was the late Lord Gendran's supporters, enforcing a curfew set by a dead man." I openly glared at the council now, politics and tradition be damned. These obstinate geezers needed to know the truth. "And those supporters? They bore blades with coiled serpents at the hilt." Spit flew from my mouth at the last words. So much for controlling my temper.

This time, I allowed the silence to stretch. Allowed each man to think before launching into the inevitable power struggle.

Terrin looked hesitantly at the assembled court. "Gentlemen, there is someone who would benefit a great deal from rebellion in our realm." He gave the council a pointed look.

I tried not to roll my eyes. This was why I didn't want to share my findings with the court. Of course they would see a snake and assume the Viper was involved. As if the Ophidians were dumb enough to use such obvious weapons.

"That slithering *bitch*," Doric spat, as predicted. He was shaking his head. "I suppose it was only a matter of time before those serpents started lusting after our kingdom again."

The Viper craved the Serpent's Crown, that was for sure. And she *would* start a rebellion in Naqad; it was exactly what the Ophidians wanted. But the Ophidians weren't behind this, I was sure of it. I gnawed the inside of my lip, tracing a circle with my perfectly manicured amethyst nails over the engravings in the table, wondering how to convince the council.

"No one has seen her since the war. Are we certain that the Ophidians still exist? The attacks on our villages have been few and far between," Lord Henry Lopaegra, Master of Coin, pointed out from behind rounded spectacles.

Attacks that were not the Ophidians' doing to begin with. But I was not about to tell the council that.

"My spies report that they lurk among us, no longer sequestered underground. They plot our destruction under our very noses." Terrin painted a bleak picture.

I pursed my lips, drumming my fingers to hide their twitching.

"If the Viper is hunting mages, we must act quickly." Lord Doric spoke with finality, as if a mere fortnight ago he had not been perfectly content to allow Gerome to embark upon his own personal witch hunt.

My fingers ceased their drumming, clawing into the table once more. The demon within me spit a forked tongue at the lord.

"To Galeston, then," Terrin agreed. "The mages from Malnova will have fled there."

"That's the mage stronghold; the Viper wouldn't dare," Brom protested.

"If she wants to wipe out the mages, that's where she will go. Don't underestimate her power, general. The Viper's power defies nature itself." Doric's voice grew haunted, his eyes glowing orbs as he spoke. Those orbs turned to me, pinning me in my seat.

"Is it wise to assume the Viper's involvement?" I interjected, voice wavering.

"I don't blame you for fearing the Viper, My Queen. But we must face her now or risk her growing stronger." Terrin reached over, as if to pat my hand, but thought better of it. *Good.* I cursed my damn voice for betraying me. Now the council thought I was some scared child, afraid to face the big bad monster.

"When do we leave?" I attempted a neutral tone. If I could not sway them, at least I could oversee their foolishness.

"Tamariya, the council can handle overseeing a protection unit. The place for the queen is here in the palace, ruling. Besides, you have a wedding to plan. Do you really have time to traipse off to the mountains?" Terrin smiled softly.

The fire within me sparked at his words. As if my marriage to that *prince* was my highest priority. I had let my guard down, and now the prince's rage mixed with my own as murderous intent raged in my chest. "You witnessed my effectiveness in the war. What happened in the square should serve as a reminder," I offered. "I am a capable monarch, not an ornament for a throne." The words felt ashy in my mouth, like a child pleading with them to bring me along. The flowing sleeves of my dress threatened to swallow me. I couldn't breathe deeply enough in this fucking corset. *Last time I ever accept a gown from Doric.* Aya's seamstress would never do such shoddy work.

"The rumors of unrest will only grow if you parade across the kingdom after marching into Malnova and beheading its overseer. Lord Kendyr will think he is next," Lord Venrylst said as he arched a brow, looking down his long nose.

I tried to find Brom's eyes, but he wouldn't look at me. Bastard. General Brom Balenek had not only seen me fight, but he *knew* me in the war. He knew what I was. I often wondered why he'd never bothered to tell anyone. But above all, Brom was direct. It matched his sharply cropped hair and pristine weaponry he always wore. I swore the man spent every moment he wasn't training or fighting polishing his swords.

I knew if anyone were to challenge Doric on this, it would have to come from Brom. But he was avoiding my gaze entirely.

I supposed Doric had a point. A monarch's job was to rule, not chase rebels. My face started to redden, and I felt the beginning of tears prick my eyes from the embarrassment and frustration. I was foolish and overzealous, and I had only proven it by rushing into Malnova to handle a situation that I should have left to the guard, or even the royal army.

"It is decided, then. Her Majesty will remain in the capital while we move on with our forces to the other regions," Doric stated. With his words, a ripple echoed across the room; there would be no disagreement. It was a level of influence I had never been able to master, striking me harder than any insult borne from a man's lips could have.

I barely listened as they began discussing the latest trade routes, our tax system, and how we would make up for the missing Malnovan harvest this year. We had plenty of stores, so it was a simple discussion. The councilmen simply liked to hear themselves talk.

They seldom asked for my input, and I was happy to keep out of the discussion. They had been at the helm of the kingdom since before I was born; they did not need help from a twenty-three-year-old child queen.

At last, the men had finished their mundane debate. Doric gave me a glance for courtesy, and I nodded my approval. I cast my gaze to the windows to hide the roll of my eyes.

The meeting was adjourned. The others lingered to chat, but I took my chance to slip out. More often than not, they discussed, in a less than savory manner, their wives and mistresses, and I was too exhausted to plaster a politely interested look on my face while my stomach rolled about, folding in on itself.

Walking toward my quarters to change into my training leathers, I turned the meeting over in my mind. I would never adjust to what it meant to be the queen. To be a figurehead, not a warrior. Not for the first time in my life, I wished that my parents had had more children before my mother died, so that I could be left to do as I pleased. My fists balled up at my sides.

Pausing at one of the many bridges connecting the castle halls, I gazed into the stream trickling below my feet. For a moment, I let myself imagine what it would be like to stumble from my perfectly worn path in the stone and pound my fists against the banister. To rip those breezy curtains from their perches. To dispose of the council and run things the way that I wanted, without this blasted tradition getting in the way.

Brom Balenek had led Naqad's armies since I could remember. Some of his captains knew me from the war, but I wasn't willing to put decades of loyalty to the test by displacing their general. Lord Terrin Speelstling's network of spies rivaled Aya's. Perhaps Aya could replace the old lord, but not without an uproar from the others. And then there was Lord Doric Venrylst. My father had touted Doric's diplomatic abilities so often that I could nearly recite every relative of his and their holdings, not to mention the many cousins he had married off to foreign dignitaries. The lord had the ear of nearly every lord in Naqad, and several in Amyara and Etrusca. Come to think of it, one of his cousins may have married the king of Por. It was a small island, but a nation, nonetheless. No, to displace Doric would cause not only an uproar at home but also one across the continent.

Doric Venrylst was not all bad. He was a complete ass, but he had advised me on which courtiers' influence mattered most, which lords to avoid when the alcohol started flowing, and explained some of the more dubious lords' political leanings. If he felt a monarch's place was on the throne, who was I to disagree?

I would stick with my father's council. They were cantankerous, curmudgeonly old men, but they would be the rope that tethered me to my reign. I supposed I could kill them all in one go and be done with it, but that would spark a war I would never be ready for.

EIGHT

Three Years Ago: The War on Hel

"She's lucky she's the king's daughter."

A deep voice chuckled. "Perhaps we're the lucky ones."

If it were possible to growl in one's sleep, I would have. Something about that voice set my teeth on edge.

My mind lost its grip, and I drifted into obscurity again.

When I awoke for good, the smell was the first thing I noticed. The putrid stink of burning flesh jolted my mind back to the surface. Screams were next, followed by hushed soothing tones. Then I felt the brush of scratchy fabric around my legs. Slowly, my eyes batted open.

I lay on a bed, tucked into the corner of a vast tent. There was more space around my bed than the others—their best attempt at privacy for a wounded royal in the infirmary. The other beds laid in scattered rows, most of them filled by moaning soldiers. I recognized a few near me as nobles I had grown up with.

If I were a better person, I would have cared about their various conditions more.

Instead, I pulled my elbows underneath me and pushed myself up.

Blood rushed to my head, and I swayed. Small, yet sure, hands caught me, and I looked up relieved to find the dark, velvety eyes of my second.

Aya smiled. "Glad to have you back." She helped me right myself, and once she was confident that I wasn't going to fall over again, she released me.

"They worked on you for ages, you know," a blonde figure chastised from the shadows.

"I've been awake for moments and you're already criticizing me. Gods, can't you leave it alone, Calliope?" I sighed, running a hand through my gnarled hair. "What would you have me do, not fight?"

Her stormy gaze crinkled. "You were reckless."

I would not stand for this, especially not moments after waking up from nearly dying. My previously annoyed expression turned flat. I met her turbulent eyes with empty ones.

"I will remind you who you are speaking to, soldier." I spoke slowly. "I do not need to justify my actions to you, nor anyone for that matter. I suggest you use more discretion when expressing your tedious opinions on morality, lest you lose the ability to do so." My words dripped with poison, a guarantee.

Cut out her tongue now; make an example.

No, now was not the time. Nor the tent. But Calliope needed to learn her place. We were not innocent ladies, and she was no damsel. She was a warrior for the gods' sake. I'd had enough of her pretending that we were something we were not.

Aya had not moved since I'd chastised her partner. She was frozen, a torrent of fury followed by calm understanding flickering back and forth across her expression. Even Aya knew that I was right. I prayed she would talk to Calliope later; the last thing I needed was for the blonde warrior to force my hand.

Calliope had never liked what I was, what any of us were, and her relentless morals were growing tiresome. We were trained killers, and we acted like it. Except for when my father was around. He knew what his daughter had become the day his wife died, but we had never once discussed it.

And there he was, making his way slowly through the infirmary tent, grimly addressing each of his wounded subjects as if he cared deeply for their sacrifice. I wasn't sure if he had felt a real emotion in the seven years since my mother passed.

I certainly hadn't seen even a glimmer of remorse when he watched them snatch me up for "training." He had to have known what they would do to me. What I would become. And when I did return to Naqad three full years later, he had barely said a word to me. The four years after that were spent in near silence.

Until the war. Until he needed something from me. Until he could no longer deny what I was.

Now he approached me slowly, as if I were a wounded animal. He wore my face, with his high cheekbones, slightly sunken eyes, and strong nose. Even his auburn hair fell in waves around his face, much like mine. The resemblance twisted something in my gut, enough that I avoided looking at him for too long.

It felt wrong that I would look so much like this stranger, and yet my only token of Helvettica Amunet, the late queen, were my glowing emerald eyes. They were striking enough to unnerve most people, and that was precisely how I preferred it. Each time someone shied away from meeting my gaze, I felt a warm pang, a reminder that I had the same effect on people as she once had.

My father came to a stop just beyond the circle of my cabal. "You seem to be well enough," Alaric Amunet commented carefully.

I clutched the bedsheets between my knuckles, suppressing a growl. "I am well enough."

"Nothing fatal, then." He shifted from heel to heel. It almost made me smile. No one made the king nervous. No one but his impossibly dangerous daughter.

Good. I could bring his realm crumbling to the earth if I wished to. My father was no fool.

"Nothing fatal," I repeated. He was here for a reason. I cocked my head slightly, inviting him to get on with it. Would he be delivering another ineffective scolding? Or did he need something?

Judging by the way he was shifting, I guessed he needed something. He was free with his criticism and always quick to let me know when he disagreed with my *lifestyle*. It was one of the few times we ever truly spoke openly. Well, he spoke openly.

He was hesitating still. I took a gamble. "What do you want?" I asked flatly.

His brow bunched, and he stopped his rocking. "To check if my daughter and the heir to this nation is alive," he spat, fire beginning to brew in his eyes. A part of me hated that fire. Hated that he could fell an entire forest with his gift while I could barely light a candle.

I chuckled. "Ah yes, the great line of succession. What a loss it would be for Naqad if I were to expire before I could rule."

His fingers flexed at his sides, sparks flying between them.

My eyes lit with mirth. *Let him come for me with his fire gift.* "What did you really come for, Father?"

He stared at me for a moment longer, brown eyes nearly petulant. He cleared his throat.

Is my father, the great king, nervous?

"Our fearless princess lives." A booming voice spoke from behind my father. Brom Balenek materialized in the infirmary, having crept up on us despite his massive size.

I could practically hear the king's jaw clamp shut as the fire in his eyes dimmed.

Catlike, I cocked my head to the side. Whatever the king had to say, he did not want to say in front of his war general. A slow smile spread across my face.

This is going to be fun.

My smile turned genuine when I turned to the general. "I'm told it is no small feat, but live on I shall."

He winked. "We must be sure to thank the Healers responsible."

The king's jaw had not opened. In fact, it was clamped tighter than before, his face nearly purple. I supposed my familiarity with the commander of his armies should unnerve him.

This was a gift indeed, to awaken in the infirmary.

"We are all pleased to see that the princess has lived, despite her recklessness." The king's words oozed from his lips, all traces of purple gone from his face.

I smirked, amused at his attempt to scold me in front of the general. "We can't all hide behind lavish command tents. Your soldiers need to see *someone* fighting."

The king's expression soured. He cast a quick glance at Brom. "I need to speak to the Viper," he said warily.

I snorted. *That's the best he has?*

Aya's eyes flashed. Even Calliope narrowed her eyes.

"That's not an option." The amusement left my face as I sobered.

"Everything is an option—this is war." He crossed his arms, gaze holding mine steadily.

I sighed. "Your request is tiresome. The Viper Queen does not wish to meet with the King of Naqad. She deals only with me. Name your grievance, and I shall pass it on." It was almost too easy, this game of ours.

I dared him to dismiss the general so he could speak plainly or attempt to scold me again. Crossing words with my father brought a light to my eyes that few other things could. There were so few people left who would spar with me in such a way. This game was all we had.

"Very well," he conceded. "Will you deliver a message?"

I nodded, intrigued.

He pursed his lips. "Tell the Viper that she's needed on the front lines. Her people fight without heart; it is clear they have no leader here."

"Seems hypocritical." I nodded to the bloodied sword coated in the black gore of the helmai at Brom's side, then raised an eyebrow at the pristine blade sheathed at my father's waist.

"At least I am here." His mouth quirked to the side, as if amused by the accusation. His arched brow mirrored mine.

My brows drew together. "You know why the Viper is not here: to reveal herself to you would mean her death. The moment this war ends, and she and her Ophidians have ceased to be useful to you, the Naqadians will come for her, just as they always have."

What kind of game is he playing? My father knew all this. Why come here just to ask for something he knew he could not have?

My gaze fell to Brom. Perhaps the general's presence was not as accidental as my father wanted me to believe.

"But you will ask her, yes? Unless you are implying that you speak on her behalf?" the king probed.

My eyes were practically slits. "No," I said slowly. "But understand, you send an emissary to ask her the impossible. She will laugh in my face."

His eyes twinkled. "I doubt that. She understands the impact that one more big push could have in this war. Tell her, General Balenek."

Brom's eyes shifted from the king to me uneasily. His gaze met mine, and his cheeks lifted, almost imperceptibly, in an apology. As if to say *I speak the truth—do not confuse me for a pawn in this game of yours.*

Fair enough, Brom. Fair enough.

"After you went down, we managed to push back the mutated helmai. One more strong push and we may have this war won. Their numbers are waning. Whoever summoned them cannot summon more. I think that's what these mutations are, an attempt to kill our spirits while their ranks dwindle," Brom said.

I exchanged a look with Aya. We could do one more push.

"And do you think the Viper will imbue vigor in our troops?" My brows were high.

"I agree with the king, Princess."

I grit my teeth. Of course he did.

"Perhaps it is worth a visit to the queen." Aya placed a hand on my arm.

I met her gaze. A million thoughts glimmered in her obsidian eyes.

"Perhaps," I acquiesced.

The king nodded, satisfied. He turned to leave.

I held up a hand. "But..."

The king paused. He sighed. "Out with it, then."

"You, too, must consider the proposal."

He scoffed. "What could you possibly mean?"

"Consider fighting with your armies. Your life for her identity. Seems fair to me."

His eyes narrowed.

My own emeralds stared back into the face that so closely resembled my own.

"Very well," he conceded. "I shall take it under advisement."

I nodded. That was the most I could hope for from him.

The king left, Brom closely behind.

Calliope released a breath when they left. Even Aya's shoulders eased a fraction. The two women turned to me.

I sighed. "I suppose we're due for a visit to the Pit."

NINE

PRESENT

"You can't be serious; you let them talk you out of going?" Aya crossed her arms, obsidian eyes gleaming with held back profanities. She frowned at me from the patch of dirt separating the grass from the training ring. Our training match was my first reprieve from duty since I had returned from Malnova, and thus our first chance to truly debrief. She began her stretches as I recounted my rush to save Katzima, her posture growing ever stiffer as I finished telling her about the council meeting.

"I'm a queen, not a foot soldier." I shrugged, trying not to let my frustration show as I ran a whetstone against my blade.

"You *lead* this nation." Deep frown lines appeared on my second's forehead. Her sharp jaw flexed against angular cheekbones.

"Sometimes leading is to show the people that all is well and their queen is not concerned with rumors of rebellion," I pointed out.

Aya arched a thin brow. "That's not the Tamariya Amunet I know. Fuck what the council thinks you should do, rule as *you* believe a queen should." She was openly glaring at me now, running her tongue along her teeth as she considered. Aya never failed to see directly through me. She could taste the falsehoods in my words as if I had etched them in the dirt before us. But I agreed with the council's decision.

"We've been over this," I said uneasily. "Things don't work the same way here. The council's opinion matters, for too many reasons to count." I turned my face upward to the sun beginning its descent, letting its rays seep into my skin as the crisp breeze cleared my mind.

Leaning back on my stool, I opened my eyes and looked around the training yard. It was empty, as was typical in the evenings. The rest of the guard would be busy managing the evening shift changes. Aya's prowess with a blade wasn't exactly a secret at court, but I preferred not to advertise either of our skill sets. Most of the castle believed she was a skilled maid I had befriended during the war. Rumors swirled that she was a personal guardian of sorts. I allowed them to flourish. A guard was harmless compared to a spymaster, especially one not sanctioned by the council.

"Perhaps their opinions matter too much," she pressed, head tilted to the side.

I sighed. "I know what you're going to say. It's not possible. We have a Protector at court." I struck the whetstone again, harder.

"You don't know that." Aya's eyes narrowed like an annoyed feline. It would have been fitting if the woman's shape-shifting abilities extended to animal forms. "It's unnerving the way you bend to them at council."

I frowned, considering. But I *agreed* with the council. "Their logic makes sense. Listening to reason does not mean that someone is clouding my mind," I insisted. Besides, I checked the study every morning to ensure that the Protector's candle had been replaced. Only my father and I had ever known the secret code we used to ensure the mage who protected us from magic of the mind was present at court.

Volcanic rock turned in her eyes as she studied my reaction. "I haven't heard a whisper of the Protector," she grumbled.

I wasn't surprised that my second had her suspicions. "And you're not supposed to. The entire point of a Protector is for them to remain hidden. It means they're doing their job well." Dealing in secrets for most of your life tended to leave one rather paranoid. Aya had witnessed espionage in nearly every corner of the realm. Her ability to change her appearance allowed her to blend in at nearly any court.

"Then, ignore the council and do as you please. You're the queen," Aya challenged, shifting the conversation. She raised her blade to begin her warmup exercises, slicing and cutting her imaginary enemy.

"Who says this isn't what I want?" I shot back my customary answer to the old question. I stood, sword sharp at last, and picked up a training blade like the one Aya wielded. "Ready?" My brow arched my own challenge.

She scowled at me but nodded. We moved to the center of a ring sketched into the dirt but stopped when we saw a familiar blonde head ending in a thick braid sauntering up to us.

"Room for another?" Calliope asked.

Aya grinned. It was rare that Calliope was able to break away from her duties as Captain of the Guard to join us for training. When she wasn't patrolling or managing her soldiers, she was praying to her sun god, Solna. The guard had forsaken nearly all the Drazurcan ways by the time I met her, trading her fur-lined tunics and battle axes for smooth Naqadian leathers and a heavy broadsword. Her singular braid, worn in the Drazurcan custom, and her worship of the deity were the only ties Calliope allowed herself to her old life. Not that I knew much of her old life—I had not bothered to ask, and she had not bothered to tell me. We preferred it that way.

"Can you please tell Tamariya she's being ridiculous letting the council tell her that she can't go with them to investigate this rebellion?" Aya demanded.

I launched my attack, uninterested in this fruitless debate.

"What's their reasoning?" Calliope asked cautiously. Despite their relationship, she was relatively fair when Aya and I squabbled, albeit endlessly moral. I supposed I owed her some begrudging respect. My blade arched through the air, poised to strike Aya's gut.

"Some bullshit safety concern, inciting panic, blah, blah." Aya breathed out with a quick exhale as she parried my blow and returned one of her own. "Bottom line is, they can't tell their queen what to do."

Calliope considered as she swung her blade at me too, darting in right as Aya retreated, keeping me on my guard. "Safety is a bit far-fetched; I'll give you that," she said between gritted teeth as I caught her sword and forced her back.

"Perhaps the point of being queen is trusting your advisors to carry out your wishes," I suggested as I got them both on the defensive, drawing my second sword.

"I know queens who have ruled without any council," Aya spat as she pounced once again.

I sidestepped and swung. "I cannot be *her*," I barked.

Calliope lunged toward me, forcing me to break from my standoff with Aya. She was on the attack now, and I had no choice but to match her blow for blow. "It would send a message across the realm." She exhaled, whirling her sword in a wide arch.

I parried her thrust and swung back on the offensive, dodging blows from both women. "So you think I'm a loose cannon too?" I challenged. Something about Calliope agreeing with the council reawakened my desire to sniff out this rebellion myself.

Calliope laughed and stepped back. "I've always known you were a loose cannon, but it's not the people who will panic if you turn your attention to the rebels." She shot a glance at Aya in between swings.

Aya launched at me again. "That's a good point," she said, in sync with Calliope. "An official visit from the queen could legitimize the rebellious lords or tip off their financier."

I stepped back. "Neither of you think I should go?" I swore, they were insufferable.

Aya stopped her assault and smiled, eyes twinkling. "I said an *official* visit."

I smiled slowly. I should have known my second would never advocate for a hands-off approach to ruling. Being in hiding would give us a better vantage point to see what was truly happening. Not that we were going.

Calliope frowned at both of us. "Need I point out the inherent danger of three women traveling solo through Naqad?"

I rolled my eyes, thrusting both blades inward to prove my point. "Are you actually implying that the captain of the Royal Guard cannot protect her mage queen and assassin handmaiden?"

"Now you're a mage?" Calliope parried my thrust easily. She snorted. "When was the last time you touched that precious gift of yours?"

I growled, abandoning Aya's attack to force the captain on the defensive. Sparks flew on the dull blades. I wasn't sure if they were entirely natural.

The captain had the nerve to laugh.

I grit my teeth.

"And how much energy did it take to summon that spark, *your majesty*?" she goaded.

I launched myself at her.

Aya stepped between us, attempting to head off my assault. The problem was that Calliope was right: my fire magic was mere sparks, the true power lurking beneath untouchable. Aya landed a blow to my arm. I swore, barely feeling the dull throb the training sword left behind. I had allowed myself to get distracted. I had to prove Calliope wrong. I was no easy target.

Calliope smirked. I had fallen for her bait. *Impatient as ever.* I breathed heavily.

"Not saying we're going, but what would you tell the rest of the guard?" I asked Calliope, pretending that I hadn't just lost my temper.

I dashed back in and sliced at them both. They met my blow just in time, in unison and with enough strength that I was forced to take several steps back to avoid colliding with the ground.

Calliope took advantage of my retreat, striking relentlessly. "I'll send half of them to guard the traveling council"—she paused as I caught her blade and flung it out of her hand with my sword— "and the other half will remain here, guarding a decoy. I'll tell them I went with the council, at your behest. Gods, I hate that trick," she grumbled as she caught her breath and went to pick up her sword.

"It wouldn't be the same child you used last time, would it, Aya?" I came at her with both my blades, ready to finish the job.

She read my overzealous posture and sidestepped me, catching me at the wrong angle, sending one of my swords spinning. She smiled. "What? You didn't enjoy Annabeth's inflated sense of self-importance for months after as much as I did?" She struck, quick as an asp, and I could barely swing my blade around in time to catch her. She was the quickest of the three of us, and Calliope was the strongest.

I stumbled back, letting go of my blade, just briefly enough so that Aya relaxed, thinking she had won. Springing forward, I caught my blade and pinned Aya, sword nestled across her throat. I was the best performer.

She glared at me but dropped her sword. "I yield. You win," she grumbled.

I laughed as I climbed off her. "Maybe one of these days you two will finally best me."

"Speaking of an overinflated sense of self-importance..." Aya rolled her eyes. "But Annabeth will be ready this time. She's been working on her swordsmanship and may even be able to pass as you if you get attacked on the road."

It had taken my second nearly a year to find a Shifter she could trust. Annabeth, like Aya, could alter her features as she pleased. It had been an agonizing year, truly trapped within my airy prison. Since then, we had only used her for short forays into the city and the neighboring villages. A trip to Galeston would be entirely too long to leave a decoy at the helm of my kingdom.

"It's too long." I shook my head. "It will never work."

"The council will be away, and no one close to the queen will remain in Egryt," Aya insisted.

Calliope crossed her arms. "The council leaves tomorrow morning; the guard has already been alerted. Think on it, Tamariya."

I supposed I could take the evening to mull over their plan.

"Fine. I will consider it." I gave them a grim smile.

That smile faded as I realized what awaited me this evening. "And I am off to dinner with the prince. I suppose I should bathe." I looked down at my leathers, drenched in sweat after our sparring session.

Aya snorted. "As enthusiastic about your betrothal as expected."

I rolled my eyes at her as I linked our arms, strolling back to my quarters, leaving Calliope to return to her guards.

I turned to my second as we walked. "The prince may pose a threat to our plans."

She cast a sidelong glance my way. "Men like that rarely pay much attention to women. He's met you twice; I doubt he would spot Annabeth. When I lived in Etrusca, I met his father, King Dahlm. He rules his kingdom with an iron fist; I imagine his son is every bit as arrogant as he."

TEN

Back in my chambers, I sat in the tub, surrounded by delicate jasmine, and stared at the ceiling. My stomach turned as my mind replayed images of the Malnovan villagers that I hadn't been able to save, laid out on the square, some screaming, some already bled out. In the moment, I had relished the shock on the soldiers' faces when they realized I was formidable, but now, I only felt disgust. I flinched as I recalled knives twisting into stomachs and then felt my own blade slicing clean through flesh. The sweet floral scent turned bitter, and I had to grab my stomach to prevent its contents from ending up in the tub with me. I took deep breaths and counted, steadying my breathing.

The last thing I needed was to relive this cursed ritual. The prince was waiting for me, and I could only pray that he wouldn't ask questions about the nausea he felt from me. With any luck, he would chalk it up to nerves. This newfound conscience of mine insisted on making my body revolt after each bloodshed. It would never get easier, taking a life, no matter how many I killed, or how guilty they were. It was pathetic.

I held my head in my hands and forced myself to stay in the bathtub, breathing. I would give anything to be *her* again. Of course, I could never admit it to anyone, but I missed her.

Someone knocked on the bathroom door, then Aya's voice called out to me. "Ry? Are you almost finished?"

I sighed. "Yeah, give me a minute." I hauled myself out of the tub along with a wave of red water. I shook my head. No, the water was clear. My mind was especially cruel this evening.

When I opened the door, Aya was clearly trying to hide her concern, her eyes looking anywhere but at me as she turned from the wardrobe, thumbing through potential outfits.

"I sent the other ladies out before Doric could send them another order to put you in an absurd dress." Aya clucked, shaking her head.

My eyebrows rose. "It's traditional Naqadian court attire."

"Those gowns are horrendous, and we both know it." Aya turned back to the wardrobe, pulling out a shimmering piece. "Now, how about this? These flowing sleeves are all the rage in Amyara, and the lining is made of Cordaenan silk."

I studied the gown she held out. Aya knew the fashions of Palegos well, especially Amyara, where she had lived at court for several years. In her three decades of life, my second had lived what seemed like a dozen different lives. If she were not such a gifted sleuth, she would be the most sought-after designer in the realm. The emerald silk was a departure from the usual amethyst they placed me in. As if the entirety of the gown was not different from what I normally wore at court. But the fabric corset barely had any boning, and the sheer sleeves were truly gorgeous. Finally, a gown I could breathe in. The longer I stared at the garment the more I itched to try it on.

"This is a private dinner with your betrothed, not an appearance at court. I think it's best to appear as yourself, don't you?" Aya placed the gown on the bed and began undoing its buttons and ties.

I grinned. My second was right, as always. She helped me into the gown, then stood next to me holding a massive diamond necklace—one of the crown jewels. A delighted gasp tumbled from my mouth.

"Comfort doesn't have to mean without glamour." Her eyes were glittering obsidians as the stunning piece settled between my cleavage. She smiled at me in the mirror.

Once she was satisfied with my appearance, she turned to the mirror herself. Pursing her full lips, she watched as her short bob receded into her head, until her jet-black hair was cropped closely around her ears. On anyone else, it might have made her seem boyish, but the short hair combined with her sharp cheekbones gave my second a beautiful fierceness.

My gut twisted as I watched her work her magic with such ease. She was perfecting the look, adding some hair back in places and taking more away in others. The hollow within me seemed to grow.

If only I had been able to talk to Katzima in Malnova. Despite my protests at the council meeting, Katzima was a true witch, a mage with a natural healing gift who had studied and shaped her magic to perform spells and enchantments that had nothing to do with healing. If anyone could figure out where my magic went, it was her. I would have seen the witch sooner, but Galeston was several days' ride from Egryt and disappearing from the palace had been an impossibility. I ran my hands against the smooth silk of my dress. It wasn't an impossibility anymore. Aya and Calliope had a plan. The council would be gone.

I shook the thought from my head. A queen's place was ruling her kingdom, not investigating dissent.

But *Cieri*, I missed my magic.

"I heard about a beautiful stranger visiting a Malnovan pub and making quite the scene," Aya said as she clipped her earrings into her lobes.

I whirled around. "You did not."

"No one recognized you, but I gathered enough to know who it was. You need to be careful," she warned.

I winced. "He had information I needed."

"Was he hiding it under his tongue?" she challenged.

"I've been known to do worse," I retorted.

Her eyes widened a fraction at the return of my old fire. She smiled. "Fair enough. As long as *Marcus* knows his place, we shouldn't have an issue." She narrowed her dark eyes. "He does know his place, doesn't he?"

I didn't answer. That was a good question. Did I even know Marcus' place in my life? The thought of him sent a burst of warmth through my chest. A warmth that I prayed never left me. My hand pressed into my temple. Marcus had sent word to me after the ball. Of course he would know about the betrothal, but I had no way of knowing how he had taken the news.

As I tried to figure out how to arrange my face, we stepped into the hall. A cool breeze trickled in through the open windows, chilling me from my daydream.

I settled on an amused smirk as we walked down the hall. It was a far cry from the serene smile I usually had plastered on my face. About damn time. *Act like a lady; you're dining with your betrothed.* The voice could fuck right off.

"You look like you're in pain," Aya offered.

"Well, how should I look?" I snapped.

"Like a queen who just saved her people from another slaughter."

"That feels like a lifetime ago." I set my mouth into a grim line. In truth, I had only been home for a day.

We rounded a corner and entered my private dining room, a room equally as ornate as the rest of the Egrecian palace. A marble table was placed in the center, set with fine cutlery. Arching windows overlooked the bay, and the crashing of the palace waterfall was a calming backdrop. Usually, the room filled me with a serenity I could find few other places in the castle. But I had been forced to invite this hulking statue of a man inside.

He rose as I entered, to his credit. He was several inches taller than me, no easy feat, and his broad shoulders made me feel small, a sensation I hated more than anything. It worked to my advantage when I was masquerading as a lady at court, but around the prince, I fought a snarl. His piercing blue eyes were, unfortunately, directed right at me.

The pale scar on my left ring finger throbbed, his anger rising in my presence. My jaw worked in annoyance.

"My love." He bowed, barely. *Love.* I balked at the word. What I had with Marcus was love. This, this was a betrothal by fire. Silver clunked on his fingers as he extended his hand to grasp my gloved one. His lips brushed my hand, stubble pricking my skin through the silk, his eyes pinning me in place.

I gave him a placating smile. "Prince." I inclined my head, refusing to be the first to look away. The voice remained silent. It was a welcome reprieve, a sentiment I doubted he would echo.

He led me to a seat at the head of the table and slid the chair out for me like a gentleman would. I sat, laughing to myself. As if anything about our relationship were courtly. He took his seat opposite mine, a mockery of equals. I placed my palms on the table, willing my jaw to loosen.

"Out with it," I snapped. So much for composure.

"I beg your pardon, love?" The prince had the gall to look confused. Even as his eyes burned and my hand was still ablaze; I would not play this prince's game.

I ripped my glove from my hand and thrust my finger into the air so he could see the pale scar. "I'd like to know what I've done to earn such ardent hatred from one who wishes for my hand in matrimony." I kept my finger high, like a madwoman. But I was mad. His emotions down the bond today had driven me to the brink.

His expression did not change, but the anger burning a hole through my finger marginally receded, as if the prince had pinched the hollow cord that tied us together.

"I can at least control some of what I cast down the bond," I retorted. "You, on the other hand, have clearly never felt a lick of magic in your life."

The burn on my finger spiked. The Prince of Etrusca was not a mage. Even someone with a weak gift would be able to control the bond to some degree. At least I had one less thing to worry about from him.

I grinned. "We are going to have such fun, aren't we?"

"Careful." A growl.

My answering smile was positively savage. I allowed my amusement to trickle down the bond. "I've seen things that would curl your toes, Prince."

Another burning spike. "I fear it is you, *My Queen*, who does not know nearly as much of the world as you boast." His knuckles were white as they clutched his fork.

Eyes flashing, I glanced to where Aya waited beside the door. Her eyebrows raised almost imperceptibly. The prince hadn't a clue who he was talking to. And he could never find out.

"Are you going to learn to control that bond or not?" I demanded.

"Would Your Majesty like to teach me?" He speared a square of meat as if it were an enemy on the battlefield.

Teach him? Like we were some kind of friends? Absolutely not. "I will send a magic tutor for you tomorrow," I clipped.

"How gracious." *Bastard.* I didn't owe him a moment of my time more than I deemed necessary.

I turned to my plate, not feeling the necessity to continue engaging with this brute. The scent of fresh herbs wafted to my nose, making my mouth water. Warm butter exploded against my tastebuds as I brought the flaky fish to my mouth, olives and tomatoes popping on my tongue, the perfect complement. The kitchens had really outdone themselves. I savored the flavors, determined to enjoy my meal in peace. The sauce was new, some spice I didn't recognize. Likely fresh off a ship from Amyara, the palace chef's favorite region for herbs and spices.

"It's a pity you rushed home from Malnova—you could have saved us both the lifetime of misery and ignored my suit." The prince peered up at me from his vegetables, and the fire in my finger replaced my cool curiosity.

I took a drink of my wine. "My business there was finished." I stared at him, waiting for him to ask his question. I had a feeling it had more to do with why he was in Egryt than he was letting on.

"The council sent their queen to kill Gerome Gendran." It wasn't even a question. *An accusation?* A breeze trickled in from the window, raising the hairs on the nape of my neck. There was something eerie about the way the prince's anger had abated.

"Does your highness doubt his queen's abilities?" I arched a brow.

"Simply the necessity for them. Isn't a queen's job to rule?" He sounded just like Doric. I was starting to understand why my advisor favored this prince so much. The remaining fish before me was suddenly much less appealing.

"Gerome Gendran was a murderous tyrant whose corruption could be quelled by the hand of the queen and the queen alone. The people must know the crown stands behind them." I met his stare, daring him to call me on my bluff. Of course, the court would put out a similar story, so it was hardly a lie.

"There are many at court who would argue that the mages are not people at all." He said it matter-of-factly, as if he were commenting on the sea breeze. My nostrils flared as I tried to get my breathing under control, resisting the urge to pull my lips back in a snarl.

A soft pitter-patter sounded behind me, and my shoulders loosened. *Rain, at last.* I closed my eyes for a moment, allowing the soothing sound of the storm to wash over me, breathing in the fresh scent of the rain.

"Those courtiers seem to have forgotten who won us the war," I countered carefully, raising my fork to my mouth, the effects of the rain settling into me.

"Quite the contrary. They remember exactly what the mages did in the war. My father especially." His eyes glittered.

I chewed carefully, considering the thinly veiled threat. "Perhaps his memory is not so fresh." I pointed my fork at him, eyebrow quirked.

"And what exactly would you show him?" he purred. He angled his head, and the candlelight played off the straight line of his stubble, sending his cheeks into sharp contrast. It gave him a haunting look that had every bone in my body screaming to run. But I was not a person who ran. Not from the Etruscan prince. Caryk was up to something. And I intended to find out precisely what it was.

I kept my face neutral as I answered his question. "That the might of the mages is not to be trifled with." I shrugged, willing my hammering heart to slow.

"And if there are no mages left in Naqad? I imagine that would make your nation rather exposed." I froze. I couldn't have heard him right. Was the prince admitting to masterminding the entire mage hunt? Was he traveling to Galeston next as we suspected? I could not accuse my betrothed publicly without proof, but I could head him off in the mountains.

"Then, let's pray to Cieri that the day never comes." I took a long sip of wine. "After all, the Naqadians are soon to be *our* people."

His eyes glittered. "As they will. And we shall be their protectors." His lips quivered as a flutter of amusement danced along my finger.

The prince was playing at something, that much was clear. At least I could use the marriage vow to protect Naqad from Caryk and his father. If the mages survived that long. I tapped my slippered feet against the cool marble floor.

"There is another matter I wished to discuss with you this evening." The prince sat up straight, the smirk erased from his face.

"Go on, Prince." I drew each word out, a silent dare lurking beneath them.

"Your *companion*." Lightning flashed across the sky, lighting up the room for a bleak moment, followed by a rumble of thunder.

I arched a brow. The prince was not about to bring Marcus into this. "You said yourself this would be a loveless union.""You were careless in Malnova."

"You could not possibly know about that." I drummed my fingers against the table.

"And yet, I do." His fist slammed against the table, a twisting heat splashing across my finger. Was the prince jealous? That would not do.

I pushed up from the table. "Let's get one thing clear, *Prince*: I shall do whatever with whomever I please. Your opinion is not of my concern, merely the gold you promised my council upon our arrangement." Fire coursed through my veins. I did not care if the Etruscan felt it. Let him feel how serious about this I was.

He stood, mirroring my posture. "You *will* be discrete."

I prowled around the table, taking my time, allowing his words to echo through the small dining chamber as rain pounded against the castle. I stopped before him, chest heaving. "You"—I paused— "shall not give orders to your queen." I enunciated each word, allowing the threat to linger upon every syllable. A snarl twitched on my upper lip. The sky cracked open once again, lighting up the room, driving my point home with a fierce rumble.

He glowered, teeth grinding together, anger boiling against my finger. I pushed back with my own fire. It was answered by a flash of lightning across his eyes.

I did not need a standoff with this prince to demonstrate my power. Some dormant part of me lifted a sleepy eye. There was precisely one person whose company and I craved, and every moment I wasted in the Etruscan's presence was one I could not spend with Marcus.

"This conversation is done. I shall bid you good evening." It was barely polite, but after those accusations, what did I care? My half-eaten dinner lingered on the other side of the table. My stomach rumbled in protest, but if I stayed in this room a moment longer, I would drive a dinner knife through the prince's chest. It would be far too bloody an affair.

Instead, I allowed myself to fantasize about how my dagger would feel sliding across his corded muscles. A brick loosened in my resolve. The pattering of rain was fading, the fearsome storm gone as quickly as it had arrived.

"Of course, My Queen." He nodded and offered his arm to escort me back to my rooms.

I tried not to flinch. But I had been rude enough this evening. To decline now would only result in a bigger mess to clean up tomorrow. He felt like a hot coal beneath my hand.

This close, I could smell him. He oozed privilege, fresh and untarnished, the way all these high lords wanted you to think they were. I knew enough about humanity to know that no one's soul was as clean as they wanted you to think. Caryk Cazaar was no exception.

"It truly is horrible that no one knew Gerome feared magic with such vigor until so many atrocities were already committed," I commented, monitoring his reaction carefully. I must be possessed. But my blood trilled, anticipating his response. I was not done crossing the prince.

"Truly curious," he mused, giving away nothing. My anger flared. He smirked.

Shit. I was projecting down the bond. *Who's the novice now?*

"Perhaps he had someone covering up for him, making sure information wasn't getting out." I made a mockery of feigning innocence. There was no point in masking my anger—I had lost all control of the bond.

"Maybe," he said casually, "your *people* aren't as loyal to you as you think."

The fire within me quenched at the absurdity of his accusation. I almost laughed. He didn't know my network of spies at all if he thought that I could ever believe that. My spies were the only people in this court I trusted without question. Marcus would not betray me for all the riches in the world, and Aya's loyalty was blood-sworn.

"Perhaps the traitor is closer to the crown than we think," I crooned, my tongue flicking over my teeth. Letting the prince know I was on to him was surely courting disaster, but I longed to wipe that smirk from his lips.

"Closer indeed," he murmured, unperturbed.

I was spared from crafting a response as we had reached my door.

"Goodnight, Prince." Would he be so calm if he were plotting the demise of my realm? Perhaps.

He smiled, blasé as ever. "Sweet dreams, My Queen." He bowed and turned to leave.

I quickly entered the room and closed the door before he could change his mind and take our battle of wits further.

"That was... intense," Aya commented.

I unclipped the crown jewels and handed them to her. "He's insufferable. I swear he offered his hand in marriage just to piss me off."

She shrugged. "Do you think he's hiding something?" Her eyes searched mine for an answer that wasn't there. I often wondered if there was anyone that Aya ever trusted fully, even me.

"I'm nearly sure of it," I admitted. "I assume Calliope told you about the blades the soldiers from the square wore?"

She nodded. "Serpentine hilts. Fine make."

"Do you think Gerome Gendran procured those himself? His castle was in near ruin."

Aya considered it. "It may explain Etrusca's involvement. Perhaps they mean to take over the continent by wealth alone."

Coin had toppled regimes far richer than mine. If Caryk were truly involved in this, our betrothal could not continue. I supposed we could rush a wedding to stop him with the marriage vows, but did I really want to live out my life married to that prick? Ending a betrothal once the bond was set was nearly unheard of. I was courting a war with Etrusca no matter how I looked at it.

"We need to go to Galeston." I whirled from undressing to meet my second's gaze. If tonight's dinner had shown anything, it was that I could not sit idly by while the Etruscans attempted to undermine my regime.

A small smile appeared on my second's lips. I swore her eyes glowed. "We'll leave tomorrow, after the council departs."

I nodded. My shoulders sagged. Something within me had changed tonight. I couldn't quite place it, but I had a feeling that my days of being a deferent ruler were behind me.

Aya sensed my exhaustion and turned to leave the room.

"Send him in," I ordered before she disappeared into the shadowy hall.

My back was warm against his skin. His arm curled around me in a protective hold. I smiled and leaned into Marcus, nestling my head into his other arm as I examined the way his brown skin glowed next to my peachy arm in the morning light. My heart fluttered at the sight of our arms pressed together. With Marcus, I wasn't a queen, I was just a woman. For a moment I let myself imagine that I was a farmer's daughter, allowed to wed a merchant's son. There were no kingdoms to rule, no lies, there was only us. The sun was warm on my face as I pretended that this was our house, and we were late for morning chores but didn't care because we were lost in each other. We got lost in each other every morning; it was a miracle we got anything done.

"When do you leave?" he whispered against my cheek, and I was jolted out of my daydream.

"Just after the council. In a few hours," I said quietly, sad that he had broken my reverie.

"Why so soon?" There was an ache to his voice.

"If the council is going, I need to be there. They don't know what I know." I sounded as miserable as I felt. I'd told Marcus last night about the trip to Galeston and who I suspected was involved in Lord Gendran's rebellion. "Are you seeing anyone?" I blurted.

I could feel his chest raise a bit and his head lift off the pillow behind me in surprise. "Why are you asking me this?" he asked cautiously. "You're the one who's engaged to the helmai's spawn." His voice held a bitter edge to it. He hated the Etruscan prince about as much as I did, albeit for different reasons. My heart sank. What right did I have to even ask the question?

"Sorry," I whispered. "You deserve to be happy."

"Ry," he breathed, and turned my body to face him, cupping my chin. "*You* make me happy." His eyes were pools of molten gold as they searched mine intently.

"You know what I mean," I responded, refusing to let him distract me.

"Yes, and I meant what I said." His gaze was resolute, curly hair flopping into his eyes as he refused to look away.

I sat up, frustrated with him. "What do you think is going to happen in a few months when I wed the prince? He made threats last night. Sooner or later, he's going to figure out how to follow through." I lifted my eyebrows, eyes begging him to see sense. I did not answer to the Etruscan, but he was no fool. It was only a matter of time before he found a way to exploit our relationship.

"So?" Marcus wrapped his strong arms around me again and pulled me into his chest. "Let him think whatever he wants—I'm not going anywhere." He smiled into my tangled hair.

"You would want that? To be with someone with whom you could never walk around the garden holding hands? To live in the shadows, a paramour? To never have children?" My voice was breaking thinking of what that would do to him.

"For you, I would do anything," he said softly, caressing each word. "You're my missing piece." He was looking into my eyes so earnestly it made my heart ache.

"You have to go," I whispered, and slipped out of his grip.

The light left his eyes, and his smile fell. "At least think about it?" he pleaded.

How could I say no to the man whom I loved with all my heart? The man who made me whole too?

"I will," I agreed. Of course I would think about it. "You must promise me that you'll stay here. Be my eyes and ears in the city. Let me know if our ruse holds."

He was silent as he dressed and drew his cloak around himself. Finally, he nodded. "I will." His amber eyes were cracked. I knew it pained him to leave me, but I needed him here.

"Goodbye, Marcus," I said, and leaned up to press a kiss into his soft lips. It wasn't long enough. It would never be long enough. His lips were home, and I wanted to nestle in them forever.

He broke off the kiss, holding my face in both hands as he breathed onto my lips. "I love you, Ry. Be safe out there."

"I love you too," I said breathlessly, fighting back the tears prickling the corners of my eyes.

"I'll see you again soon," he said, a promise in his eyes.

I nodded, and he opened the latch on my window, slipping out and through his secret route. Dread scraped in my stomach. Something about his departure felt final, so I said a silent prayer to Cieri and imprinted our last moment in my mind, pleading with the goddess to keep him safe.

ELEVEN

THREE YEARS AGO: THE WAR ON HEL

Thick tree roots intertwined with the cave walls, arching overhead and providing us a natural path to the Pit. Green tree pythons hung from the roots lazily, unaffected by our presence. There were so many snakes in the caves today that I could barely make out the candles hidden in small alcoves. I strained my eyes in the dim light, attempting to discern if the candles were lit.

A faint glow shone from the wall to my left from behind a nearly solid wall of green scales. Carefully, I approached the lounging snakes and stretched out my hand to part the scaly curtain.

The pythons recoiled from my touch, as if I had bitten them.

"Disssune, disssune," I murmured to the snakes—an apology.

The serpents left me alone, readjusting their intricately hung bodies so that none touched my skin. In the gap they left, a candle burned brightly.

The candle was not there to light the path to the Pit—no one who traveled these caves needed light to see. The candle was a signal: the Protector was here.

My shoulders relaxed a fraction. Protectors were a powerful, yet rare, kind of mage. Rare enough that kings paid small fortunes to keep one nearby and went to great lengths to keep them hidden.

The Ophidian's Protector was charged with keeping magic of the mind from entering the Ophidic Court. Their identity was unknown to all, Viper included, save for the mage who administered the Protector's oaths: Katzima. While the witch was not an Ophidian herself, she was our bridge to the mages, responsible for handling any binding or transformation rituals, and the only outsider we allowed into our order. Katzima had searched a long time to find a Protector powerful enough for the Viper Queen's court—even longer to find one willing to join the order.

When in residence, the Protector would stay hidden, scouring the minds of all Ophidians present, searching for signs of the meddling of Illusionists—mages who could trick the mind into seeing things that were not there; Dreamers—those who could enter dreams and place false prophecies into the mind; or Allurants—mages who could control and influence the minds of any who came into close proximity. Mind mages were rare, but a court as powerful and secretive as ours could not afford to take chances with even the greenest Ophidian.

If anyone entered the proceedings with an overly addled mind, the serpents would bring them to a room where they would stay until the Protector could finish working on them. Digging through someone's mind and undoing enchantments was one of the more challenging magics. It took almost as much skill as it did power to be an effective Protector. Nothing like my blunt, destructive gifts.

Aya came to stand next to me, remarking on the good it would do to be near the Protector after all the mages we had encountered in the fighting.

I grunted my agreement. Magic was slippery, and you could never be too careful.

She stared for a moment at the pythons, her palm open, as if she would reach out and touch them.

"Come on, these caves give me the creeps," Calliope grumbled from behind us. She shifted from foot to foot, the opposite of her usual demeanor. The soldier was not comfortable around the Ophidians the way that Aya and I were.

I chuckled. "No need to keep your voice down; they will know we're here soon enough."

Calliope glowered in response.

The soft hiss of sliding scales, accompanied by the occasional hiss of a disturbed serpent, followed us through the caves as we walked. The walls nearly glowed with their slithering bodies. As we approached the center of the cave, the Pit, the number of snakes increased until the cave wall was not visible at all.

Candles flickered from the Pit, making it look like the docile serpents were writhing on the walls. I smiled. We entered the cavernous chamber. Hundreds of Ophidians were assembled, scales covering their cheekbones, arms, and a few ankles I spied peeking out from too-short pants. Their scales ranged from bright, inexperienced bottle green to emerald, to several darker, forest greens. As Ophidians rose in rank, their scales darkened to demonstrate their prowess.

Some of the darker-scaled Ophidians raised hands in greeting as I passed. I nodded to them, a cruel smile twisting across my lips. Others averted their eyes, stroking the pythons that lazed across their laps. Some sat on the floor among the snakes, a python's fangs sank into their arms, eyes nearly closed as they fought through the pain of the venom.

Not only did the green tree python help transform them, dosing their venom— if they could handle the pain—combined with the magic in their veins, gave the Ophidians great strength. The ritual was gruesome, yet necessary. Ophidians healed quicker than humans, so the fang markings never lingered long.

Over the low murmur in the cavern, a stream gurgled at the front of the Pit. Tall grasses and a few trees framed the stream, kept alive by the magic of Herbal mages turned Ophidian. As we drew closer, I spied the slow-moving body of a green pit viper.

I smiled.

We continued to the stream. The chatter in the crowd grew quiet as my cabal marched forward.

"Bosssale, mys acress," I crooned to the vipers. *Hello, my darlings.*

Aya, Calliope, and I turned to the assembled Ophidians. The room was now silent, save for the gurgle of the stream behind me.

I smiled broadly at the crowd, then looked at Aya. Her scales shone, darker than the elder Ophidians. The light danced off her obsidian eyes; if you looked just right, you could see her slitted pupil. It was why the spymaster often got away with using her snake eyes on the surface. I turned my head to Calliope next. Her scales gleamed just as dark as Aya's, despite the distaste that she fought so hard to hide twisting her features.

My gaze returned to the Ophidians assembled. My second and third took several steps back, sinking into the corners until I stood alone at the center. One of the pit vipers had traveled from its grass to my ankles and now wound its way lazily up my legs. I stretched out an arm for it, and it draped itself across my shoulders, turning its yellow gaze on the Ophidians.

The viper's scales were bright, like that of the snakelets after their first transformation. I imagine we created a striking image: the viper's luminescent body against the dark green, nearly black of my scales. Black with the blood of the many I had killed and the gift that coursed through my veins.

Magic flowed easily from my body, the Black Gift no longer caged within my mortal frame. Here, I did not have to hide. Black mist covered the cave floor below me, winding into the tall grass and between the gathered Ophidians. My eyes nearly closed as I reveled in my power.

I stroked the viper's scales idly as I gazed around the room. It did not recoil at my touch the way the pythons did. Instead, the blood within my veins called to the serpent, signaling that I was one of their own, for I was the Viper Queen, ruler of the Ophidians, and this was my realm.

"Bosssama, Ophidianss." I called the court to order. *Welcome, Ophidians.*

"Essmos tyo ssamahaar," they responded in unison. *We are yours to command.*

The serpent across my shoulders hissed its agreement.

"My heart is troubled today." My words echoed around the chamber. Despite the lightness of the words, my eyes were narrow, the promise of retribution glittering within. My gift hummed, elated at the prospect of serving its purpose. It would be obliged soon enough. "I hear reports, accusations, of your lackluster attempts at fighting." I bared my teeth. "And I've seen it for myself." I finally allowed my fury at my father's accusation to consume me. My Ophidians would not be found wanting on the battlefield.

I stepped toward them, beginning a slow walk down the aisle. "You are a league of trained killers," I hissed, my tongue catching on my elongated canines as my blood sang. "So tell me." I stopped halfway through the room. My gift pooled as I assessed a pair of Ophidians before me: twins sporting emerald scales. The woman had pale sage-green eyes; the man's eyes were warm and earthy. Experienced enough comrades for there to be no excuses for their inability to execute a simple order. Members of my personal battalion.

A malicious grin spread across my face as I leaned in. "Why. Aren't. You. Killing. Helmai."

"They cannot be killed," the pale-eyed woman spat.

I recoiled, hissing, and the viper around my shoulders did the same. It hovered, poised to strike on my command. There were so many ways to handle her disrespect. While the viper venom would not kill an Ophidian, it made for an excellent torture device. Meanwhile, my gift twirled around her, caressing her face, practically begging me to let it loose. I had fought beside this soldier, she was an Herbal, incredibly useful in our fight. She needed to pay for her outburst, but not with her life.

While all Ophidians were trained killers, I belonged to a different category entirely. From the moment my mother died, I had been imprisoned, beaten, and forced to fight my way free, sans magic. I had not rested a moment until Katzima was sure that I was better, faster, and stronger than any Ophidian to ever live. And I was a mere child. Only then was I allowed to drink the viper blood. The viper blood, in place of the python, not only made me their leader but also doubled my power, both physical and magical. There was not a being alive stronger than I — as long as the viper venom coursed through my veins.

My lips twisted. Perhaps I would use my gift to teach them all a lesson. Camaraderie in battle did not earn anyone the right to speak so freely against me. Constricting the mental grip on my magic, I met her gaze. Her chest began to rise and fall faster. Her eyes bulged. Then her mouth opened in a gasp. Her skin began to gray. My smile deepened.

"She speaks the truth!" a voice shouted from behind me. I released my grip on my gift. The pale-eyed woman gasped, clutching her throat as her skin returned to its previous color. Her twin patted her shoulder.

Slowly, I turned my head to the speaker and met his eyes—nearly as black as Aya's. I constricted my gift once more. This time, I did not hesitate. I watched as the light in his gaze winked out, and he fell to the floor.

"The helmai are killable," I stated. "Most magics do not work against them. Only the physical kinds: Elemental, Herbal, and Wild." I continued my walk to the back of the room. "They are not living, so my magic cannot kill them. They are born from Helfyre, so our fire cannot kill them. But they can be killed. You know this already, so why do you fight with the vigor of elderly humans?" I demanded.

The pale-eyed Ophidian's twin stepped forward. "My Queen, if I may?" he enquired.

I nodded, subduing the fire in my eyes. Despite my rage, I needed to know why my forces were failing.

"Don't we *want* the helmai to take out as many humans as possible in this war?" Ives, that was the twin's name. He was newer to the order but one of the sharpest recruits. He and his sister were well respected, as evidenced by their evergreen scales so soon after their induction. I could not dismiss Ives's concern.

My eyes narrowed, and I cast my gaze around the room. Others were nodding their agreement. So the Ophidians *were* pulling their punches. I fought the urge to close my eyes. In the near decade that I had led them, the Ophidians had not been easy charges. When I was thirteen, the gift had thrust itself upon me the moment my mother took her last breath, leaving the Ophidians with no choice but to follow a child. I had to keep them in constant check. Power was the only way to earn their respect, and luckily for me, I had a plethora. The Naqadians had made themselves our enemies over the centuries, constantly hunting mages and threatening the continuation of magic. Once we ruled Naqad, the mages would finally be safe, our creed fulfilled.

Squaring my shoulders, I addressed the room. "If the helmai win this war, there will be nothing left to rule over. We must help the humans win, and *then* we will take Naqad. We cannot defeat the helmai ourselves."

I returned my slitted gaze to Ives. He would be a fool to continue to challenge me. My gift snaked toward him, thirsting for more. But he was smart. He simply nodded, peace said, and returned to his seat beside his sister, Rohesia.

Walking to the front, I addressed them all. "Patience, my serpent friends. It will all be yours when the war is over."

The Ophidians hissed their approval, the serpents gathered on the floor joining in. With the Ophidians' vigor renewed, this war would not last much longer.

TWELVE

PRESENT

"You're staring."

Heat crept up my cheeks. I knew the man standing before me was my second in disguise, but I couldn't help but ogle the perfectly chiseled jawline and eyes that seemed to reflect the night sky, even as the sun was high. Aya Jesper was the most talented Shifter I had ever met. She had managed to transform her lithe, feminine frame into a broad-shouldered, strong-armed *man*. It was hard to pull my eyes away. Guilt splashed through me as I thought of Marcus. I really should not be staring, even if it was just Aya.

"She's *taken*," Calliope growled next to me, blonde braid flicking in the crisp autumn breeze.

For once, I heeded Calliope's warning. I gave her a sheepish grin and returned my gaze to the palace gates before us. To the guards perched upon walls, I appeared to be foraying into the city with two of my most trusted guards. We had to pack lightly, concealing our bags cleverly within the saddles and my skirts.

I wore an artful gown, designed by Aya herself, with sweeping skirts and billowing sleeves that would appear elegant and regal from a distance. And she had managed to do it without a corset. The dress even had a slit in the front that revealed my travel leggings, allowing me to ride comfortably.

"Stop fidgeting," Aya muttered to Cali as we neared the gates. "We've done this dozens of times."

Aya was right: we had done this dozens of times—forayed into the city with Aya disguised as a guard. We had tried to enter the city with the three of us undisguised before, but since Aya was a well-known lady in waiting, it had been a disaster with every guard we encountered insisting another guard join us. I found that two guards drew no questions. But we had never left the city.

We cleared the palace gates and made our way down the winding waterfall path to the city. As we passed the cascading water, mist sprayed our cheeks, the refreshing scent of fresh rain filled my nostrils, and I smiled. The water was a welcome cold, awakening my insides, uncoiling the tight grip I'd held on my demeanor since returning to Egryt. The escape to Malnova had been a blur, but I had been *free.* I looked down the cliff face separating the palace from the city, allowing my gaze to travel to the woods that stretched beyond.

The city had been carved into a small mountain that rose up like a cliff against the coast, with the palace at its apex, the city dwellings woven together below by ample bridges that allowed passage across the waterfalls and cascading rivers. To the south and west, the city filled the cliffs, evening out to a bustling harbor, while to the north, the city gave way to the Venile Forest. I prayed we would make the trek undetected.

The prince must have slept in, or perhaps was in shock from our conversation last night, for there was only a tiny flutter on my finger telling me the prince was still breathing. Figures. I wouldn't be so lucky for him to be murdered in his sleep.

The end of the palace path loomed before us, and then we were in the city. Citizens bustled around us, paying us little mind. We traveled into the city often, as did the other nobles. A few merchants gave us pleasant nods and curtseys, but no one stopped for long. We neared an alleyway, and in sync, Aya and Calliope turned their jackets inside out, another of Aya's designs, trading the Royal Guard insignia for simple brown leathers.

I pulled the string tied around my waist, and my cascading skirts turned inside out, becoming a sturdy cloak. Aya was truly a genius.

As a unit, we moved through the city. I kept my hood drawn, eyes on the road ahead. Soon enough, we reached the gates that opened to the road north. The doors were flung wide, open to traders and travelers. We slipped through with the crowd, no one sparing us a second glance. The guards were focused on scanning the faces of traders entering the city, not monitoring those who left.

My back began to ache, and I realized I had been holding every muscle taut. I breathed in, forcing my posture to relax as our distance from the city grew. I kept my hood drawn, in case any passersby noticed us, but they were too focused on drawing their cloaks in from the wind and shielding their faces from the biting breeze that grew as the sun began to wane.

The grassy plains quickly gave in to the Venile Forest, and we scanned for places to make camp.

"This looks suitable," Calliope said as she surveyed the forest around us. We urged our horses into brush, farther from the trading path, where the underbrush grew thicker; it would provide good cover from the road. After dismounting, we navigated the horses through until it emptied into a clearing.

We said little as we made camp. The routine was like coming home, the three of us on the road together again. That was how it had been during the war. The three of us, together, trying to keep two nations from killing each other.

Aya had returned to her preferred female form since making camp. I took the first watch as she and Cali settled into their bedroll. I muttered something about it only being fair after they had spent the previous night preparing, but the truth was I feared what nightmares might befall me on the road. There was always the chance that I would wake up as something else entirely. *She* had not plagued me since my coronation, but the farther we traveled from the capital, the more I could feel her stir.

Best not to risk it. I settled with my back against a tree and stared into the surrounding forest.

We had been heading north, deeper into the mountains toward Galeston. If someone were hunting down all the mages, their sanctuary would be the best place to start. It was hard to picture Galeston as anything but the glittering jewel oasis that had offered my reprieve from my mentor's grueling lessons.

The last time I was in the city was before my coronation. Katzima had made hot tea for me while we sat around her hearth debating the merits of bringing the mages into the war.

My memories of Katzima felt hazy, but the ache in my chest was sharp. I missed the older woman. It felt as if each encounter we'd had of late had been colored with tragedy. I frowned, searching for a different memory.

Her olive hands covered mine as she corrected my grip on the pestle.

"Now, child, if you want the herbs to muddle, you must grind them like so. Otherwise, they'll lose all potency, and you'll merely bring a man to his knees when you meant to kill him." She tsked as she leaned over where I sat.

My cheeks heated as hot anger bubbled in my stomach. I was thirteen years old and possessed more power than this entire village combined. I knew how to muddle herbs for Ophidia's sake. I thrust my chin up to let her know just what I thought of being called a child.

As I opened my mouth, the raven pendant on her necklace flickered in the firelight. The anger evaporated on my tongue as I studied the ornately crafted feathers.

"Why do you wear it?" I whispered for the thousandth time.

Katzima smiled and laughed softly. "Why does this necklace fascinate you so, child?"

"It's a symbol of evil," I said bluntly. "And you are good." I stared up at her, wondering if this would be the time I would finally get an explanation.

Instead, she smiled and said, "And who decided that?"

I frowned. Everybody. The world. Ravens were symbols of evil to mages just as serpents were to Naqadians. Everybody knew that.

The witch saw the struggle on my face and laid a gentle hand on mine. "In time, I will tell you, my dear, but not before you are ready to hear it." The crow's feet crinkled around her eyes, and I knew that was the most she would say on it until she was ready.

Deep within me, my power stirred, urging me to Galeston. I reached for it, some foolish part of me praying that leaving Egryt would be all it took to return it to me. It was like pulling an endless rope. I could *feel* my power, but it wasn't there. I wanted to scream. Instead, I clawed my fingers in the dirt. As the gritty earth scraped my fingernails, something occurred to me. Something I hadn't tried in years.

With a glance at the camp, I crept slowly into the woods, calling out. "Bosssale, mys achress." *Hello, my darlings.* "Vees a myn." *Come to me.*

I repeated the mantra as I scanned the brush. Pit vipers were rare, but my darlings had their own underground networks and could move at uncanny speeds when called. Finally, there was a slither in the brush. *They came.* Relief flooded me. I sank to my knees, holding my arm out for the viper that weaved toward me. Emotion filled me, spilling out of my eyes. I had missed my friends so dearly.

Her tongue flicked as she reached me, gliding easily up my fingertips to wind herself around my arm.

"Drebees, mys achress." *Drink, my darling.*

Obediently, the serpent opened her jaw and latched onto my forearm.

The pain was blinding. Hot venom shot up my veins, setting my arm ablaze. It had not been this bad before, had it? Venom was not supposed to affect me as much as the others. I fisted my other hand in the earth, grunting. Perhaps I was out of practice, not as used to my serpent's sweet kiss as I had once been. Just when I thought I could hardly bear it a moment longer, she withdrew, slithering away quickly.

I knelt in the brush, hurt replacing the burning pain. The viper had not even stuck around to chat. What had I become? I could summon the serpents, but was I still their queen? Dread pooled in my stomach. What if that was why I couldn't access my power? What if I was no longer the Viper Queen? Had I neglected my post so thoroughly that Ophidia herself had revoked it? I closed my eyes, bracing my palms in the cool earth. If I was no longer the Viper Queen, that meant I would have to stay like this forever: a pathetic, powerless, puppet queen.

Snap. My head flew up, eyes scanning the forest around me. I stayed still, listening for the steady footsteps of an animal pattering around the woods. There was nothing. I whipped my head side to side, but the moonlight revealed little.

A whisper brushed my ear. "Looking for something, *My Queen*?" The voice was definitely male. My heart spiked. I whirled, leaping to my feet as I drew a knife from my belt. Who had found me here? A palace guard? Had we caught up to the council's entourage too quickly? Had some cutthroat noticed us leaving the city? I begged my eyes to shift, allowing me to see my assailant, but my cursed body refused to cooperate.

This was not right. I was not supposed to be vulnerable at night. *I* was the monster that lurked in the dark. And yet my racing pulse betrayed me. I would not be prey. I would *not* be prey.

"What are you here for?" I growled.

His fresh, clean scent hit me. He was no guard—this was a nobleman. I could take on a noble. I was better trained than them all. My arm ached, reminding me of the foolish ritual I had attempted. Maybe the venom would poison me. No rush of power filled me. I had failed.

"You," he breathed, as I inhaled his scent again and felt his presence. I thrust my knee up into the dark and received an answering grunt. As he sank to his knees, he fell into a patch of moonlight, and I could finally make out my assailant. Uncanny blue eyes met mine, moonlight dancing within them. The Prince of Etrusca stared at me as his mouth twisted into a smirk, deepening the cut of his cheekbones. Cool amusement splashed across my ring finger. I had been too preoccupied with my own panic to notice that the sensations from the pale scar had strengthened.

I cursed my own carelessness. My senses were full from being sequestered in the palace. Yet another way the crown had failed me. The prince *was* hunting the mages. He was going to Galeston, just as I'd suspected.

Caryk hopped easily to his feet. Before I could react, he advanced on me, placing his foot directly between my legs. I backed up, bumping into the rough bark of a tree. The hard muscles of his chest pinned me. A snarl started to work its way up my throat. My pulse raced. Was he going to kill me for getting in his way?

"Missed me so much you had to resort to stalking?" I spat. A small waver slipped into my voice. *Fuck.* Heat rose to my cheeks, and I thanked Cieri that the prince couldn't see it.

"What are you doing out here?" He pressed closer, a shadowy lock of hair falling across his eyes, his chest heaving against mine. A strange emotion tingled at my finger, one I couldn't quite place. Murderous intent?

"Does it matter?" My lip curled. His head was angled down toward mine, making it hard for me to breathe. Why was he so close? There wasn't enough air in the space between us.

"Of course it does; my betrothed stowed away without so much as a goodbye kiss." I could practically see his eyes glittering.

"A kiss, you say?" With a flick of my wrist, my dagger secured a position beneath his groin. Magic or not, I would not die in these woods.

"Apparently not." His body stiffened against me, voice rough.

"Your concern is noted. Thank you, *Prince.* Now, run back to Egryt before anyone notices your absence." I straightened as best I could against the tree, hissing the words through gritted teeth.

His shoulders twitched. "Don't mistake my interest as concern for you, your majesty. I wish to know what you are up to." He spoke slowly, enunciating each word. The prince could not know our plans.

"Exercising my horse," I shot back. I didn't care how obvious the lie was. It was none of Caryk Cazaar's business what I was doing in the middle of the woods, half a day's ride from the palace.

He brought a hand to rest on the tree. "I'm not leaving until you tell me."

"Or I could kill you right here, problem solved," I suggested, feigning indifference while my pulse refused to quiet. I feared *no one.* So why couldn't I find my usual icy calm? It was the venom, it had to be. It was affecting me strangely.

"Kill your betrothed? You may be Doric Venrylst's puppet, but you are no fool." It was almost a compliment. But the prince didn't know me. Not the real me. The queen he knew wore dazzling ball gowns and brought out her sharp tongue to torment overzealous suitors. She could wield a blade, but she always did what was best for her people. He hadn't seen the other part of me. He hadn't seen *her.*

I would kill him. It would be easy. Caryk may be strong, but I had been besting opponents far more skilled than him for almost a decade. But I had agreed to marry him. Naqad *needed* Etrusca's money. We had to rebuild. And we couldn't rebuild unless I went through with this betrothal.

As much as I itched to sink my blade into his flesh, there was another part of me that recoiled from the prospect. Cursed betrothal bond. It was already addling my mind.

I exhaled, lowering my dagger. "Fine. I won't kill you tonight, Prince. But the only way to find out where we're going is to come with us." I shoved him off me, and he relented, moving out of the way. If the prince came with us, we could keep an eye on him. If I couldn't kill him, I could at least ensure that he didn't kill any more mages on my watch.

"Fair enough." I could hear the shrug in his voice. How was the prince so blasé? It was as if this was his plan all along. "With *us*?" he inquired.

"You didn't seriously think I was out here alone, did you?" How stupid did he think I was? Or maybe he truly had no idea what we were really doing.

"I didn't know any of the royal entourage would disobey direct orders from the council."

I grit my teeth. "I am the Queen of Naqad, in case you've forgotten."

"Are we going to pretend that Lord Doric Venrylst does not rule Naqad? Is that why you snuck out of your own capital?"

He was wrong. I didn't sneak out because of Doric, I snuck out for my people. Because someone needed to be seen ruling. My lack of freedom as monarch had nothing to do with the council.

He took advantage of the silence to press further. "What, you don't trust your own advisors?"

"Of course I do," I answered fervently.

"Then, why risk your life to chase after the council?" He glared.

"Risk my life?" I was incredulous. Did he really think I was so incompetent that sleeping in the woods would kill me? Had I not just returned from another *solo* voyage?

"These woods are treacherous. There are far more dangerous creatures than me lurking here," he warned.

"Like me," I said quietly, enraged at his disregard for my competence.

He laughed. The bastard had the gall to laugh. Somewhere in the back of my mind, I wondered how the prince had learned that we were following the council, but my rage consumed me beyond caring. I would not stand for this.

Venom blazing in my eyes, I spun into a roundhouse kick that hit him square in the stomach. The prince stumbled back, and I grabbed his arm and twisted, forcing him to the ground, then placed a knee on his sternum and held him in there, staring into his eyes.

Bright, orb-like eyes lit up in shock.

I repressed a smile. Teasing and gloating was not what I needed now. I needed to wear the mask I feared the most, the one that always lurked just beneath the surface. I needed to become *her*.

I leaned down so he was staring directly into my eyes, mere inches between us. "Now that we're travel companions, let's get one thing straight," I said in a low, quiet voice. "I am no one's pawn. I heed the court's well-earned council from their many years running this country. That does not make me their puppet," I spat as I slid my knife out of its sheath and caressed his perfectly trimmed beard with the blade. I was tempted to put a nick in his precious facial hair.

"I am not the person you think I am, nor am I the person the rest of Naqad thinks I am. I will flay you alive if you cross me." My voice was deadly as I leaned closer. "Killing you would be rather inconvenient, but I am not above it. If you insist on coming with us, I will tolerate your presence, but do not think for a second that you have won." I breathed the last words into his lips, a lover's caress.

And then I let him see the cold, unflinching killer in my eyes. I let him see the bodies I had buried and the ones I had left there for all to see. I let him see the madness that sometimes controlled me and the demons that haunted me. At dinner, I had only shown him mere glimpses, but now, I let him see all of me.

His expression was entirely unreadable as I lay on top of him, pinning him down, forcing him to see the monster beneath the jewels. I should have been annoyed that he didn't look afraid, but instead I was filled with an odd comfort. At least one person in Naqad didn't immediately run from who I really was, although he was pinned to the ground. Even Aya took a step or two back when I opened the cage.

He understood who I was and what I had done. The expression he returned was one of respect.

I staggered off him, unsettled. The prince had surprised me. My anger dissipated as I stared at Caryk Cazaar, unsure what to make of him for the first time since meeting him.

He sat up slowly and looked at me, questions forming in his eyes. He opened his mouth.

I stood and turned away before he could ask them. The lingering sensation on my ring finger told me I was not ready to hear them.

"I'm not sure even you understand all that you could do," he said quietly, an odd lilt to his voice.

I spun, eyes blazing again. "Believe me, I know what I'm capable of." My lips pulled back from my teeth, daring me to show my fangs. Oh, how I longed for my fangs. I felt a rush of emotion start to prick the back of my eyes. I shoved it down as quickly as it came. Not here. Not in front of *him*.

The prince stood slowly, his face impossible to read in the dim light. He took a step toward me, silver rings glittering on a hand half extended.

I shook my head and turned to walk back to camp, not particularly caring if he kept up. My mind whirled, but I couldn't seem to focus on one thought.

I manned my post for several hours more before waking Aya for her shift. I refused to wake Calliope—she was an unbearable grump upon waking. My second cast a skeptical gaze at the prince, but I shook my head, too tired to explain now. She nodded, understanding our silent code.

In my bedroll, I rehashed the encounter with Caryk. An odd guilt filled my stomach as I thought of Marcus. I had been too close to the prince. And he had made me feel... I didn't even know the word for it. And that feeling from the betrothal bond. It was irrelevant. I shook the memory off, forcing myself to think of Marcus' arms encircling me. I enveloped myself in the image, savoring the warm memories of our last morning in bed together. It was in Marcus' safe embrace that sleep finally found me.

THIRTEEN

My blood sang with the sweet sensation of freedom. Fury burned behind my eyes at all those who had kept me captive. A hand shook me awake. I sat up, hissing. Who dared to interrupt me?

The insufferable Calliope Torino stood over me. I snarled, reaching for my power. It blazed through me, begging to be released. This would be the last time that pious blonde crossed me. Thrusting the Black Gift out, I willed her to her knees.

Nothing happened. No mist swirled. My power was gone. Where was my gift? This body had failed me. Calliope tilted her head, then shrugged and walked away. She dared walk away from me?

I leapt up, grabbing a dagger. I did not need magic to kill. Before she could turn, I was upon her. At the last minute she whirled, shock in her storm-cloud gaze.

"What the fuck, Ry?" Her features twisted as she ducked, drawing her own blade. "It's not exactly time for a sparring match, is it?"

Kill. Kill. Kill. I needed the sweet release of fresh blood upon my hands. Maybe that would bring my gift back.

"Tamariya? Oh fuck. AYA." Calliope was calling for help. What a fool. She'd be dead before anyone reached her.

"Tamariya Amunet." I whirled toward the voice. Aya. Of course she had answered her lover's call. I snarled. I could kill them both. It would be easy.

"Tamariya." Calliope spoke. I turned.

"Tamariya." The voice was Aya's.

"Your mother knew that you were stronger than this."

"You're stronger than her. Your mother believed in you."

I whirled, shifting my stance between each of my adversaries. Something was pushing at me, clawing its way out. No. No—it was too soon.

"Tamariya."

"Naqad needs you."

The Naqadians could perish. I did not wish to rule them. Why weren't they dead by now? The thing inside me pushed harder.

"Marcus needs you. He loves you." Marcus.

"Your mother believed in you. She knew you could beat this."

"Come back to us, Tamariya." The voices were getting farther away. She *was clawing her way back. No, no, no. It was too soon. I was supposed to have more time.*

I gasped, panting. Cool hands shook my shoulders. My clothes clung to me in pools of sweat. I looked down at my hands—one of them clutched a dagger. I opened my palm, and the dagger clattered to the earth.

I looked up, and there was Aya, shaking my shoulders. "Wha—" I stammered. I tried to take a step, but my legs buckled. Aya caught me, knees crumpling as she lowered me to the ground.

"Here, drink," she commanded. A flask was thrust into my hand. She helped me raise it. Dry wine flooded my senses. I savored the feeling on my tongue, allowing it to bring me back to the present.

"It happened," my second murmured. "You almost killed Cali." There was a hint of accusation in her voice, though she fought to hide it. Her eyes were guarded.

Calliope stood on the other side of the clearing, her lips twisted in a snarl but eyes still wide in fear. I closed my own eyes.

"I'm sorry, Cali," I whispered.

"You weren't yourself." Her words were clipped. She turned and walked from the clearing, likely to pray to her sun god for the strength not to murder me.

"What in Hel's name happened here?" Caryk emerged from the trees, two rabbits slung over his shoulder.

My jaw dropped. "Are those rabbits?"

"As if me bringing food is the strangest thing to happen this morning. What happened?" The prince's jaw feathered. I feared it may burst through his cheek if we delayed much longer.

"N-Nightmares," I whispered. "From the war." I wasn't sure if I was in shock from Ophidia's visit or that the Prince of Etrusca had just brought me a rabbit. At least the prince's appearance saved me from feeling too sorry for myself.

He nodded, taking in my sweat-soaked state. "I'm sorry to hear that. Those gruesome days haunt many of my nights as well."

I blinked. There was no malice or bravado in the prince's face. He was studying me, as if committing every feature to memory, a crease appearing in his brow.

"Er, thank you," I managed, the prince's weirdness bringing me fully back to the present. I moved to stand, and Aya took my arm to help me up.

"Perhaps there had been a Protector in the palace after all." She speculated, loud enough for only me to hear. I met her concerned gaze with a bleak one of my own. Ophidia was back. Whatever, or whoever, had been protecting me was done. As I had always feared. At least I knew one thing: I was still the Viper Queen.

One good thing arose from the events of the morning: neither of my companions challenged my decision to bring Caryk along. Perhaps they agreed that it would be easier to keep an eye on the prince's scheming with him close by, or they simply feared Ophidia's resurgence. I was grateful to avoid the conflict either way.

We continued on our path, exiting the Venile Forest. Before long, we were in the foothills of the Borgonas, the mountain range that housed the mage sanctuary.

The prince drew his horse up next to mine, a crooked smile upon his lips.

I sighed. The silence from the prince had been a gift, but I should have known it would not last. I looked at him with wide eyes, refusing to speak first. It was petulant, sure, but I didn't care. This wasn't court.

He arched a brow. "The Borgana Range? You're heading to Galeston."

I kept my face neutral. There were few settlements through the mountains, and very little reason to travel this way except to visit the town. I wasn't exactly surprised the prince had figured it out.

"Would you like a medal?" I asked dryly.

"Would you care to tell me why?"

"Since you seem to have all the answers, why don't you tell me? Why do we travel to Galeston, all-knowing prince?" I hoped he didn't see through my snarky façade. In truth, I hadn't considered a good lie to tell him.

A glimmer of amusement trickled through the betrothal bond. Caryk was getting better at hiding his emotions. I wondered if his rage still burned, concealed in some dark corner of his mind.

"I'll give it my best shot, then." His eyes reflected the sun itself. "You're visiting the mages, investigating this hunt that Gerome

Gendran appears to have begun." He shrugged, as if it was a wild guess, but the tension down the bond betrayed him.

I weighed my options. Our plan was fairly obvious, that much was clear. But I didn't care much for the truth. Leaning in conspiratorially, I answered the prince. "We seek an audience with the Viper Queen. I once convinced the Ophidians to come to Naqad's aid; perhaps they will do so again."

Caryk blinked. "The Ophidians? You truly believe they will help you?" His incredulity was insulting.

My eyes widened, as if we were not discussing the monsters of Caryk's bedtime stories. "They exist to protect the mages. Everybody knows that." This was too fun. The prince's face contorted.

"They're ruthless killers, hiding behind the guise of a creed. You must know this," he exclaimed, hands abandoning the reins to fling wide.

"They'll protect the mages," I reassured with a smirk. It was almost funny how ardently he hated the Ophidians. While few of them dwelled in Etrusca, there were enough that the Etruscans housed no more love for them than Naqadians.

"They'll take your country down in the process." Caryk's face was somber, a deep seriousness echoing down the bond. At least I didn't have to worry that I had given too much away last night. The prince had no idea how wrong he was.

"Perhaps." I was toeing a line. To react further would be to rouse suspicion, and the more naive the prince was about my true nature, the better. Losing control last night had been necessary, but I would need to keep my anger in check as long as the prince was close. Unfortunate, considering the farther we traveled from the capital, the wilder I felt.

The remainder of the two-day ride was rather uneventful. Caryk kept his thoughts to himself, and we were thankful for it. Except for Aya. She kept consistent conversation with him the entire way. I wasn't sure how she could stand him for longer than five minutes, but I was grateful. Several times, I had turned in my saddle to catch the prince staring at me, a line forming between his brows, as if I were some riddle he was attempting to discern. After a while, I stopped turning around, afraid to find out if he was still staring. As Cali and I discussed our plans, the lush forest grew sparse, and the soft dirt of the well-trodden trade route turned into pebbles underfoot.

On the second day, we had to dismount our horses several times to navigate the increasingly large boulders as we got closer to the mountain town. On those climbs, I caught myself getting out of breath. I really needed to train more often, or I would turn into the ornament I masqueraded as.

We sat around the campfire in a cave just a few hours walk from Galeston, discussing our plans for tomorrow as we finished dinner. Thankfully, I was spared from brushing elbows with Caryk, as Aya and Calliope sat on either side of him.

"Please tell me you aren't planning a grand entrance like you did in Malnova," Caryk said dryly, picking at the remains of the rabbit I had caught.

"Of course not. That was different," I said with a scoff, taking a slurp of mead. "Besides, we haven't even figured out who to behead yet." A wicked smile spread across my face as I beheld the prince.

"Ry," Aya said softly, shooting me a warning look. Her interference was enough to jar me.

"Only joking. We have no idea if the mages in Galeston have been ruthlessly slaughtered yet. That's what we're here to find out," I said, relaxing my smirk into a neutral expression.

Calliope nodded. "Tomorrow, we ride into the city in the middle of the day. We can blend in with the other travelers passing through on their way to Etrusca. We find lodging, we eat, we drink, we act normal. We observe."

I wanted to hiss at Calliope. What business did she have telling the prince our plan? Not that it was all that elaborate, but still.

Aya shot me a look, and I could almost read her thoughts. *Don't start on this again,* she said. *You're lucky she's talking to you at all.*

I narrowed my eyes but let it drop.

Caryk studied us. "We just sit there and watch people—that's your grand plan? Don't you think someone will recognize that the queen is sitting at the tavern bar?" Honestly, he had a point. Blending in had been much easier as princess, and during the war, everyone was too focused on staying alive to pay a misplaced royal much mind. But I wasn't going to admit that.

"People see what they expect to see," Aya murmured, saving me from responding.

Caryk turned his luminescent eyes on her, mouth set in an unreadable line. "Present company excluded, of course."

FOURTEEN

THREE YEARS AGO: THE WAR ON HEL

Just a fortnight ago, I may have laughed about the farce of a crown designed to look like a coiled serpent being placed atop my head. But today it felt more like an executioner signing my death warrant. The crown of serpentine amethysts floated down the aisle toward me. Orange afternoon light seeped in from the arching stained windows, casting a glow over the crown.

My father had done me the courtesy of getting himself killed in the fighting so that I didn't have to execute him myself. Of course, he was following my advice to inspire his soldiers with his hand in battle when a helmai had struck him down from behind. The blow had been so swift that none of his guards had time to react. The blade ran right through his heart, as if the helmai knew precisely where to strike so that even the royal Healers could not save him.

I smirked. In an ironic sort of way, he *had* inspired his soldiers to win the war. His death was the turning point we'd needed to spur on our tiring armies.

The crown's death march continued. The two men holding it were somber. I should have laughed in their faces. But the great fangs protruding from the crown stopped me, their dullness creating an eerie contrast from the glittering jewels.

I wanted to set the room ablaze with a spark of flame. Seeing Doric's and Terrin's faces as I ruined this coronation would surely be worth it. They seemed to be pretending like magic didn't exist anymore; now would be as good a time as ever to find out why. But wasn't that what everyone expected from the psychotic warrior princess? Perhaps today I would surprise them and behave myself. How dull. Besides, a legitimate throne was much easier to hold onto than a seized one.

The floating serpent had nearly reached me. My heart raced as I shifted my gaze around the room. Most of the guests assembled in the coronation chapel looked just as uneasy as I felt. I thought I would have more time to cultivate a reputation of sanity before I wore this crown. Would my mother have approved of my plans? She had married my father to bring peace between our people, unity. Not to bring about the destruction of Naqad.

But she had not seen the suffering I had, had not seen the gross mistreatment of her people after they handed the Naqadians their victory over Hel's forces.

The priest was lifting the crown above me. *Cieri*, my knees were starting to hurt. This dais was not meant to be knelt upon.

"Tamariya Amunet, Princess of Naqad, do you swear to protect this nation and its people from threats both foreign and familiar?"

"I do." Did I? I was supposed to have years to sort this out.

"Do you swear to put the needs of this kingdom and its people before your own?"

"I do." I supposed it depended on how you defined my needs. There were a lot of people in Naqad. I happened to be one of them, too. As did the rest of my mother's people.

"And do you swear to uphold the laws of Naqad to the best of your ability?"

"I do." *Not.* I fully intended to break the laws of this kingdom. Regularly.

Lord Doric Venrylst shifted next to me, as if he could sense my train of thought. I resisted the urge to smirk. *I am going to reign fire upon this realm.*

The priest, somber as ever, placed the crown on my head and said, "Then, rise, Tamariya Amunet, Queen of Naqad."

The crown felt like lead upon my brow.

"Smile; you're their hope now," Doric whispered encouragingly in my ear.

I rose and smiled. It wasn't my usual feral smile either, it was full and bright, the smile of a ruler who would lead her people into prosperity. I wasn't entirely sure where it had come from. The crowd erupted into applause, and I felt their earlier skepticism dissipate. Drums banged in the distance; I could hear people celebrating in the streets.

What fools.

FIFTEEN

PRESENT

My mare trudged up the incline of the mountain as it grew steep, and I fought to remain astride. I looked over to Aya and Calliope, and the adept riders lay almost flat against their horses' manes. On my other side, Caryk looked like he was riding through a summer valley instead of facing the biting winds that threatened to whip us off the very face of the mountain.

The vantage point of the city made it nearly impenetrable. However, it also dissuaded many traders from braving the climb. Those who did trek up the mountain were rarely disappointed. The mage's sanctuary was unlike anything I had ever seen. I remembered visiting it in my youth.

Sparkling rivers flowed next to the streets, ending in cascading waterfalls where children would play in the pools beneath. The fresh water flowed by nearly every home, giving every citizen access to clean water. We didn't even have that in Egryt. Gardens blossomed in every front yard, and the markets were alive with colorful fruits and vegetables that should not have been able to grow at this altitude. The storefronts glittered with jewels and stalagmites that rivaled even the royal jewels my mother often wore. Many of the country's rarest treasures came out of Galeston, and it was all because of the mages, whose lives were entangled in the very threads of the city.

Anticipation fluttered in my stomach as my horse made the last few steps into the city. It had been years since I'd laid eyes on Naqad's glittering jewel, but the city had barely been touched in the war. Even the helmai army had not attempted to attack with such a disadvantage.

We passed through the city gates, and I almost fell out of the saddle. The city, once abuzz with activity, was nearly silent. People shuffled to and from dark shops with drawn curtains. No wares glittered in the windows, and I didn't see signs of a market anywhere. Even the air seemed thicker, heavier, even this high up. And then I noticed it.

The river was nearly black with muck. It still turned and flowed along the pebbled walkways, but it wasn't the frothy cascade of my childhood. Where children had once delighted, townspeople now skirted the water lapping over the stone barricade, casting uneasy glances in its direction.

My stomach rolled, threatening to bring up my lunch. The mages hadn't abandoned the city, had they? I supposed it was smart, if word was getting around that they were being hunted down. They were sitting ducks in Galeston after all. My heart raced. I wasn't entirely sure I believed my own theory. Closing my eyes briefly, I threw up a rare prayer to the gods that nothing had happened to them. To the woman who practically raised me. That we hadn't been too late. I tried not to let my hands shake as I gripped the reins tighter. If Katzima was gone, I had no hope of regaining my magic.

Cali was barely able to contain her shock as well. Her eyes were bulging, but she kept her mouth set in a firm line, her stormy gaze focused on Aya—the calm figure leading us through the winding path of homes and shops. What had once felt like a magical garden now threatened to swallow us whole. A glance toward what used to be the Mage Quarter revealed only charred outlines, ghosts of a bustling town. There was a slight stiffness to Aya's spine, the only indication that she was surprised by the state of the city.

Caryk was unperturbed. The absence of a tug down the betrothal bond confirmed it. For all I knew, the prince had never set foot in Galeston before now.

There was one tavern on the main square that still appeared to be open, so we guided our horses over, fighting a wind that had begun to pick up. There we would wait, and watch. There had to be evidence in this city of what had happened to the mages.

We chose a table against the far wall of the dimly lit bar. I kept my hood up, lest anyone look too closely and decide that I bore a striking resemblance to a certain royal. Aya and I sat facing the room, the less observant of our group sitting opposite us. Caryk shifted in his seat, uneasy. I smiled sweetly, daring him to complain, fighting a scrunch in my nose against the yeasty, almost sulfuric scent of the tavern.

He glowered but quickly sighed, giving up. "If we're going to blend in, we'll need drinks. Anyone hungry?" he asked as he stood, dark hair falling into his eyes. Eyes that assessed us warily when we didn't answer. I could have sworn the prince rolled his eyes at us, but he turned and strutted to the bar before I could confirm. There were a few other patrons here, gazes deep in their tankards, thoughts far away from this town. The wind howled against the flimsy tavern doors as a man in a torn jacket talked quietly with the barkeep, stopping abruptly when the prince approached.

"Do you know why Galeston used to be so beautiful?" I asked no one in particular.

"Something to do with the rest of the world leaving them alone," Calliope grumbled.

Aya didn't offer her usual smirk. Instead, she looked at me gravely and said, "The mages. Lord Frydrik Moscar liked to pretend that he had created a flourishing trading post, but he knew that the city would be nothing without them."

I studied Aya. She had never mentioned visiting the city before. But Aya had lived many lives before coming into my service. I nodded. "We didn't have to hide here. For once, we got to show the world the good that magic could do."

Aya frowned. "I'd like to know where the mages went. My sources told me they were still here." To an outsider, she appeared completely unperturbed. But I knew my second well. Her eyes narrowed slightly as she contemplated what she would do to the informants with the gall to lie to her.

Calliope scoffed. "If you can even call them mages anymore."

I glared. "Explain."

The blonde woman tilted her head, considering, the crow's feet around her eyes wrinkling. "The Ophidians have been taking their strongest for generations. There's hardly a mage left with more than a spark of power." A slam of wind thwacked against the shutters as if to say *we will not be dismissed.*

"They volunteer to join the order," I pointed out quietly, ignoring the uncanny behavior of the wind.

"Do they?" Calliope challenged.

I pressed my lips together, mouth set in a firm line. Clouds turned in Calliope's eyes as she refused to back down.

"I've never told you the story of how I came to join the order." Cali drummed her fingertips against the table. "I was *taken.* I was not asked, a choice was not given to me. I was yanked from my bed in the middle of the night and stolen from my parents, all because of my *strength.*"

A shiver passed through the tavern. Calliope did not volunteer to join the Ophidic order. My mouth was suddenly dry. Where was the prince with our drinks?

"Strength." She scoffed. "If a child with so common a gift was stolen, do you think that someone like Rohesia joined the order willingly?" Rohesia was an exceptionally gifted Herbal. She could entrap an enemy in her vines with a thought. And she had been an Ophidian since she was a child, as had her twin.

But we had not done that during my rule. The only new Ophidians I had accepted were volunteers, like Aya. Calliope's hatred of the Ophidians was no secret, but I'd had no idea it ran this deeply.

"Then, why stay?" I asked her, genuinely curious.

She swallowed. "Someone has to look after them." Another rattle of the shutters.

"Who?"

The storm in her eyes had quieted, but I was under no impression that it was any less deadly. "The others like me."

I refused to consider what she was implying.

I looked at my cabal and said quietly, "What if the mages didn't leave Galeston?" It was a pathetic attempt to pivot, but hopefully the question would distract the women.

Calliope's eyes widened slightly. Even Aya's lips twitched in surprise.

"This city is nearly in ruins," Aya said in a low voice. "If there were any mages left, how could they have let this happen?" Her obsidian eyes searched mine, almost accusatory.

"The Ophidians weren't here to protect them," I murmured. "If Frydrik Moscar started hunting them the way Gerome Gendran did, they would be easy targets, even in their numbers. Everyone knew who they were. They could have gone into hiding to protect themselves." I tried to keep the doubt from my face as I prayed to the gods that I was right.

Aya tilted her head slightly, likely considering the information she had gathered. I could see Calliope's stormy eyes contemplating the difference that the Ophidians could have made.

"We should have been here," Calliope whispered, looking up at me, accusatorial. "We have one job, one purpose, and we couldn't even do that. What's the point in ruling a kingdom if you can't protect the people in it?" she demanded. Were those tears glimmering at the corners of her eyes?

I often forgot the decades that Calliope and Aya had lived without me. Both had seen acquaintances and lovers come and go that I would never meet. I wasn't the only one who had people in this city I feared for. The word stung behind my eyes, and I startled. I did not feel fear. I could not afford it.

"Cali," I started.

"Don't give me some bullshit about keeping the peace between our people," she snarled, lightning crackling in her gaze. "You were never interested in peace. I thought that ruling Naqad was making you a tolerable human being, but doing nothing while the people you've sworn to protect die, is a different kind of evil." Her lips were pulled back, the dim light glinting off her teeth. Her canines were elongating, pupils beginning to narrow.

Her words struck me as if she had pulled out her broadsword and slashed it across my face. Calliope and I had hated each other for years, but that was when I was a different person. I was better now. I wasn't *her*. I didn't kill people for the thrill of it. I kept my temper under control. How could she think that what I was now was just as bad. Evil? I was aware that I wasn't much of anything these days, save confused. I sat there and stared at her, my mind racing, unable to form words.

"Cali, you know that's not fair," Aya whispered in a gentle tone she reserved for the blonde warrior.

"Isn't it?" Calliope demanded, a promise of retribution in her eyes I had not seen before. "She is the reason we were not here to fulfill our duty. Because we were protecting *her* as she sat in a palace, surrounded by her jewels." The guard's eyes were narrowing, pupils constricting in her fury.

"We don't even know what happened to the mages. There's no point in placing blame for something that we don't understand," Aya said levelly.

I was faintly aware that Calliope was on the fringe of ruining our carefully crafted anonymity. Smoky tendrils thrashed in my mind, demanding to be unleashed. I couldn't be *her* again. She was all the worst parts of me, manifesting as a power-drunk killer. I tried to calm her down, breathing deeply. The memory of my knife pulling slowly across flesh replayed in my mind. I savored it, drinking in the feeling.

Guilt crashed in, threatening to pull me under. Where was Doric Venrylst when I needed him? He had always been able to pull me out of my spirals. He may not have known what I truly faced, but one word from him would set me back on the right path.

I grabbed my elbows, my dirt caked fingernails digging into my flesh. There were other hands on me too.

"Ry, come on. Snap out of it. She didn't mean it," Aya's quiet, but urgent voice echoed in my mind.

A faint grumble sounded in the background.

"Look up," a voice hissed.

My head snapped up. A low mist hung over the room. Some patrons were noticing, looking at it in confusion. A dark-haired man at the bar studied the mist. My eyes flew wide. *Shit.* I took a deep breath. Then another. Slowly, I withdrew the fog. People around the tavern blinked and shook their heads as if they had imagined it. As the mist receded, so did the fog in my mind.

I looked up at Calliope. "Thank you for letting me know what you really think of your queen. Get out of my sight before you get your wish and *she* returns," I said with deadly calm.

Calliope's eyes crackled with raw lightning, but she pushed her chair back and nodded to Aya before leaving the tavern.

"I should go with her," Aya whispered. "Make sure that she doesn't do anything stupid."

I nodded. It wasn't Aya's fault that her partner hated me so much. I didn't blame her, honestly. I was intolerable. But I would have imploded if Cali had continued much longer. Aya knew that too. The wanderer would make a far better queen than I. The pair would get their room for the evening, and tomorrow we could pretend as if this exchange had never happened.

Caryk returned from the bar, holding four drinks and some food. It was the first decent-looking food I had seen in days. My stomach growled. I fought the urge to bang my head against the table in impatience.

Mercifully, Caryk registered the look on my face but didn't comment on Aya's and Calliope's absence.

"To the gods." The prince raised his tankard, smiling grimly. Then he downed the mead.

I scowled, rolling my eyes.

Caryk continued to drink deeply.

I stared at him, transfixed for a moment. In the palace, you took polite sips. You drank an appropriate amount, never to get drunk. To be drunk was to make a scene. Memories flickered in my mind as I recalled indulgences I had once allowed myself.

The prince finished the tankard, slamming it down on the table. I looked at him for another moment, considering. Then I grabbed my own tankard and took a large gulp.

The lukewarm liquid burned as it went down my throat. My chest warmed as the bubbles filled me. I got about halfway through the tankard before I had to set it down. When I looked up, the prince's piercing eyes were fixed on me.

I arched a brow.

A grin spread across his face, transforming him in a way I had not seen since the night we met.

"What would you say to a drinking game?" the prince asked, mischief dancing in his eyes, lips quirked to the side.

"You can't be serious." I shot him a withering stare. I would not play drinking games with this usurper. Besides, the prince hated me. There was no way in Hel he wanted to play a drinking game with me.

He shrugged. "You need a distraction, and we need to find out as much as we can about Galeston."

I remained silent, studying him. Did the prince know what had caused the mist? *The mist.* A thrill ran through me. My magic was back. I didn't feel it lurking under my skin the way I used to, but perhaps it was simply taking its time reemerging.

He took that as an invitation. "Every time someone walks in, we take turns making up a story about who they are. Then we go talk to them and find out. If you're wrong, you drink." His eyes danced, daring me to join. Daring me to have fun.

I considered. I supposed I could pretend that I didn't loathe the man before me for a couple of hours, or that he didn't loathe me. It wasn't like I had to be friendly with him forever because of one drinking game.

What he proposed was simply information gathering. With a bit of a twist. Who said that we couldn't enjoy ourselves while on a mission? We'd probably blend in better if we were drinking anyways. Calliope wasn't even here to ruin the fun. My chest tightened at the thought of my friend. If I could even call her that. Our relationship had always been complicated. And that was the last thing I wanted to think about tonight.

Returning my thoughts to the prince, a smile tugged at the corners of my mouth. I grabbed what remained in my tankard and downed it. "I'm in," I said, reaching for another.

SIXTEEN

Several rounds later, the prince and I had each done our fair share of drinking. Despite myself, I was grinning.

A broad-shouldered man sauntered into the tavern. Dirty, blonde hair fell to his shoulders, matching the distressed tunic he wore rolled up to his elbows. The man's face was fixed into a permanent scowl.

"See the dirt on his trousers? I think he's secretly a mage, and he just came to the tavern after a long day tending to his roses," Caryk whispered conspiratorially, a slight slur to his voice, hand hovering above my waist.

"What does tending roses have to do with being a mage?" I protested, finishing off my third tankard.

"You know… he's an Herbal. He grows flowers," the prince explained, a flush in his cheeks as he gestured to the room.

I giggled, trying to picture this mountain of a man nurturing a rose bush to life. The Herbals I knew did not spend their time tending to delicate flowers. "You're on," I said, raising my tankard.

Caryk pushed back from the table, raising his eyebrows at me in a way that said *you'll see*.

"Wait." Without thinking, I reached out and grabbed his wrist. He froze, and the moment hung between us. Under my fingers, his pulse raced. I swallowed. "You can't just ask him if he's a mage."

A smirk bloomed on the prince's lips. "You think me some kind of fool? I'm just going to ask about the roses."

I rolled my eyes in response, sipping my drink as I watched the prince approach the brawny man. Caryk gestured wildly while the man wore a deep scowl. My shoulders shook with laughter as I watched the exchange. The man's teeth were bared now, and he turned his shoulder away from Caryk. An actual giggle escaped my lips.

The prince returned to the table, the picture of defeat. I howled with laughter as he turned wordlessly and drank heavily from his tankard, finishing it off.

"At least you're not a poor loser." I grinned, clinking my tankard against his.

"I have far too many flaws to be bad at that as well, love," he said between drinks, beer running down his stubbly chin.

I snorted.

"So you admit it: I have flaws." He sighed, placing the drink in front of him, pretending to look forlorn.

"You've been nothing but a pain in my ass since the coronation," I retorted, arching a brow.

He feigned shock, pressing a hand of glittering rings to his chest.

I smirked. "I liked you when we first met, you know. Before I could feel how ardently you hated me."

His gaze darkened. "I do not hate you, Tamariya." He looked at me intently, the humor fading. My cheeks heated.

The booze must have gone to my head. "Then, why have you been so angry since we bonded?" I whispered, terrified that his answer would break the spell that tonight had cast over our... friendship? I didn't dare call it that. More like a tentative alliance.

I was not drunk enough to believe that one game would create any sort of trust between the scheming prince and me, but I would be lying if I didn't admit that some part of me yearned for that companionship. Guilt instantly pitted in my stomach at the thought. I had companionship, I had trust, I had *love*. I had all of that with Marcus.

I shook my head. It was a fool's question.

The prince continued to regard me, his eyes drinking in my face, as if the answer somehow lay there. Perhaps he would credit the pink in my cheeks to the alcohol. "That... is a question with a very complicated answer," he said carefully, an odd look in his eye.

I didn't know what to say to that. I sighed, the spirits suddenly weighing on me. The prince noticed the change and sighed too.

"The things I wish I could tell you, Tamariya." He forced a smile. An emotion I knew too well rimmed his eyes. A confirming pang throbbed in the thin scar on my ring finger. The prince was lonely. Perhaps Caryk was not the plotter I had assumed him to be. But that didn't mean I had to be satisfied with his cryptic answers.

I grimaced, grabbing my jacket. "By all means, don't rush to share it all at once." If he really wanted to tell me so much, he would. Probably some bullshit scheme he and his father had cooked up.

He placed a hand on my arm, halting me. "This isn't exactly how I imagined my life to turn out either, you know."

I looked up at him in surprise. "You're a second son. You can do whatever you want."

"I thought so once as well," he said bitterly. With a grim smile, he released my arm.

My head was spinning. I wished I hadn't had that last tankard. I could barely comprehend his words.

Perhaps that was why I furrowed my brow and said, "You offered your hand to me. No one made you introduce yourself to me at the ball."

"That wasn't the first time we met."

The crisp night air hit my face as we exited the tavern. I stopped for a moment, frozen. I tried to think back, but my memories were so damn foggy.

"We met before that night at the ball?" I said thickly, cursing myself for letting him deflect my accusation.

"A tale for a time when we stop lying to each other, love," he purred, back to being infuriating. We were only a few paces to the inn now and I'd be able to retreat into my own quarters.

I rolled my eyes. "Gods, please tell me you're as drunk as I am."

"I did lose more than you. Only difference is one of us is out of practice." He winked and patted my arm. Heat spread from where his hand rested. Something about the gesture... no. It couldn't be.

"Caryk." I stopped in my tracks.

He turned to me, eyebrows raised. "What?"

I pursed my lips. "We didn't... how we met..." I trailed off, unable to finish the mortifying sentence.

His brow crinkled for a moment before realization dawned on his face. He laughed. "*Cieri*, Tamariya, no." He shook his head, hand dragging down his stubble. Then his gaze darkened, his entire expression changing. "Is the competition so vast?" he inquired, a single eyebrow raised, a dare in his gaze.

I blushed. I was not ashamed of how I had chosen to enjoy myself. Perhaps I was a little ashamed of *who* I had chosen to enjoy myself with, but the prince didn't need to know that. My mind scrambled to come up with a clever retort.

His gaze heated as the silence lengthened, eyes framed in long, dark lashes, roving my face as he took a deliberate step forward. My heart raced. I reached out and touched the hard leather of his jacket.

Someone exited the inn, turning our attention to the door. I snapped out of the trance, practically jumping away from him.

"We better get our rooms," I mumbled.

He nodded, and we stepped into the inn. I examined the wood-paneled walls and tried to focus on the gray-haired innkeeper sitting before us.

The prince's gaze bored into me, demanding I address what had just transpired between us. I ground my teeth together, took a deep breath to unclench my jaw, and sauntered up to the innkeeper to request us two *separate* rooms. Aya and Cali would already have their own, leaving me to bunk solo. A bitter taste filled my mouth, that I quickly dashed. The couple deserved time alone after being on the road for so long. A pang echoed in my chest as I thought of Marcus and my order for him to remain in Egryt.

The old man obliged us graciously, happy to have visitors in this barren city.

How long will his inn remain, with Galeston in such a state? My heart sank for him.

As we walked silently through the nearly deserted inn, the prince's massive frame was unavoidable. Turning a corner, his hand brushed mine. Heat shot up my arm, lighting my right side on fire.

I squinted through the dim light to the grainy flooring. I couldn't trust my gaze not to give me away. It was the alcohol, surely. Tomorrow we would be back at each other's throats, and he would resume his plot to steal my crown.

At last, I reached my room. Without a backward glance or a whispered good night, I inserted my key into the lock and nearly fell into my room. The door slammed quickly behind me.

I exhaled, leaning against the hard wooden frame. My thoughts were a scrambled mess. I tried to make sense of them, but only one phrase echoed in my mind. I couldn't let myself think it, so it circled my thoughts, prodding me each time I let my guard down.

An image of a blood-soaked monarch flashed across my vision. Her sharp teeth were dripping with crimson, and her slitted pupils gazed without feeling. I blinked, and she was gone, replaced by a beautiful woman, whose heavy crown sat atop soft-curling auburn hair, the harshness of the crown at odds with her warm smile. Her eyes were equally as vacant as the murderous queen's, cold calculation replaced by blissful ignorance.

I blinked, and the doe-eyed beauty was gone. I was alone, cold wood pressing against my back. I had been many things in my life, was probably on my way to becoming something else entirely, but there was one thing I had always been certain of, since the day I watched that bright-eyed boy slice his arm open and drink the python's blood.

I was a monster.

Bred for exactly one purpose. Calliope's accusation had only proved it. But my magic had returned. The mist was faint, but I had seen it. A coldness settled over me as I realized what that meant. I could no longer hide from it, from *her*. I was the Viper Queen, and it was about time I started acting like it.

My thoughts drifted to Marcus, encased in turmoil. He did not know what I truly was, and I loved him for it. With him, I got to be the best version of myself, a benevolent ruler, a caring friend. Before

Marcus, there had only been the blood. And the killing. Our time together since the war had been the most precious gift.

But then there was Caryk. Something about Caryk was... different. When I was around him, I felt lighter, my head clearer despite the alcohol. After tonight, I was nearly convinced that he could never be the one hunting the mages. But why had he followed us from Egryt?

Perhaps a lifetime hitched to Caryk Cazaar was not the death sentence I had thought. Once we made the marriage pact, our vows would become binding, and betrayal would be nearly impossible.

Shaking my head, I unraveled myself from the ball I had created against the door. The travel was getting to my head. We had barely slept the last few nights, and I needed to rest. I rose and made my way over to the bed. Upon closing my eyes, I fell asleep almost instantly.

A circle of hooded figures surrounded a trembling boy, watching as his knife slid shakily across the throat of a young girl. Her screams turned into contorted gurgles until she was silent. Her body fell to the ground as the knife dropped from the boy's trembling hands. A raven-haired woman knelt calmly over the dead girl. Light from the massive bonfire flickered off a silver chain dangling from the woman's throat. She

stood, holding a bowl, and handed the knife back to the boy. He was barely a teenager, only a few years older than me.

I took a half step back, gripping my mother's tunic, hoping the shadows cast by the flickering fire would shield me from view. She laid a comforting hand on my shoulder and squeezed. I tried to relax.

Dark hair fell over the boy's face. His hands trembled as he stretched out his forearm. The dark-haired woman held his arm gently and nodded, then he gulped and brought the knife to his own arm. I gasped as dark liquid oozed out of him and into the woman's bowl.

Another woman approached the boy, this one clad in fighting leathers, carrying a satchel. My heart raced.

The warrior reached into her satchel and pulled out a writhing form. The boy's eyes grew wide, and he stumbled back. I squinted into the flames, but I couldn't make out what she was holding. She took another step toward him, holding out her arm. The creature was coiled tightly, its sharp hiss finally reaching my ears. The warrior kept one hand on its neck, carefully avoiding its fangs. The raven-haired woman stepped up and began to uncoil the serpent. As she stretched it out, I could see the reflection of the flames on the creature's scales. Its hiss, frantic now, echoed through the clearing as it thrashed in the women's grip.

"Is that a viper?" I whispered, looking up at my mother with wide eyes.

She chuckled softly. "There is only one here who carries viper blood in their veins. That is merely a regular python."

My eyes were as large as the plates we had used for dinner this evening. I turned them back to the boy. He reached out with the knife and sliced it down the python's body. The raven-haired woman reached with the bowl to catch the blood. As the droplets fell, she sprinkled something else into the bowl, chanting an incantation I couldn't quite hear. A knot formed in my stomach at what my mother had implied would happen to the blood.

The massive bonfire crackled and the logs within started to shift. The woman did not flinch as the flames next to her stretched to the sky, and it seemed like the logs were following. I couldn't take my eyes off the crackling fire. As it waned, I realized it wasn't logs at all, but a man. A man who was completely on fire. He had been seated before, giving the illusion of a bonfire, but now that he stood, I could see that he was the fire. His face was obscured, but nothing about his stance suggested he was in pain. Gods.

The burning man, the raven-haired woman, and the warrior joined hands, encircling the boy. Somehow, the flames from the burning man did not engulf the others. The dark-haired woman handed the boy the bowl, and the three began chanting.

The boy drank from the blood-filled bowl while the chanting grew louder. I felt my dinner threatening to make a second appearance. My mother squeezed my shoulder again. As the chanting reached a shout, it abruptly ended. The boy fell to the ground. The mages released their hands, stepping away from him slowly, murmuring another incantation. Silence. Not a single person gathered around the fire made a sound. I looked frantically from person to person. I hadn't paid them much mind before, but now I wondered who these people were. Was this some kind of mage ritual my mother had brought me to witness?

A crack snapped my attention back to the boy. He lifted one arm, then another, pushing his body up. He stood, hunched over. Then he raised his head. Glowing, serpentine eyes met mine, a slit where his pupils were supposed to be. The flicker of the flames cast a shadow on his face that I swore made it look like scales rimmed the edges of his temples and cheekbones. Around the fire, several mages had withdrawn their hoods, and the same scales shone on their faces. Theirs seemed darker than the boy's.

I was sure I spied fangs sticking out from someone's mouth. I snapped my eyes back to the boy. He smiled, and indeed, two long, pointy teeth protruded over his bottom lip. The fire around the burning man roared bright white, highlighting his bright-green scales.

The stories were true. Ophidians were real. And they were just as terrifying as the stories said.

My legs began to shake. I blinked, and the boy had transformed back to normal. He wasn't a boy anymore though. The cut on his forearm had healed. His cheekbones were sharper. He was cute. *No wonder nobody believed they're real; they looked just like us. The boy gazed right at me, and I saw his striking eyes, uncannily bright even in his human form. Like he could tell that I didn't belong in this cabal. Not yet anyway.*

SEVENTEEN

I awoke with a start, eyes wide. Whipping my head around, willing my vision to adjust to the dim light, I felt something stirring in the walls. A deep, forgotten part of me called to it, beckoning the demon within. Half asleep, *she* strained to the surface. My skin prickled with the transformation. That was enough to snap me out of my slumber. I shoved *her* back down, remembering my oath to Calliope.

My body sagged. At least I still had control. *She* would not win, not tonight. Demon quieted, I could still feel the stirring in the walls. No one was in the room, but something was here in the inn. If it was anything like the demon I carried, it would need to be dealt with.

Grabbing a long tunic and my shortsword, I stepped into the hall, nearly blind. The whispers continued, not in the walls this time but from down the hall, accompanied by the scraping of scales. They weren't whispers — the sound was soft hissing, like a pit of adders. Ophidians. They were in Galeston after all.

I tiptoed down the hall, following the hissing. It grew louder, and cool human voices laced in with the menacing cadence. If they were here, why weren't they protecting the mages? Unless they had been the ones to run the mages into hiding.

They were in the room on my left. Based on the sounds and my ability to sense them, there were a lot of them. Footsteps sounded just on the other side of the door. It had been a long time since I'd had any contact with the Ophidians I was supposed to be ruling.

I needed to know, and there was only one way to find out. With a breath, I shed the sweet persona I had worn for years. Perhaps I had shed her days ago, but now I allowed myself to bask in the freedom. My power answered with a purr. It was there. I could feel it pulsing within me.

I reached for the doorknob. Unlocked, as the Ophidians' hubris dictated. A cool sneer decorated my pale face as I stepped slowly into the room.

Half a dozen pairs of glowing, slitted pupils blinked at me from faces edged in scales of various shades of green. My eyes widened slightly at the brightness of some of them. These adders could not be more than several months into the order. Who was creating new Ophidians?

"New recruits?" I said, hiding my surprise behind a smirk.

They blinked at me for a second longer until the Ophidian with the darkest scales approached me, leering. "Give us one reason not to feast on your bones, *human*." The words were breathy, the Ophidian's tongue flicking against her teeth, making her words trail off in whispers.

I smiled toothily, willing the demon out of her cage. "I wasn't aware that you had resorted to eating your own."

The pear-green scales on her forehead crinkled in distaste.

"Whose orders brought you into this city?" I enunciated each word with deadly calm. Where in Hel was she? My body refused to transform. I should be able to shift now. If my magic was back, I should be able to shift. *She* came back, for Cieri's sake. Unease settled in my stomach.

The Ophidian laughed, her comrades following her. Green as they were, these Ophidians were in their snake forms, faster and stronger than any human's body, even one as trained as my own.

Your body used to be *well trained.*

"Rebels, then," I said quietly, buying myself time to think through a strategy. They were young and unorganized. Were they members of some rogue Ophidian force? Had *they* forced the mages into hiding? I hadn't spent three months of my childhood magicless in an Etruscan prison to be outwitted by a pit of snakelets. If I could not shift, I doubted my magic had truly returned.

The female rolled her eyes at me.

"How dare you," I hissed, weaknesses forgotten. I would not stand for this.

"We couldn't care less what a human queen thinks of us," she drawled, resting a scaly hand on her hip.

They're so new to the order their scales have barely even lost their glow. "I will not allow a *snakelet* to disrespect her queen." My eyes narrowed.

"Kill her," the snakelet ordered, more authority in her voice than those bright scales should have warranted.

My mouth cocked to the side in a crooked grin. Let them try.

The snakelets lunged at me one by one, as expected. I dodged the first easily, his hips giving away his strike well before he moved. I sliced my blade upward. His intestines splattered against the cool wood.

Wet droplets coated my face. I smiled.

"*Bitch,*" the commander hissed, charging me herself. Her words only enraged me further.

She was smarter than her predecessor, but I blocked her easily with my blade. I spun, pulling a knife from my leg holster and landed a slice across her face.

She screamed. Untrained indeed. I would have been whipped for screaming like that during training.

Another charged me, and I lashed out, my sword finding its mark. Another scream.

A hard fist collided with my abdomen. I gasped, whirling to the source and striking out with a knife.

I missed. A sharp pain pierced my side. I did not cry out.

Staggering back several steps, I stood, chest heaving, as the Ophidians converged on me. They had figured out how to move as a unit. *Shit.*

Reaching for the well of power within me, I filled the room with black mist. I allowed its illustrious tendrils to circle the snakelets, beckoning them into its embrace. I smiled sweetly. Now was as good a time as ever to find out if my magic had truly returned.

"Goodbye, snakelets," I crooned, yanking on the tether to my magic.

The Ophidians continued to creep toward me. I pulled on my magic again, flexing that mental muscle. They continued their approach.

Shit.

Panic welling inside me, I clawed and screamed at the part of my mind where my magic was housed. Begged it to do something, anything. I pressed the full force of my will onto it. Nothing happened. The Ophidians stood, my mist nothing more than decorative swirls.

A dull ache throbbed in my chest, threatening to erupt. Eyes darting between the Ophidians, I tried to remember how to breathe.

Are you a warrior queen or not? I shook myself. *Get your shit together, Ry. Katzima did not bless your magic so that it could become a crutch.*

Dragging the spit from my mouth, I lifted my gaze. A snakeling with scales as bright as a lime bared its fangs, preparing to strike. I threw my leg out under it, felling it easily. The snakeling popped back up, but I was there, pounding my fist into its skull. I felt my knuckles split under the pressure.

They were all in their Ophidian forms. I had to be smart about this. Even unarmed, they were lethal.

I spun, flinging an elbow into an approaching form. My blow landed, followed by a rewarding grunt. But I had left my stomach exposed. Another fist to my ribs had me doubling over.

A hard boot collided with my head, and I began to teeter. Shifting my weight, I rolled forward, out of the snakelings' reach. Springing to my feet, I tried to catch my balance. The snakeling I had felled was already getting up again, its body having healed itself. I staggered but held my ground.

I felt a shift in the air and adjusted my body, but I was too slow. Another fist collided with my cheekbone, followed by a sharp coppery taste filling my mouth. I spat the blood out, trying to grin, then swung out with a fist but missed this time. My reward was a swift kick to my side that sent me tumbling to the ground.

My fingers closed around one of the many knives at my belt, and I struck out, the blow drawing blood. The snakeling backed up a step, and I was able to fend off another with my legs. I had to get vertical again. I tried to push the throbbing in my head aside, but the alcohol I had consumed earlier was catching up to the blows I had taken.

Another swift kick to my back and I was on the ground. Blinding pain erupted on my head, and my vision began to blur. My jaw slackened. I fought to get my arms under me, but they refused to move. I lay there as my eyelids closed against my will, and fist after fist connected with my body. It was ironic really that this would be the way I died. Unfortunate of course, but I supposed I had never been meant to live a long life. *The great Tamariya Amunet, reduced to a pile of flesh in a snake's den*, I thought bitterly.

Haze filled my mind now as sweet reprieve beckoned me. I was drifting into it when I heard a crash followed by a vaguely familiar hiss. "You fools..." My fading mind could only catch fragments "...who that is?"

And then there was nothing.

EIGHTEEN

My own shivering woke me. The stone was cold on my back, and I could barely feel my fingers. I was still in my nightdress, but the sheath that I kept strapped to my thigh had been removed. My gaze lifted weakly to the room around me. Based on the acrid smell, I was underground. The water seeping into the opposite wall confirmed it.

The room was a simple stone square with a small window in the top corner that let in the faint moonlight. Shackles dug into my wrists, leaving red marks behind. I fought to remember what had happened, but my head was so foggy.

Had Aya been drawn to the Ophidians as well? If I vanished, would Calliope even care to look?

Anu's ass. I had been a fool. I brought an entire race of trained killers to their knees as an adolescent, and now I was a puppet who let things happen to her. A puppet who was sitting alone in a prison cell, and the gods only knew why. Not for the first time, I wondered if I had chosen the wrong throne. My eyes were heavy, but the sharp biting from the chains kept me from drifting off again. Slowly, I struggled to sit up. My back roared from lying on the cold stone. There was a good chance no one knew I was here, and no one was coming to rescue me.

I closed my eyes briefly, calling to the person who I knew could make it through this, the person who I had shoved so deep inside me I could pretend like she didn't exist most days. Until she had taken over in the woods. Lately, Ophidia had been fighting harder each day to emerge. I stopped fighting her.

My pain didn't matter—the grogginess was merely an inconvenience. I started gathering the chains around me, positioning them so I could strangle the first person to walk through that door. As I gathered my feet under me into a crouch, footsteps echoed down the hall. My muscles tensed. The door slid open. A familiar figure with flowing dark hair and piercing blue eyes walked in.

Doric's protégé would have hesitated. She would have seen his familiar face and remembered the moment we had shared last night. She would have asked questions before striking. Good thing she wasn't here.

I leapt, soaring through the air to wrap my chains around his neck. He merely stepped to the side, knocking me to the floor, but the chains caught me, throwing me back. I started to gather myself again, but two guards in unmarked uniforms rushed in and grabbed hold of my chains. One of their sleeves pulled up, revealing green scales. *Disloyal snakelets.* They dragged me into the wall. I snarled. A serpent smiled back at me.

"I would apologize for the cell and chains, but it appears that you've already proved them necessary," he gloated, eyes glittering predatorily. He prowled closer.

I spat on him, baring my teeth.

He laughed. It was cold and unfeeling, all of the warmth from last night gone. Instead, white-hot pain seared my ring finger, and an anger that was not my own consumed me. Somewhere in a deep corner of my mind, a girl wondered if she had imagined it. She would have blushed remembering her foolish behavior and juvenile thoughts. I sneered at the memory of her.

"This will be so much easier for both of us if you cooperate," the prince hissed. A muscle feathered in his jaw as his rage continued to roil through me. Hurt bloomed in my chest. Last night had meant nothing to him.

Foolish girl. I had never been interested in the prince's affections, and this only proved that my instincts had been correct.

The pain was blinding, traveling through my ring finger, splicing into my heart. Was this what happened when someone betrayed the betrothal bond?

A crack formed in my murderous exterior, allowing my emotions to trickle in. He was right: I had failed my people miserably. I spent the first three years of my rule locked away in my palace, twirling around in flowing gowns, convincing them from my cozy fortress that everything was well in Naqad. Letting Doric make the decisions about my kingdom for me. The fog crept back into my head. I could barely see Caryk in front of me. My knees buckled and I fell. What had he done to me?

NINETEEN

Ice rested against my cheek, seeping into my cuts as if its crystals would heal me. Someone had saved me. A burning sensation radiated near my wrists. I opened my eyes, expecting familiar obsidian and gray eyes to blink down at me in concern. Instead, a fuzzy outline of leathery boots blended into dark stone. I hadn't left my cell. My heart sank.

"How much did you give her?" a man said in an annoyed, clipped tone. *Caryk.* The sound of his voice punctured my chest, filling me with horrible emotion. I was a fool for letting the prince get so close.

"She fought back harder than we thought so we had to keep dosing her—that should have been the last of it," a gruff voice with a familiar accent said from behind me, and I jolted, causing a searing pain in my head. I knew that voice. The scaled arm of one of my captors flashed before my eyes. These were *my* Ophidians. My own order had betrayed me. They would burn. I would destroy them all if I ever got free. And I *would* get free. If only to exact my vengeance.

I tried to sit, my head screaming. I could feel my extremities again, not that it was a pleasant realization. At least I could move. I pulled myself into a seated position leaning heavily against the wall. Unflinchingly, I stared at Caryk, my eyes steely emeralds, forcing every ounce of hate I felt for him into my gaze. I forced it down the bond; finally, he'd get a taste of his own medicine.

"What do you want?" I spat, green fire blazing in my eyes.

"Time," he said simply. The gaze he fixed me with was the very same one he wore that day in the grand ballroom when he beheld me on the dais. And then the pain started again. The prince's rage completely unbridled.

"Why?" I whispered as I grit my teeth through the pain. *Why* did the prince hate me so much? The pain continued, past my heart this time, searing into my skull. My hands fisted at my sides, and they thrashed against the wall, fending off the agony.

I was panting, barely able to breathe. "Why... are you... doing... this?" I huffed. Caryk Cazaar had turned my Ophidians against me. He had usurped one throne and was attempting to destroy the other. And now I was being tortured. For what?

"For the good of the realm," he answered, his face a stony mask.

The prince had turned the Ophidians against me. *The prince.* Something clicked in my mind. An Etruscan prince had no claim over my people. Unless he was one of them. But that was impossible. I had never seen Caryk Cazaar in the Pit.

"Show me your fangs," I whispered. It was a risk, but there was no way the Ophidians would have turned on me for a *human*.

He laughed. "As if you're in a position to be making demands." *I was right.* If Caryk was an Ophidian, then he knew exactly who I was.

"You've kidnapped your own queen," I accused, doing my best to arch a brow while focusing on my breath. The pain ebbed a little when the prince spoke. Maybe I could keep him distracted long enough to focus.

He frowned. "I had to get you away from them somehow," he murmured.

"I could think of several better ways to go about it," I hissed. Bright white light shone around the edges of my vision. Whatever the prince was doing to me, I would not survive it much longer.

"I have your attention, don't I?" he challenged, the agony abating momentarily. "Where have the mages gone?"

"Even if I knew I wouldn't tell you," I ground out. Traitor. He was an Ophidian, they all were. They were supposed to be protecting the mages, not hunting them down. Dread scraped my stomach as I realized what had become of the order in my absence.

His frown deepened. "He's messed with your head more than I thought." The words were barely audible, and I wasn't sure if he intended for me to hear them. His jaw hardened, and the throbbing returned to my head.

"Go to Hel," I spat.

His luminescent eyes dared me to cry out, to scream. I would not. I would die before he knew the pain that he had caused me. More importantly, I would die before I told him a word about the people who had practically raised me.

I wasn't sure if I could open my mouth without screaming anyways. I met his poison-soaked stare with a venomous one of my own, willing his death with every part of my soul. The dungeon took on a misty haze. Now would be an excellent time for my magic to start working again.

My stare was death incarnate. He would die—they would all die for this. With every last bit of my will, I envisioned his body crumpling to the floor. The mist thickened.

One of the men holding my chains fell. An arrow zinged through the air and hit the other in the heart. Blood splashed my face as he fell to the ground. My chains loosened, and I lunged at Caryk, clawing at his eyes, and kicking anything I could feel. It was nearly impossible to tell what I was doing through the ringing in my mind. I struck out like a feral beast until I heard a shout.

"Ry!" I flipped toward the sound in time to see a knife careening end over end through the air. I caught it handily, palming it and thrusting backward at an Ophidian trying to pull me off Caryk. More men had come in the door chasing after my savior, who I didn't have time to thank, as someone yanked on my chains. An angry scream erupted from my lips as my body hit the ground. I held onto my knife with one hand, grasping the chain held by my captor with the other. I wrenched my bindings, and he fell into my dagger, sagging to the floor. His blood sprayed me, its coppery tang on my lips awakening something within me.

I spun, daggerless, arm held high, and caught another guard around the neck with my chains. Long fangs protruded from his jaw as he hissed. I slit his exposed throat, edged with bright-green scales.

A sharp pain erupted on my forearm, forcing me to release my grip on the Ophidian's neck. I threw my dagger in the direction of my assailant, but he caught it. Pushing off with all my strength from my good leg, I swung my mangled leg around to collide heavily with my attacker. He dropped my blade, and I took the opportunity to slam my elbow into his face. The crunch of his bones told me I had found my mark.

I spun to face the room and beheld Caryk's prowling form, a blade in each hand. Both mine. How many of my blades did he take? Was he going to slice me open with each one before he let me die? He wouldn't get the chance. I flung my dagger at his heart as I staggered toward him, forcing him to drop one of the knives to protect himself. He flattened himself against the floor, throwing a knife as he did. It hit my bicep, and I fell to the floor. I needed to get up, to get to him before he could flay me alive, but my body had stopped.

The blow to my arm had released all the adrenaline from my body. I couldn't move any more. My head was fuzzy again, this time from all the blood I had lost. Caryk noticed my pathetic state and smiled, pushing his arms under him to stand. This was how I died. At the hands of this conniving bastard. An Ophidian, nonetheless. The irony was not lost on me.

His glowing eyes fixated on mine, and I couldn't look away. Then a boot collided with his head, and his snake eyes dimmed, closing as his head fell onto the cold stone. I gasped. The arrow, the knife. My rescuer.

Warm brown hands were on my wrists, sliding a key into the shackles. They fell away. The rough hands drifted to my face, and I watched as amber flames studied my wounds. The flames blurred, and my head fell slightly to the side.

"No, no. Don't you dare. Don't you dare die on me. Do you hear me? Ry. Ry!" The voice was frantic. I could feel a pressure on my bicep as he hastily tried to stop the bleeding.

"Ry, please," the voice begged. I knew that voice. It was a sweet song, reminding me of crowded pubs and laughter. Even in its desperation it carried the joy of a minstrel's chorus. It was home.

I was in a field walking hand in hand with a man whose skin reflected the sun's falling rays like amber glass. The sun was warm on my face, and his broad smile made me forget my pain. We could stay here forever, his hand warm and calloused, filling me with radiant joy. Why would I ever leave this place?

"Ry!" The name sounded foreign. The moment of confusion shattered my idyllic world. It was replaced by a thick fog, but the voice kept on begging, kept asking me for something. What did it want from me? I was dying. But it kept asking, demanding now, so

I fought back to that voice. Pulling the hazy curtains aside, I opened my eyes a crack.

"Ry, thank the gods." He sighed, dipping his head in relief. Through the blur, I saw tight curls falling out of a messy knot and smiled weakly.

"Marcus," I breathed, squinting at him, trying to force my eyes to work. I could feel his warm body next to mine, and I drew on his quiet strength, letting it fill me up. Letting it ground me in the present. I focused on the feeling of his bare forearm resting against my bloodied one and let the contact send spurts of life into me.

"Let's get you out of here before more come," he insisted, scooping me into his arms. I groaned as the weight on my leg shifted. It was so heavy, dangling in the air. His bicep brushed a gash in my back, and I let out an involuntary yip. Each step he took sent pain lancing down my body, but I gritted my teeth and fought the darkness threatening to overwhelm me.

TWENTY

A stream gurgled next to me, along with the distant crashing of a waterfall, as the sun's rays melted over my face, spreading throughout my body, warming me. A floral scent mixed with fresh pine wafted up to my nostrils. I inhaled deeply, breathing in the scent I only dreamt about. My body felt light. There was no more pain; I had the feeling I could jump and run for miles if I so desired.

It was a shame really, that Marcus had gone through all that trouble to save me only for me to die in his arms. I felt a pang of guilt for leaving him and my friends but dying had been so easy. Because I was dead, right? There was no other explanation for this idyllic world I sensed around me. Cautiously, I opened my eyes.

The sky was a bright and clear cerulean, the clouds puffy white passengers on a lazy cruise. I turned my head to the gurgling stream.

It was clear with brilliant orange fish jumping in and out. Following the river's path, I could see it drop off and knew where the delicate roar of crashing waves came from. Next to me was a house I would never forget. Ivy grew along its walls, ending in rainbows of flowers and vegetables under cozy windowsills. I smiled. A tiny trill of fear rushed through me. I hoped that Katzima was not here. I prayed that she had survived and was deep in hiding somewhere. Her house was a perfect replica of the one that had been destroyed in Galeston. This was certainly death, and I prayed that she had not joined me.

The sunny yellow door to the home opened, a perfect complement to the tan stone framing the house. A curvaceous woman stepped through wearing a gauzy dress of flowing blue as bright and clear as the river next to her home. She wore a heavy cream shawl, patterned like the swirling waterfall that contrasted with the raven's-feather-black of her long, straight hair. Her warm brown eyes sparkled in sockets lined with crow's feet, and the wrinkles in her olive skin flushed slightly against the crisp autumn breeze. My heart sank. Katzima was dead. It was selfish, but relief washed over me. I didn't have to go through the afterlife alone. She walked over to me and smiled.

"Peace, Tamariya," she said softly. She reached up and wiped a damp tear from my face, forehead creasing with worry.

The sound of my name undid me. I cried out and rushed into her arms, beginning to sob in earnest. She folded me into her shawl and patted my back. I sobbed for her death, for the destruction of their way of life, and for the families who had been ripped apart by the war on Hel. For the first time, I allowed myself to truly mourn all that had been lost in the war. I was dead, so what did it matter if I fell apart? No one was counting on me to rule a country anymore. There was no need for façades in the afterlife.

Katzima let me unravel, rocking me and comforting me, squeezing me tight when my weeping turned to howling and I thought the grief would overwhelm me. Finally, my cries turned to sniffles, and she took a step back, holding me at arm's length and surveying me with a critical eye.

"Some of my best work, if I do say so myself," she trilled, crow's feet crinkling.

My brow creased, confusion clouding my eyes. "Your best work?" I asked.

She laughed, and the sound reminded me of the bubbles gurgling in the nearby stream. "My dear child, did you think your body healed itself all on its own? I know you are powerful, but no one is quite *that* powerful." Her dark eyes lit up like dancers around a campfire.

I laughed too. Even in death, she was still cleaning up after me, making sure I had a working form to roam the afterlife with. "Thank you," I said, smiling. "I dare say you did an excellent job."

Grinning, she said, "Come inside. I've put some cider on to warm. I imagine it's been quite some time since you've had any."

I smiled even broader. Even among the mages, Katzima was famous for her ciders. The fruits and spices she grew in her garden were the purest and freshest of anyone's, not to mention her knack for making the nastiest medicines bearable by adding them artfully to her concoctions.

I passed over the threshold and froze. My heart plummeted, for there at the kitchen table sat Marcus. "Marcus," I whispered.

He was up in an instant, closing the distance between us. His arms encircled me as he buried his head in my shoulder.

"I'm so sorry, Marcus. *Cieri*, I'm so sorry," I wailed, tears pricking my eyes again.

"Sorry?" he asked, raising his head. "What for? For being captured and tortured by your betrothed? That's not your fault, Ry," he said with a laugh that was both soft and sad.

"No," I sniffled. "For getting you killed."

His citrine gaze fogged in confusion. "What?" He studied me, and I could see him taking in my state, noticing the evidence of the sobs that had racked my body only a few minutes ago. He looked to Katzima and understanding dawned on his face.

"Tamariya"—he drew my name out carefully—"you aren't dead. I carried you out of the cell, and Katzima found us and led us here. She said that the spirits called her to you and gave her the strength to heal you. I swear she gave you every poultice and potion she has trying to bring you back. She worked on your body for days, chanting spells, replacing your bandages. Finally, she said it was your turn to decide whether you would live or die, and she placed you outside to be closer to the spirits," he finished, eyes wide.

"But Katzima is dead. The Mage Quarter was destroyed." My mind raced as my pulse thrummed. I smelled Katzima's rich cider on the kettle and heard the rustle of the wind through the trees. A cool kiss of air brushed my skin. I drew my hands to my face and felt the flush of my cheeks. I was *alive*.

Katzima smiled sadly. "I am sorry we had to hide from you, my child, but we had to make them believe we were gone. There is an evil in this village that we could not outrun. We used the last of our strength to protect this place and make it appear as ruins to all who passed by. Only one who knows what to look for can find us."

My jaw dropped. I had no idea the mages were that powerful, or that many of them had survived the war. I supposed that was exactly what they wanted the world to believe. My blood went cold. But Caryk knew. He captured me to find out where they were hiding.

"He knows," I whispered, looking up at Marcus and Katzima with terror. And I was alive. As realization dawned on me, I rubbed my hand against my arm, searching for the hole that Caryk had gauged there. I felt nothing but the smooth fabric of the dress Katzima must have put me in. But I could still feel it, the hole. My muscles tensed, remembering their agony.

I raised my hand to my temple. I knew there wouldn't be scar but I couldn't help the nausea that followed when my calloused hands met soft skin. It felt wrong, not bearing any marks after what I had endured. What had the prince done to my mind? Katzima had healed me before, but usually I asked to keep the scars. They reminded me of who I was. There was no scar to remind me of what the prince had done.

I closed my eyes and forced myself to remember. I remembered the cold look in his reptilian eyes as he demanded answers. Shame burned my face as I recalled almost kissing him in the inn. The empty sensation as I watched my father's corpse lowered to the earth. My heart racing when I stood on the altar and watched a crown being placed on my head as if it was someone else's. The radiant joy when I twirled on the dance floor in Marcus' arms. The warmth of his body holding mine on a cool morning. The air squeezing itself out of my lungs as I stood over a pile of corpses I had created. The triumph I felt as I drew my knife slowly across a body, eliciting screams. The emptiness of my soul cracking.

I dropped to my knees as images and emotions raced around me, and I took in each one. It was like seeing Katzima again had awakened the part of me that remembered how to feel.

I felt the embarrassment after my first council meeting when I realized I didn't know the first thing about being a politician. The dread and emptiness of wanting to give up. The relief when Terrin proposed that I relinquish control to them. The loneliness of being locked away, watching my kingdom move on. I let myself feel the trill of excitement at the prospect of finding a partner to carry this burden with me and then the rush of humiliation when I saw the contempt on Caryk's face the moment I met him. I felt all of it, and I shook with sobs, processing the war, ascending the throne, and the years after, ruling in silence.

Katzima came and knelt next to me, rubbing my shoulders, encouraging me to keep feeling, keep remembering all that I had been through. The pressure of her pendant was cool against my neck. "You are strong enough to get through this, child. You always have been," she said softly, squeezing my arms. It felt like forever that I had knelt in the middle of her floor sobbing, but eventually I had felt all that I could, and the sniffling stopped. Katzima led me to the sitting room and placed me on her overstuffed couch, positioning my hands around a mug of steaming cider. "For the soul," she whispered, gesturing to the drink.

I looked down at the swirling red liquid, steam billowing off it, and inhaled. Warm cinnamon and zesty citrus filled my nostrils, sending my tumultuous thoughts to a screeching halt. The corners of my mouth tugged up. I hadn't really lived these past few years without my family. Because that's what Katzima was to me. She was the mother I had deserved and the mentor who had taught me poise and control.

I took a sip of her potion and felt the shattered pieces of my soul sliding back together. Another sip and my heart began to warm. I was becoming whole again. Whole enough to remember the reason I had come to this city, the reason I wanted to see Katzima.

"Katzima," I started, "something happened to me after the war, once I wore the crown. My, uh, gift hasn't quite been the same." I cast a glance at Marcus, hoping she would understand what I was trying to ask.

Understanding dawned in her eyes. She frowned, considering. "Let me see," she whispered, reaching out, grasping my hand between hers, muttering an incantation.

Marcus looked over at us, concern etched in his gaze. I hadn't ever mentioned a problem with my fire gift, the only gift he knew I had. I usually avoided discussing my magic with him altogether.

Katzima looked up, lips twisted in a thin line. "I'm not sure, my child. There's something there, but I'm not sure what. I'll do some research and see if I can figure it out." She nodded toward her bookshelves, overflowing with spell books, history books, any text that mentioned magic.

That would have to be enough for now. "Thank you," I whispered, hope brewing in my chest. Katzima would look into it. And I had never known her to give up on a problem. There was one other thing, something I had not brought up to Katzima in years.

"How did she die?" I asked quietly. Maybe this time she would finally tell me. Maybe, finally, I would be allowed to know my mother's fate.

Katzima's warm eyes crinkled, kind understanding meeting my pleading stare.

"Please, I deserve to know," I begged.

"Aye, you do." She sighed. "I don't know everything, but what I know is not for the faint of heart." She cast a meaningful glance at Marcus.

He swallowed. "It's Ry's mom. I can handle it."

That was enough for the witch. "Your father found her in the palace. The Healers looked at her, but there was nothing they could do. They said that her mind was shredded."

"Shredded?" My stomach turned. I couldn't imagine what that would feel like. Or perhaps I could. Was that what the prince had attempted to do to me? It was the worst agony I had ever experienced. And Mother had endured much worse before she died.

"Aye." Katzima nodded, her expression grim. "And there's one other thing, Tamariya, what I have always feared telling you."

"Tell me," I breathed.

"They never caught her killer, but it had to be someone close to your parents, with access to the palace." For once, there was no warmth in her brown eyes, only flinty resolve.

Someone close to my parents had killed my mother. Was it an Ophidian? A Naqadian who found out she was the Viper Queen? Was that the fate that awaited me one day? A brutal assassination if I took either throne too far?

But it had been someone they knew. Caryk did not know my parents—he had never visited with the Etruscan caravan. But his father, King Dahlm Cazaar, had visited regularly. He had been a friend of my father. Could the prince have returned to finish the work his father started?

I had just gotten my family back and the prince was threatening to take it all away. But I knew who he was now. He had revealed himself. He suspected who I was, but if he had known for sure, he would have killed me in my sleep.

Raising my chin, I looked at my mentor and then across the room to where Marcus had hesitantly positioned himself on the couch opposite mine.

I set my jaw, then whispered, "I'm going to kill him." I stared at Marcus, daring him to disagree. The gold flecks in his eyes caught on the light and sparkled with anticipation. He smiled, and it was a smile I had never seen before on him. It was cruel and unfeeling. We were going to exact our vengeance on Caryk together.

My brow furrowed as it dawned on me that two people were missing from this reunion. "Aya and Calliope?" I asked.

"Safe," Marcus assured me. He may not have known why, but he knew that the three of us were inseparable. I nodded, exhaling. Caryk had not gotten to them.

Upstairs, I lay on my old bed, Marcus' arms wrapped firmly around me.

"How did you find me anyways?" I peered up at him.

He made a face.

A divot formed between my brows. "What?" I asked.

"You're not going to like it," he mumbled, a slight flush deepening his brown skin. He kept his eyes trained on pink and orange beams of sunlight filtering in through the window. My own eyes narrowed.

"Tell me." I frowned. If my oldest friend wouldn't be honest with me, was there anyone I could trust?

Liar, a voice rang in my head. *As if you've been honest with him.*

He let out a dramatic sigh. "Fine," he said, lowering apprehensive eyes to meet mine. "I was following you. I had a feeling you'd need backup." He paused, studying me, smoothing my hair back.

I tilted my head to the side. "Why?" I had asked him to stay in Egryt. To keep an eye on things in the capital for me. My insides were starting to fizzle at the prospect of Marcus of all people thinking that I wasn't capable of handling myself. Hadn't I proven myself enough? But I supposed this business with Caryk was a striking example of my ineptitude.

"I know what you're thinking, and it's not that." His amber eyes chastised me in an earnest warning. "I've known you my whole life, remember?" He placed a warm hand on my cheek. He knew *part* of me his whole life. I continued to glare up at him, watching the emotion in his eyes swirl like a glass of whiskey.

Eventually he said, "I haven't beaten you in a fight since we were children. I'm no fool—I know what you're capable of. I didn't follow you because I thought you needed my protection. I followed you because I noticed the prince leave Egryt rather quietly and thought you may want backup." His eyes roved across my face, pleading.

My brow crinkled. "What's the difference?" I asked.

He sighed. "The difference, Ry," he said, eyes darkening, "is that I don't see you as someone I need to protect; I see you as an equal. I want to fight the Viper *with* you, Ry. And when this is all over, I'm going to marry you." Twin flames burned in his eyes. My own widened.

"Marcus..." I whispered. We were not equals and we never would be. It had nothing to do with royal status. As long as this darkness burned through my veins, I could never truly share my whole self with him.

"No, listen to me, Ry. Do you love me?" Those flames were burning a hole right to my soul. I couldn't lie to him, not when he held me so close, the sunset dancing off the planes of his face. He held my hand in his large one and traced a slow circle on the back of my palm.

I couldn't give him false hope, that wasn't fair. He brushed his thumb around again. But what about the truth? Didn't he deserve that much? A rush of feeling slid up my arm as his calloused finger completed a rotation. He deserved the truth. I needed him to know the truth.

"Yes," I breathed. "I love you, Marcus." Before I could say more, his palm splayed across my back, pulling me to him so that my breasts grazed his chest. His other palm cupped my chin, moving across my cheek to tangle in my waves. His eyes were honey as he stared intently into mine.

"I love you too," he whispered, skimming my lips with his.

I let out a small moan and melted into him. The kiss was slow and luxurious, as if we had all the time in the world to revel in each other's bodies. Soft, warm lips enveloped mine as he kissed me with a reverence I had not noticed before. His hand was on my waist now, thumb tracing a path underneath my thin nightshirt.

I gasped as his hands roved my body hungrily, making their way up to my breasts, teasing around the edges of my nipples. I sat up, taking the edges of my shift in my fingertips and pulling it over my head. The thin fabric slid smoothly off my back.

His eyes darkened, and a chill ran down my spine. I was transported back to a time of stolen midnights when we devoured each other with an insatiable hunger.

But tonight, we had all the time in the world. He stood, eyes drinking in the soft curves of my body, the same hunger reflected at me now. My chest heaved under his gaze, desire pooling between my legs.

A smile spread across his face, but it was nothing like his usual easy grin. The tilt of his lips was a promise.

Heat bloomed across my body along with my answering smile. It had been so long since we'd had this kind of time together. Our goodbye in Malnova had been sweet, but it was tinged with the sadness of my departure. This was a homecoming, a thank you for saving my life, a celebration.

Reaching out, he placed one hand next to me, then the other until his arms were framing me. I inhaled sharply.

Amber orbs melted into my gaze. His eyes blazed, and a muscle in his jaw flexed. "Tamariya Amunet, Queen of Naqad, I *will* marry you. I will find a way to convince the council and your people that I am a worthy match for you." He breathed the words against my lips.

My eyes widened at the fervor in his words. His hand moved to grasp the hair at the back of my neck. "I love you," he whispered.

His lips crashed into mine, melting against my skin. His other hand slid to my back, then slowly to my hip. I spread my legs, barely resisting the urge to beg him to touch me.

My lips were captive in his as his hand traced from my hip to my leg, blazing a path of desire through my center. I squirmed against him.

"Please," I whispered.

He chuckled against my lips. "Your wish is my command."

His fingers retraced their path up my thigh, this time moving to my core, and I gasped as he finally touched me, fingers sliding easily through the wetness between my thighs.

"Marcus." My voice came out as a whine.

He plunged his fingers inside me. My head fell back, and I moaned as he worked me. His fingers explored me while his thumb found my clit. I bucked my hips against his fingers, grinding them into me.

Being touched by him was ecstasy. His other hand glided to my chest, teasing and toying with my nipples. I breathed heavily, already on the verge of an orgasm. Marcus had not forgotten how to make my body sing.

Hand coming to rest in the center of my chest, he pulled away a fraction, studying me. I squirmed under his gaze, breasts splayed out before him. He smiled.

"Gods, you are gorgeous."

I beamed.

He pushed my chest, and I fell backward onto the bed. His hand stayed between my legs, but he dipped his head down, tongue finding my breasts, swirling against my nipples. He began to suck, and I moaned against him, working his hand into my throbbing center.

"Please," I breathed. "Fuck me."

"Yes, Your Majesty." I didn't know if it was the use of my title or the push of his cock against my core that caused another splash of ecstasy to course through my body. My back arched as my hips bucked against him. Each thrust was luxurious, and I reveled in it.

His hands came to grasp my wrists, holding me as he pounded into me. I could not think, could barely breathe as we melted together. This was all I ever needed.

He shifted and his cock stroked the spot I'd been yearning for him to find. I groaned, head lolling to the side. A burst of pleasure coursed through me, building quickly. Thrust after thrust until my center erupted.

As I came, he moaned, pounding hard, pleasure building within him too. I could feel his orgasm against me as his cock flexed, filling me.

He collapsed on top of me, breathing heavily. I smiled, breathing hard as well. My head spun, and for a moment I let it wander into oblivion, soaking in the release that my orgasm had brought me.

Being with Marcus made the rest of the world fade away. But slowly, my unwanted thoughts began to trickle back in.

I shifted, aiming to disentangle myself.

"No, Ry. Please," he begged, eyes scanning my face, watching as my expression changed. "Not yet." He started to sit up, but I jumped from the bed, pulling my shirt back on. I refused to get caught up in him again. His hand stretched toward me, fingers flexing as if they could grasp my hand from there.

I shook my head. We both knew this was wrong. We were wrong for each other, and the realm would pay if we were ever caught together. Katzima would never sell my secrets, but this had to end eventually, as all good things in my life did.

As my ecstasy faded, a strange pang echoed across my finger.

TWENTY-ONE

It felt like I was living in a dream, walking through the Mage Quarter with Marcus, despite the tension that hung between us. Familiar faces passed me and offered hesitant smiles when they realized who I was. The immaculate sky mocked me, daring me to find a flaw in this perfect day. The river tumbled beside us while beautifully colored fish jumped alongside sparkly humanoid forms. There was a child lifting the water to make floating spheres while her friends giggled. She launched a water ball at them causing them to shriek and laugh at their soaked clothes. The girl launched another, but a young boy threw a burst of flames from his hands that evaporated the ball immediately. The girl beamed.

While the power that mere children among the mages possessed unnerved some, it was beautiful to me. The few mages with deep magical wells had displayed the terrifying depths of their power on the battlefields, but they were not a warrior people. They taught their children to love and respect magic, to use it for good above all else. A smile spread across my face as I witnessed the joy that remained in my people, even after I had dragged them into a war with the underworld. After many long years, I was *home*.

And I was about to ruin it by spending my afternoon talking to Lord Doric Venrylst and the rest of the council. We would inevitably have to relay my capture and torture to them, and a tight knot formed in my stomach at the prospect. I forced myself to focus on the fact that I was alive and to use it as the gift it was.

We walked in awkward silence through the rest of the Mage Quarter. The air turned brittle as we passed through the mage's barrier back to the dull gray shadow the rest of Galeston had become. I grit my teeth at the contrast. Once Caryk was dead, the mages could come out of hiding and return the city to its former beauty. He had to be the one hunting them; it was why he had followed us to Galeston and captured and tortured me.

Before us, Galeston's keep loomed. It was a hovel compared to the palace in Egryt, barely larger than the castle in Malnova.

The city's defense relied on the looming city gates, so the gate to enter the keep was mostly for show. The building behind it was only large enough for a great hall and several nice rooms. Not that I would know. I hadn't dared step foot in the keep when I was spending my summers in Galeston, even though Lord Frydrik Moscar was a friend to the mages in his territory.

"Care to lead the way to my utter humiliation?" I asked dryly. At least I was dressed with some dignity today. I wore pants that ballooned out and cinched at my practical boots. Even my waistbelt had been fashioned into a weapons harness, a piece Katzima had refused to toss out after I left her training.

Marcus nodded with a grimace, leading the way through the gates. We passed through the crumbling marble halls in silence, not daring to speak lest one of Terrin's birds overheard. Despite its small size, the keep projected a former splendor. Shallow marble pools lined the halls, empty, save for deep red streaks absorbed into the rock. I tried not to think about what had happened here and to whom while we rounded a corner to one of the small meeting rooms.

As the doors opened, I was greeted by Doric Venrylst's flared nostrils. My eyes flashed, and I straightened my stance. He was waiting for me to break, to fold into submission, but I would not, not this time. Not over this. Instead, I nodded coolly. "Lord Venrylst."

His eyes narrowed. "Your Majesty," he answered carefully.

Terrin gazed at me with concern but thankfully did not say a word. I looked each council member in the eye and was met with variations of concern and annoyance. To them, I was a silly little girl who had disregarded orders and was met with the obvious consequences.

I slid my hands into my pockets to prevent them from twitching to the knives sheathed in my belt. My gift hummed within me, begging to slaughter them all. I shoved it back down, shoving *her* as far away as I could. I could not rely on my gift to save me. While I could at least feel it again, I wasn't convinced it was truly working. Besides, I needed answers, not to threaten my closest advisors.

It was General Brom Balenek who finally spoke. "You did not heed my warning." I resisted the urge to roll my eyes.

They would not speak to you this way if they saw your power. No. I would not go there. There had to be another way.

I walked slowly around the room, aiming for controlled grace rather than a prowl. Ophidia would be too happy to see me reveal myself as the predator I was. "Your warning was heard and appreciated, Brom," I said diplomatically. "However, you are not the Queen of Naqad. I am, and I am not obligated to obey you." I cocked my head to the side. "I listened to you when I agreed to the betrothal to the prince and look where that got me." I stood directly in front of Brom now, eyes flashing as I tried not to appear as if I were looking up at him. I missed the days where I could bring a man to his feet with half a thought. *You still can.* I placed a mental hand on her coiled head and shoved.

He narrowed his eyes, unsure how to handle this new version of me. "A queen with any sense would not have been tricked into a drunken stupor and captured so easily." I knew that Terrin's birds would have told them everything, but hearing it confirmed was still a blow.

My nostrils flared. My hand spasmed toward my blades.

Make it hurt. Make the pain last. No, not here. I could not rule Naqad that way. Ophidia did not rule Naqad.

Go away.

I had to play their game. After a deep breath, I said quietly, "A council with any sense would have vetted any suitor that dared come near the crown." I turned my head to look at Doric as I said the last words. It had been his idea after all. Sure, I had agreed, but only because I had trusted his judgment.

"We need to consider the possibility that the Prince of Etrusca either is the Viper or is working closely with her." Terrin spoke now. "Never mind whose fault it is, we've seen an Ophidian at last. Now is our time to strike."

I fought the urge to laugh. "The Ophidians are not our enemies," I challenged. How did Terrin know what the prince was? There had been no birds in the cellar. My gaze shifted to Marcus. How much had he told the spymaster?

"Are you sure about that, love?" a velvety voice that was both foreign and familiar oozed from the doorway. A tall form prowled in. His dark hair hung just past his closely trimmed beard where a cruel mouth twisted into a smile. Serpent's eyes turned to me, brimming with poison.

The council stood, bristling at the prince's sudden intrusion.

"Guards!"

"Seize him!"

The calls rang out through the room. No one came. Perhaps the predator before me had bewitched them with his mind magic. If the council knew what Caryk was, they had severely underestimated him.

I felt the ghost of a headache returning. I flexed my fingers.

Kill him right now.

She was right this time. He deserved it. A haze fell over the room as I smiled. But this smile did not belong to the Queen of Naqad, demure ruler. This smile belonged to Ophidia, Goddess of the Ophidians.

"My prince," I crooned, prowling closer. "I'm afraid we did not say goodbye properly when we last met."

Marcus moved to step between us, but I placed a hand on his arm, shaking my head. This was between the prince and me.

"Nobody intervenes," I said to the room.

For once, the council heeded my warning.

Caryk tilted his head to the side, blatantly scanning my body. I resisted the urge to hiss.

"Looking for something?" I arched a brow.

A brief flash of confusion softened his features. I thought I may have imagined it until he said, "Your skin does not bear any reminder of our time underground." His voice was almost wistful, like a lover's caress. It brought chills down my spine. He flexed his knife hand. My smile fell.

"Then, it's clear who the victor was," I said with a smirk. It was my turn to scan him, lingering on the scrapes beginning to heal on his face. He was an Ophidian, so they would heal quickly, but not faster than Katzima's healing magic. I wondered if his slow walk masked a limp. I hoped so.

His eyes darkened. "Who healed you?" He said it slowly, both a threat and a demand.

"I drank the blackened river water; I think it might be magical," I said with a poisonous smile, forcing down my growing panic. If he was hunting mages, I may as well have shown up with a map to their hideout.

His piercing eyes were hypnotic as he prowled toward me. The look on his face would have brought a different woman to her knees. "I would not be quick to jest if I were you," he said, glowing eyes intent on mine. "Everyone who has helped you will die… unless you come with me," he whispered, breath teasing my cheek.

A fire burned within me, and I let the madness in my eyes show. "You have wandered into *my* court. You are in no position to be making threats." I emphasized the last word, turning it into a caress.

He laughed. Nervous murmurs from the council followed his reaction. "You will not kill me," he said slowly.

"Is that a challenge?" I said with a quiet threat, seduction in my voice begging him to follow through on said challenge. The haze in the room thickened, flicking around the chairs now. I hoped the council would credit it to Caryk's mysterious power.

"If you kill me here in the middle of your court, you will never learn who is behind the attacks on the mages. Your Healer friend will die before you can uncover the truth."

The haze in the room rolled. *He doesn't respect your power. Prove him wrong. Make an example. He doesn't get to threaten the witch and live.* I balled my fists against the voice in my head. But she was right. I should kill the prince for the brazen threats.

"The council is handling such matters," Doric sneered, stepping forward to take on the prince.

"Was I speaking to you?" Caryk cocked his head in the councilman's direction, death glittering in his eyes.

"Tamariya, Caryk Cazaar is an arrogant fool who will bring nothing but destruction on the mages. Do not listen to him," Doric said smoothly.

I looked at Doric, narrowing my eyes. Just months ago, the prince had been the ideal suitor, a perfect match for the kingdom. What right did Doric have to order me around like that? My headache grew, no longer a ghost of a memory.

"I'd like to hear what the prince has to say." My gaze met the prince's. His eyes were aglow.

"Interesting," he purred. Then his mouth twisted into a smirk. "It would appear your influence is not all the queen considers nowadays, Doric."

Doric searched my face furiously, as if I held some riddle there. If I didn't know better, I would think that a glimmer of panic dashed across his face. In a blink, he wore a cool smile again.

Did I imagine that? No, it was there. Some emotion laid barely concealed just behind his eyes. I refused to consider what that could mean. It wasn't possible.

"Let me handle this, Tamariya," Doric said quietly, urging me to listen.

I refused to budge, crossing my arms in front of my chest. "Not a chance."

The prince's expression was triumphant. My brow creased. Caryk was far too gleeful. I looked between the two men in confusion. As I watched, the prince's mirth transformed. His eyes grew dark, and his jaw flexed. The pale band on my finger warmed. His hand, with its glittering rings, twitched to the massive broadsword he wore at his hip. "How dare you," Caryk growled as my finger began to burn with his rage.

Something within me coiled, responding to the prince's rage directed at Doric. Caryk's pupils were nearly slitted, piercing blue irises drilling into my chief advisor. When he opened his mouth, I could see his elongated canines. On his cheekbones, dark shapes started to take form. My jaw slackened. *Those eyes.* They had been burned in my memory for over a decade. Since the gruesome ceremony my mother had forced me to witness.

The Prince of Etrusca was the first Ophidian I had ever seen. My mind raced as I tried to figure out what that meant.

"Why are you here?" Doric demanded. I barely heard him. I tried to focus on my breathing. There was something else to the prince.

"I came for my queen," Caryk said through his teeth. My head snapped to attention.

"Get out," Doric hissed. "Tamariya, kill him."

Something within me sparked at the order. It was like my body wanted to obey the urgent tone in the lord's voice. My head cleared slightly. I had wanted to kill the prince mere moments ago. *She* would luxuriate in the feeling of his life seeping away. But something about what Caryk had said... I needed to know what he meant. "Not yet," I said, holding up a finger, intrigued by the break in the prince's cool exterior.

This time, I did not imagine the rage burning on Doric's face. The councilman was not used to taking orders from his queen. A situation that needed to be rectified immediately.

"I didn't come here to ask nicely for the queen to join me," he said, losing patience. "Tell me, where is your pet spy and her ice princess today, love?" His enraged tone had calmed to a stewing anger by the time he turned to me, chest still heaving, but the flame on my finger dulled to warmth. His fangs receding with every breath, his scales never getting the chance to fully form.

The color drained from my face as I looked at Marcus. "You said they were safe," I whispered. Marcus' skin had turned a sickly olive.

"Did someone tell a lie?" the prince said dryly, not bothering to feign concern.

"Our sources said they were safe," Marcus said carefully, amber eyes pleading. *Our sources.* I knew Marcus worked with Terrin, but he was *my* informant.

The prince rolled his eyes. "Aya Jesper and Calliope Torino reside in an abandoned inn, just south of the city. You have an hour to meet me there, or you will not see them again."

He had them. He took the two people who tethered me to this world. Calliope may drive me insane with her bloody morality, but I needed her. Without Cali, who would stop me from slaughtering entire villages? My rage blew holes in my carefully cultivated façade.

"How?" I bit out, trying not to let the avalanche tumbling within me show. I gripped the back of a chair. My knuckles were snowy white against the dark wood.

He smirked. "It appears that your *people* are not quite as loyal to you as you may have thought." His eyes glowed as he watched the impact of his words dance across my face.

I didn't have time to speculate, and my mind refused to acknowledge the prince's words. They would be dead soon enough. I could stop this. I would get them back. The prince thought he could control me by capturing my friends? He was utterly mistaken about the kind of person I was.

"Do not threaten me," I said, quiet as death.

Caryk's nostrils flared. "For each minute over the hour, your friends lose a limb. I wonder how Calliope would hold a sword without hands. Aya would make a poor spy indeed if she lost an ear or two." His eyes glittered with malice as he examined his sword.

The image of my friends bleeding out slowly in Caryk's dungeons settled the mist swirling in my mind. Aya and Cali would gladly give their lives to save our people, but I would rob them of that honor. Tamariya Amunet would not be manipulated. Every breath I took was saturated with the need to kill, to exact vengeance on this man who threatened me.

I drew the corner of my mouth up, my eyes shining with madness, death swirling on my fingertips. "You do not know me at all if you think that you or any of your henchmen will survive the night." I let the threat hang in the air.

"And one more thing, *Your Majesty*. Come alone."

Death boiled inside me. I would kill him. After I had murdered every soul he ever cared about, I would kill him slowly. Caryk turned and slithered out the door, disappearing as quickly as he had arrived.

When he was gone, I spun to face my court, quieting the mist. I prayed they would attribute the magic to the prince. It was foolish to lose control like that, but I hadn't felt my magic in so long. Even if it wasn't working, seeing its beauty filled me with hunger.

"We will get them back, Riya," Terrin said gently, gazing at me with sympathy.

"Why not just do as he asks?" Doric mused.

Marcus growled. "Absolutely not."

My eyes widened. As did Doric's, before they narrowed into thin slits.

"You save a queen once and think your opinion matters?" Doric sneered.

Marcus' cheeks darkened. My hand twitched. I wanted to throw one of my knives at the councilman.

"I will get them back, and I will do it alone," I said, raising my chin as I spoke.

Brom spoke, concern etched in his gaze. "He's an Ophidian, Tamariya. He has an entire army of mages behind him. You do not stand a chance of walking out of that inn alive."

"I am not risking their lives by bringing any of you along. You heard the prince: I will go alone. And I will be fine," I stated.

"That *prince* is corrupting our lords and causing the people to starve. Do you honestly think you can take him on alone? Naive girl," Doric said, lip curling.

Rage flashed in my eyes. I was no little girl. I had seen things in my short life that would bring each of these men to their knees. Not to mention that I could flay every one of them alive before they could lift a finger against me. For a moment, I let myself picture it. My dormant gift hummed in response. If only I could get it to work before my visit to the inn.

While the thought was comforting, they were still my council, and I still needed them to rule. And the image of Doric's or Brom's body limp against his chair snagged on my heart uncomfortably. But I could no longer allow my gratitude to overlook their disrespect. This charade that we all put on was insulting. For the first time in years, I knew what needed to be done.

"Let's stop pretending that I am some child who inherited the throne by chance," I seethed, letting my power fill the room. "Brom, despite yours and the king's best efforts, I fought in one of your battalions in the war; you know exactly what I can do with a blade. I set all of that aside to be your puppet queen, but don't you dare forget who I am and what I can do."

I gave each council member a meaningful look. "The mages are our people just as much as any other Naqadian. I will go meet the Etruscan prince, retrieve my comrades, and stop him from destroying our realm."

Doric's usually pale face was purple. Terrin looked as if I had slapped him. But Brom nodded in understanding. "She has a point," he said. "Whether we care to admit it or not, the girl can pull her weight with a sword."

Doric's eyes threatened to bulge out of his skull. My eyes zeroed in on his. I wondered if Doric knew the truth. That I was the only thing standing between the council and the full might of the Ophidians.

"She's right, Doric," Terrin said. "We need to listen to our queen." My crumbling heart thawed at the spymaster's words, caught off guard by the display of allegiance.

Marcus nodded. "We find Calliope and Aya, and kill the Etruscan prince." The pale scar on my finger burned in rage, as if Caryk had heard.

The men muttered their discomfort, but Brom nodded, followed by the other councilmen. It was only Doric who had not agreed.

I took a deep breath, pulling my anger back, composing myself. When I looked up at Lord Venrylst, a calm but resolved exterior gazed at him. The purple was fading from his face, but his long nose still looked as if he had smelled something rotten. This was the first time I had stood up to him in ages. But he was wrong this time.

I continued to breathe deeply, looking into the pale orbs of his eyes. It felt like an eternity passed before he said, "You'd better get moving, then." My shoulders relaxed. I would save my friends and deliver my betrothed's head to the council on a spike.

TWENTY-TWO

"I said I was going alone," I grumbled, as Marcus and I crouched behind a crumbling stone wall. The building beyond was an old inn, the one where Caryk and his Ophidian traitors were hiding out. The sun was already beginning its descent; I had waited nearly the full hour to come. Aya and Cali were running out of time. If they hadn't been slaughtered already. But I wanted the prince to think that I wasn't coming.

I peered around the wall again and scanned the wooden façade ahead. A few of the windows were cracked, and the grass had long been trampled over. I searched the muddy yard for tracks. There were a few sets of footprints between the inn and stables and around the yard, but that didn't mean anyone was inside now.

I was debating whether to make a run for the front door and leave Marcus in the dust when he blurted, "I was surprised that you showed them your magic. Why do you pretend like your fire gift is so small? I know that smoke in the room was you." His amber eyes tried to catch mine.

I avoided his gaze. "It's not something to be proud of," I muttered.

"You say that every time I ask you about the time they sent you to live with the mages. But I've met Katzima. She's clearly proud of you," he pointed out.

"In a sense, I suppose she is." I could see it in her eyes though. For every kind word she uttered, a world of sorrow for the monster I had become, echoed in her eyes. I bet she would unmake the monster she had created if she could. But I couldn't tell Marcus that. Nobody but me needed to bear that burden.

At least, for the moment, I was in control. The rage flickering inside me promised Ophidia's imminent return. I inhaled deeply, shoving her down with each breath. I was in control. The creeping sensation that I was waking up from a dream still lingered after the council meeting.

Marcus' eyes were molten as he looked back at me, and he must have seen the sorrow in mine because he nodded and looked away.

"Any ideas on why Lord Venrylst looked like he'd swallowed a turnip?"

"I have a theory, but you're not gonna like it," I muttered. A light flickered in one of the windows. Or it was a glare from the sun. The house was shaded by the trees in the distance, but I couldn't tell if my eyes were playing tricks on me. I needed to sneak around to the side where there were fewer windows. I wasn't sure, but I got a sense that there were more than a few Ophidians slithering within. Bloody traitors. The monster within me licked her poisonous fangs.

Marcus grunted his agreement and followed me as we slunk along the low wall. "Would you care to share your theory or leave me to imagine a motive for the pissing contest I just witnessed?"

That got my attention. "Excuse me?" I pivoted in the mud, coming face-to-face with him. Where I expected to see anger, there was only concern.

"You and Doric basically whipped your bollocks out and threw them on the table." The words were oddly gentle.

"Funny, I didn't know asserting my crowned authority would be so controversial," I said with a steely edge to my voice. I was tiring of everyone's concern.

"Sorry, sorry." He put his hands up. "But why did it bother Lord Venrylst so much?"

I sighed. "I don't know, probably the same reason everyone is on edge."

Liar. You know why. Gods, *she* needed to shut up. *She* was wrong anyways. But the way he'd acted when I had disagreed with him...

To explain it to Marcus would be to tell him everything, and I wasn't ready for that conversation. Nor did I ever plan to be. "The mages showed what they were capable of during the war; now they're being hunted. No one knows how to feel about it, not even the council."

I continued creeping along the wall.

"But the council protects Naqadians, just as you do," he pointed out, unrelenting.

"Do they?" It came out a lot more accusatory than I had intended. But the way they had acted when I'd proposed we visit Galeston had me reconsidering. What reason did the council have to keep me from the city?

"That's quite the accusation."

I stopped. Marcus nearly crashed into me. "It's not that," I said over my shoulder. "I know that they care about this kingdom and the people in it—they served me and my father well and have always acted in the best interest of Naqad. But you must admit they have quite the talent for holding onto power." I resumed my hunkered creep along the wall.

A power grab surely. What wasn't a power grab when your entire life was court politics? We were coming up on the side of the inn now. I hadn't seen any other flashes of light in the window. "Maybe I imagined that light," I murmured. "Time for you to go." I looked at Marcus.

He was studying me with an odd look in his eyes.

"What?"

"The council does what they do because it's best for the kingdom. You know that, right?" Deep shadows masked the rest of his face, but his eyes were like hard leather.

A crease formed in my brow. "Of course. Like I said, I know they care about Naqad as much as I do." I turned back to the inn. "Now, get out of here," I said impatiently.

We were wasting time sitting out here talking.

He grabbed my arm. "I'm not letting you go in there alone."

I rolled my eyes. "You do not *let* me do anything, Marcus," I hissed, eyes narrowing on his hand. "The prince expressly told me to come alone. You following me this far has already put my friends in danger." If the situation weren't so dire, I would have smirked at calling Calliope a friend. More like a personal moral watchman.

"There are too many of them, Ry," he pressed, warm eyes worried. "You're going to get yourself killed." His concern was genuine, but it echoed hollowly in my chest.

"I can handle myself," I growled. Marcus had no idea what I was capable of.

"I don't doubt that, but I see the look in your eyes. You aren't planning to meet Caryk. You're going to kill them all."

I remained silent. I was creeping around the inn for a reason, and it wasn't because I was about to give into the prince's demands.

"Tell me that you plan on walking out of there alive, and I'll leave."

I glared. He couldn't possibly understand. I needed Aya's astute observations to handle the council's ever-changing alliances. Even Calliope, and her incessant moral compass, was essential to my humanity. Without them, I was not a queen, I was not anything. No, if they died, I would become something else, something hardly recognizable as human. I could not leave that inn without them. Naqad did not deserve the chaos that would ensue.

"That's what I thought," he spat, eyes ablaze. "Someone needs to look after you too, Ry. I'm coming." I had never seen this look in his eyes before. I didn't have time to explain it to him, to explain why he should let me perish. Why, if he knew the truth, he would not be looking at me with such intense heat. He would not be able to look at me at all.

"Fine," I said through my teeth. "Let's go, then. The side entrance." I took a few deep breaths, calming my budding unease before glancing around the yard.

Seeing nothing, I gripped the stone wall and flung my legs over it, moving swiftly to the windowless façade. Marcus joined me. We crept along to the back, ducking under windows, and advancing hastily. Perhaps the prince was laughing to himself as he watched us, but I hoped his attention would be fixed on the front entrance.

We came to the back door, and I tried the knob. The door swung open. My heart plunged. This was too easy. Caryk had been expecting me to disregard his summons, and I had fallen right into his trap. There was no going back now, so we slipped silently into the room. For once, I was grateful that Marcus was one of Terrin's spies. He moved nearly as silently through the room as I did.

We entered a sitting area. The plush leather couches were faded and ripped, the bookcases bare in haphazard places, picked over by those searching for quick kindling. The sun was setting now, casting long shadows off the old furniture. Other than the disorder, the room seemed clean. There was no dust. My heart flipped. Someone had been here.

Something moved in the far corner behind a couch, and a dark bolt zinged toward me. I ducked, flattening myself to the floor behind an overstuffed chair, and pulled Marcus down with me. I drew my long knives and motioned for him to cover me. He nodded, drawing an arrow from his quiver.

Peeking my head around the chair, I searched the room with new eyes. Eyes that refused to adjust to the dim light. I gritted my teeth, still unable to shift. I sent my senses out into the room, feeling for any sign of life, as I held up my palm to Marcus, careful not to turn my head. There were five of them. At least my gift could do that much. It was something, but I dared not rely on it for more.

He pointed to the smoke swirling around him and then to his eyes. Pulling my power back in, I rolled behind another couch, making my way to where I knew someone lurked in the hall. I sprang up behind them, drawing my blade across their throat. As they fell, I caught them and gently lowered them to the ground. Bright-green scales rimmed their face. Ophidian, and newly created too. No wonder they were so slow. *They're traitors, all of them. They deserve what's coming to them.* For once I agreed with the monster.

I cast my gaze around the room from my new vantage point. The chairs and sofas were arranged to overlook large windows into the woods beyond the inn. Curtains framed the windows, one set brushing up to where I knew Marcus perched, the other ending in shadows. I drew a smaller knife, balancing it on my palm as I waited.

A dark blur moved between couches, and I flung my knife. A grunt confirmed I had hit my mark.

I had given up my position. I ducked just in time as an arrow came flying my way. The attacker was charging at me, so I swept my leg out as they approached, plunging my long blade into their back on the way down. A hiss sounded as they fell.

Springing upright, I slipped into a corner behind a large trunk. Another assailant dashed across the room, and Marcus disposed of them quickly. Surprise splashed across my cheeks at his speed with the bow. Ophidians were quicker than the average man; it was no easy feat to catch one.

That made two, and a third was injured. But how many more had crept in, blending with the shadows? I supposed there was one way to find out. I stood up, making myself clearly visible, and felt three arrows stir the air. One, barreling right at me. I easily dodged it. Two, not so lucky this time, the arrow skimmed my arm. I barely felt it. Three, Marcus' arrow buried itself into the chest of another attacker. I smiled.

I launched myself across the room, hurtling into the other Ophidian. They fired arrow after arrow at me, but I knocked them away with my blade, breathing death as I sliced into them, a swift kill. I whirled to face the room.

Marcus had drawn his sword and was trading blows with another, its fangs getting dangerously close to his neck. Another Ophidian pounced on me. I parried their sword with one knife, striking out with the other. This one's scales were darker—I wondered how many kills they had under them. They jumped out of the way. I faked a lunge in, and they reacted, jabbing into where my heart was seconds ago. Smirking, I took the opening and sliced their chest open. The Ophidian stumbled back. I knocked their sword away, finishing with a final blow to the chest.

Looking up from my conquest, Marcus had killed another one, but two more were taking their place. So much for only five. A blade swung through the air, headed for Marcus' chest. His sword parried blows from the other assassin. I drew another knife and hurtled it at the Ophidian. It hit him square in his back, and he fell, dropping his sword before it could find its mark. The other turned, and Marcus used his distraction to finish him off.

Carefully, I stepped over to him. We stood in the middle of the room, back-to-back, scanning for any more assailants. The room was quiet. There was a hallway in the back, the one where I had slit someone's throat, and two more closed doors at each end—I had no doubt that more hid behind each.

Marcus pointed to the hall with a raised brow. I nodded. We crept down the hallway, covering each other. The inn was crawling with Ophidians. More traitors than I could have imagined. Red clouded my vision. It wouldn't be that hard to kill them all, but I couldn't believe that this many had defected. My control on my gift began to unravel.

The front door stood at the end of the hall. From here, a communal dining area lay to the left and another sitting area on the right.

In the middle was a wide staircase. The waning sunset cast shadows on the stairs, hiding the upper levels from view.

"They're up there," I whispered to Marcus.

He gave me a startled look but didn't question me. As we ascended, I released the dampener on my power. We didn't dare light a lantern, so Marcus couldn't complain about the swirling mist. It had been years since I had really flexed my power, let it spill out as I did now. My head felt clearer in the absence of the constant need to quell my gift. My hands of smoke spread through the halls like a blanket. What I felt made me smile. There were bodies in nearly every room, some stirring, some perfectly still. I could not take them all out at once, not without accidentally killing my friends. We would have to search every room.

At the top of the staircase, my hand brushed Marcus', signing what we needed to do. I felt his agreement, completely unaware of the predator now stood beside him.

Ophidians were emerging from the rooms, coming to see what had happened below. Before they had time to figure it out, we were on them. Two corpses hit the floor, followed swiftly by a third. We crept through the hall, seeking out the others. Few others came to investigate.

We made our way through every room on the floor, ensuring that none housed Aya or Cali. Upon opening a few rooms, we found Ophidians who hadn't bothered to investigate the commotion. I could feel Marcus stiffen after each kill, but I reveled in it. I had not had my power open this long in years, forgetting the draw it had on me, the urges it instilled.

Each kill fed the beast roaring inside me. It wasn't long before I was drunk on it. *Cieri*, I had missed this feeling. On the third floor, waiting Ophidians filled a sitting room. As bodies lunged at us and struck one after another, my grip on my power loosened, and I struck out with it. Nothing happened. *She* howled. For all its smoke, my gift still wasn't working. I quickly dispatched the assailants, sobered by my gift's impotence. The room was empty again, save for Marcus and me.

My power's presence didn't feel like a release anymore. It was maddening trying to keep it at bay, to keep it from doing what it was made to do, while knowing if I released it, it would not succeed. I pulled it in all the way, and the mist cleared in the sitting room and in my head. I could feel Marcus turn toward me in the dark. Before he could say anything, I headed for the door and whispered, "We need to keep moving. They know we're here." He followed me out.

"Wait," he whispered when we reached the door. He glanced back and forth along the hall. "This doesn't look right. The second floor was longer."

I looked. I couldn't be sure, since my gift had clouded our view, but in the waning sunlight filtering in from a hall window, I swore he was right. Marcus walked back into the sitting room, right over to the far wall. He began feeling along it and tapping on the bookcases. I joined him, running my hands along the baseboard, feeling for any unevenness.

Behind an ornate table, I found an edge in the wall. I pressed my hands into it, but nothing gave. With my knuckles, I gave the wall a small tap, my rings clacking. Hollow. Feeling along the wall, I splayed my hands out, pressing, searching for anything. There was a picture frame in front of me. I cocked my head to the side and reached out to lift it. It did not budge. My brow creased. I tried each side of the frame. When I pulled the bottom up, I heard a click, and the wall swung inward.

I tapped Marcus, and we peered inside. It was a narrow hall that veered immediately to the right. I went in first, not daring to announce our presence with a light or my mist. Carefully, we crept along, feeling the wall next to us, keeping one hand on our weapons. The hall turned sharply left, and a soft glow shone from the end of the short passage. As we approached, we stood with our backs to the wall and peered around the corner.

There was nothing except for another hall, the glow getting stronger at the end of it. Wherever we were headed was designed to make escape difficult. In the glow, the wooden walls became clearer. Haphazard dark splotches covered them, streaking in some places. I swallowed and forced myself to focus on the light and not allow my imagination to envision Aya racing through these halls, bloodied hands grasping at the wall. My paralyzed power rumbled at the vision. We moved forward, stopping again at the corner.

This time, I inched around the bend, and my knees buckled. The room was tiny, small enough that the missing square footage would go unnoticed to most. Marcus had a keen eye, I had to give him that.

Pools of scarlet dotted the floor like the rain puddles I used to play in with Marcus as a child. My vision clouded. *They will pay for this.* The stench of human waste hit me as I walked into the room. My gaze traveled to the far wall, where two sets of manacles hung. They were empty, but the blood dripping from them was fresh.

Black mist erupted over my eyes, and the room was cast into a complete haze. My heart raced. My mind whirled. I wouldn't go there. I wouldn't go there. I *couldn't* go there. *Kill every last soul in this building.* I would. After I found my friends.

"Ry," Marcus said quietly.

"No."

"Ry," he said, softer this time, reaching out to me with a bloodied hand. "This blood looks fresh."

"No," I said again. I couldn't breathe. I couldn't think. "No." I had to breathe. I had to think. I would not accept anything until I saw their bodies. They were alive, and I would find them. I had to find them. The mist thinned. "The prince wanted them alive—this doesn't make any sense. He knew I wouldn't come here to talk." I was grasping at straws, trying to convince Marcus as much as myself. It didn't make any sense that the prince had left the very place he'd instructed me to meet him.

"He's an Ophidian; he's ruthless. We can't trust how we think he would act," Marcus argued. The pit forming in my stomach morphed into a fire.

"They are not gone," I said, teeth gritted and eyes blazing. "Let's get out of here so we can go find them." I turned around and left the room. The stench was overwhelming, and I couldn't think with pools of my best friends' blood glaring at me from the floor. I would come up with a plan when we were somewhere I could breathe, when the mist swirling around me could still. I rushed around the first two bends, the narrow hall feeling even smaller, a growing feeling of panic rising in me at the prospect of what could be lurking after every turn.

Approaching the entrance, I stopped. I had to get myself together. I didn't flinch at the sight of blood. I had seen people tortured before my own eyes and barely batted a lash. Hel, I had *done* the torturing and been barely bothered. My time masquerading as the Queen of Naqad had softened me.

I took a deep breath, then another. My friends were alive. I had to believe that. I would find them. My hands shook as my mind raced. If I found their bodies instead, the inn would burn, along with every last soul remaining in it.

I faced the wall, ready. But as I turned, I noticed that to the left of the door, where I thought there was a solid wall, was another door. I pushed on it. It swung open, revealing a dark abyss. Slowly, I placed one foot in front of the other. I inched along the stone and felt Marcus doing the same from behind. My next step faltered, and I almost lost my balance. It was a staircase, and we were going back down into the inn. Blindly, we shuffled down the stairs, clinging to walls and masking our footsteps as best we could. Each step took an agonizingly long time to traverse.

I stumbled again as I took another step and hit solid ground. Another step and I was butting up against another wall. I felt around and encountered wood on each side. A dead end. My hand closed on a latch on the wall in front of me. Another door. I reached for Marcus behind me, and I grazed his hand, signaling what I had found. I did not dare speak. The inn was still crawling with Ophidians. We had barely killed half of them.

I turned the knob, bringing my head to the crack as I opened it just enough to peek through. Nothing. Marcus brushed my hip with a question. I opened the door a crack farther and saw a tree. My shoulders sagged. I opened the door all the way and stumbled into the night air, the sun a dash upon the horizon.

Leaning against the exterior of the inn, I inhaled the crisp air. We had found a hidden exit, but now we had to find the prince. Truthfully, I wasn't sure where he would have gone. I was formulating a plan in my head when I turned to Marcus and the night sky lit up in a blazing orange. It came from the north. My blood ran cold when I realized what lay directly north of the inn.

"No," I whispered. "The mages."

TWENTY-THREE

Caryk had found the Mage Quarter. And he was burning it to the ground.

Aya and Calliope were still his captives, and I had to find them, but what if they were never at the inn? What if it was just a distraction so Caryk could attack the mages? Were Aya and Calliope even alive? Was it too late to save the mages? Everyone I cared about was going to die. I had to do something. I had to choose.

I was frozen in place. My second and third were the closest thing I'd ever had to sisters. But I hadn't given up my kin to save them. I would die to protect their secret, and I was willing to let others die for it too. Why did I feel so differently now? Why was the need to save my friends burning a hole through my chest?

"Ry?" Marcus put his hand on my shoulder, a thousand tiny torches flickering in his eyes.

I looked up at him. I let the warmth from his hand sink into me, steadying me. I filled myself with his quiet strength. "We have to save them," I whispered.

"Who?" he asked breathlessly.

My gaze shifted from his face to the fire raging behind him, illuminating the sky. "My people," I breathed. My sisters would understand. We had devoted the last decade to protecting them. All three of us had promised to guard them with our lives. I needed to respect my friends' oaths and my own.

Hardened emerald eyes shifting back to Marcus, I squared my jaw. "Run."

I barely registered his surprise.

I let myself feel it now, the terror that my kin, that Katzima, was hurt. I let the fear propel me forward, taking control of my legs as the adrenaline coursed through my body. Marcus ran at my side as we sprinted through the yard, hurtling the stone wall.

We darted through the vacant street, and I let the tug in my soul drive me home. After flying down an alley toward the main street, I saw the people of Galeston. They were screaming, running in and out of buildings, desperate to find refuge from this second siege.

They had no idea who the real target was, who had remained hidden among them for years while they suffered in poverty. I wondered if they would join the prince's crusade if they knew. *Ungrateful sycophants.*

We dodged women, street carts, men, and children, as we raced along the main street. Smoke tore at my lungs, filling my nostrils as I struggled to breathe. I ducked into another alley as I felt the pull tighten. The mages were losing. I could feel it. The fire that had always been lit in my soul was dying, slowly ebbing out. All while the one on my ring finger was burning brightly, evidence of the prince's involvement. We were getting close. We had to get there in time. I *had* to get there in time. I could save them. I could save them all. That was my job. I was their protector. I was the one person they never had to fear, and I had led the predator right to them. It was my fault that the prince was even in this city to begin with.

Each step brought me closer to them. I was only a street away now. At the intersection, I would turn and be able to see the Quarter. Marcus was no longer at my side. I glanced around and did not see him on the avenue. He must have gotten lost in the chaos. It was probably better that he didn't see what I did to Caryk's army anyways.

The entrance to the Quarter loomed around the next bend. I was only a few paces away. One step, two. I rounded the corner and looked ahead. The entire street was ablaze. Children were crying in the street, some shouting for their parents, some leaning over still bodies, pounding their fists. Mothers were carrying babies in their arms while sprinting for safety, away from the Quarter.

I continued down the avenue, gathering my power around me, searching for the attackers. I would *make* it work today. My power was mine to sculpt.

There was chaos, but less than what I had expected. As I got closer, I could see why. Bodies littered the ground, the smell of acrid flesh ripe in every direction. Some burned so deeply I could not tell if they had belonged to a man or a woman, some with large gashes in their necks or chests, some so covered in dried blood that I could not tell what had killed them. Swords caked with entrails littered the ground. There were small bodies too, fallen behind larger forms, some charred while clutching onto one another.

I let my rage loosen the grip on my power. He had killed them. This fire was not natural; he had used their own power against them. My vision was red as I stalked down the street, the haze from my gift thickening. I sensed little life as I moved through the Quarter; it only fueled my fury. I turned, navigating the street using my power and ran to Katzima's house. She had to have gotten out.

She was a survivor. They all were. My family was made of *survivors*. A fire could not kill them. The mages were not gone. Caryk's army could not kill them. And where was his army?

My gift guided me closer to her house, and I eased the fog back enough to see through. The house I had left this morning was a pile of rubble. The hearth where Katzima had made me cider was the only discernible landmark. But the river behind the house still had the faintest blue tint. The grass and flowers were charred, but some of the trees retained their green. Frantically, I searched the rubble, moving ash, some of it burning my skin. I dug and dug until my fingernails were caked with soot. I stretched my gift out, straining for any sign of life.

There. Where the entrance to the garden used to be, I could sense a faint light. I ran over, feeling around in the ash. My hand connected with something soft, followed by a tiny moan. Lifting the rubble away, I began to make out a feminine form. She was completely black with soot, but I could see the delicate raven's necklace at her throat. She opened her eyes, and their usual obsidian was dulled to a soft coal.

"Katzima, I'm here," I whispered, holding her head, tears pricking at my eyes. "You're going to be okay."

She smiled at me weakly and moved her head to the side, just barely.

"You will not give up, do you hear me?" It was then that I noticed the burns. The soot was so thick on her face that I hadn't seen them at first, but they traveled from her cheeks, down her neck, covering her arms completely. She had been inside when they burned her house to the ground. I looked at where we were: the entrance to the garden. She had been trying to get out, but in her old age she wasn't fast enough.

My stomach turned.

"Ry-ya," she huffed.

"I'm here," I mumbled, eyes beginning to burn.

"The... ra-ven," each word was a fight to get out.

The raven? Her necklace? It bobbed, flames flickering off it. Was she really going to use her last words to explain the ridiculous necklace? Her fashion choices weren't exactly last words material.

I began to chastise her. "Katzima, I—"

"The sym-bol." Her coal eyes managed to ignite one last time, burning into me and demanding my attention. "Evil... tu-rned to go-od." Her hand made some attempt to flick in a last gesture as the fire left her eyes.

The light didn't return, and her eyes stared vacantly at the sky.

No. No. No, no, *no*. This wasn't possible. I had just gotten her back.

I glanced around frantically — the trees had charred, and the river had turned black. My body shook with sobs. She was gone. Katzima was gone. My teacher, my mentor, my mother when mine could not be. My heart dissolved, and I couldn't think, I couldn't move. My mind was blank as I tried to understand what had happened. Who I was. How was I supposed to exist in a world without her?

Her raven's necklace caught my eye. I removed it from her body and clutched it in my hands, tracing the curves. The delicate necklace did not belong at this scene, and it did not belong with someone like me. Evil turned good. That must have been how she saw herself. She kept it close all these years as a reminder of what a witch could become. I would bury it somewhere worthy of Katzima. Tears streamed down my face as I held it.

I looked out at the blackened river and felt the return of a different emotion. The grief was ebbing, being replaced brick by brick with a cold, empty rage. I clasped the raven around my throat. All who played a part here today would pay. I would hunt them to the ends of the earth. I would not rest until every single one of them was gone.

I would bring down this entire city, my entire kingdom, to make it happen.

It felt like a giant had lifted its hand from my shoulders. My power flowed through my veins, bursting with a promise of death. It wasn't until now that I realized it had been moving through molasses. I let it consume me. I fed it my rage, and it grew and thickened, until I was kneeling in a swirl of dark mist, practically invisible from the outside. Until I became *her*.

I felt a glimmer of light approaching, and footsteps crunched on the soot as they made their way through the rubble. I barely held enough control to keep it from devouring whoever approached. Not before I saw their face. I wanted to look in their eyes as the life left them. I hadn't used my gift to kill in years; I wanted to savor this first time. I let the mist ebb until I could see his face. Reptilian eyes greeted me. Soot-stained cheeks topped with dark hair. He looked like the angel of death. Too bad the job was already taken.

My lips twitched, and my power collapsed in on the Prince of Etrusca, squeezing, devouring, destroying everything that he was. For what he did, I would make it slow and painful. He would suffer. My power coiled around him and constricted, draining the life from his body. But the prince only stood and stared at me. A pink flush remained behind the rubble on his cheeks. The obstinate bright blue glint remained in his eyes. His broad shoulders faced me squarely as he towered over where I knelt.

I hurled my power at him with everything I had. My rage blasted into him, my gift taking control. It flowed out of me in waves and with it, I felt my anger ebbing. After a few more minutes, it was dull enough that I could hear my thoughts. My mind was relaxing with each torrent of power that escaped me. It was like the cloud that had been living in my mind had finally cleared.

But Caryk remained upright. I frowned. *Kill him.* I could feel my gift, raw and real. I had forgotten what true power felt like. Curious, rather than vengeful, I reached my gift out and stroked it along his body, searching for an opening. The smolder he returned did not belong among the smoke and burnt bodies. I reeled.

"Done yet?" he said quietly, peering down at me.

I glared at him. My mind was clear, and he was a dead man. But I had to be smart about it. I had to play his game. Knees still resting on a pile of ashes, I drew a knife, dangling it in front of me seductively. I returned his smolder.

"My gift may not work on you, but I have other means of exacting revenge." I simpered, blinking slowly up at him.

His gaze followed to where I knelt. To whom was at my side. If I wasn't fixated on him so intently, I would have missed his eyes widening a fraction. A flicker of something behind them. A tug on my finger so brief I could have imagined it.

"No last words?" I taunted.

He brought his eyes to mine again. "You mourn the witch."

Irritation ignited in me again. "This will be the last time you underestimate my malevolence," I promised.

"Oh, I've never doubted your capacity for cruelty, love," he said darkly, eyes aglow.

"You should be dead," I said flatly.

"I would imagine if you stuck that knife in my heart I would die rather quickly," he commented mildly. The thought was comforting. I needed to get off the ground. He was taking slow steps toward me now, stalking his prey. "But... that is not what you meant. Tell me, love, what is your gift?"

"You already know."

"I have known what you are from the moment I met you. The creature lurking beneath was not so easily concealed."

"The council bought it," I challenged.

Anger sparked in his eyes at the mention of them. Interesting.

"Perhaps not as well as you think," he muttered.

My brows drew together. They could not possibly know who I was.

"Do you honestly believe they would allow one who wields the Black Gift to sit at the helm of their kingdom?" he demanded.

My eyes narrowed, refusing to accept his words. He was bluffing. No one could have known what I was.

"Who?"

He smiled, and fangs slid out. Slits replaced the round pupils, but his eyes remained a piercing blue. His cheeks and forehead darkened, scales replacing skin.

The blood drained from my face. Caryk was an Ophidian. This, I had known. But I had not seen his scales clearly before. Scales that shone such a dark green they were almost black.

Scales that would rival the Viper's own. Which meant the prince's rank in the order was near mine. Impossible. I would have known who he was. I would have seen him.

I snarled, launching myself up from the earth. As I sprang, my body transformed, allowed into its true form at last. My canines lengthened, and I could feel my pupils contracting. The world shifted around me, and I could see so much better in the smoke and darkening sky.

It felt as if the air propelled me forward as I moved in this form. I breathed in ecstasy as I drew my twin knives from their sheaths, then sprang on top of the prince. Caught off guard, he fell to the earth.

I hissed, pressing one blade into his throat, hovering over his heart with the other. "Do you see the scales on my face, you fool?"

He smirked.

"How dare you?" I roared. "How dare you defy your queen?" I began to press on each knife, ready to end this usurper.

"You don't have a clue what you're talking about," he spat back, fangs bared. His anger twined with mine, twin flames burning a hole through my control.

My hiss deepened. "How dare you break the single oath *you* swore? How dare you lay a *hand* to the people you vowed to protect?"

He did not balk. He stared into my eyes for a moment, searching. His body relaxed. "I did not do this to our people," he whispered.

"Your scales suggest otherwise," I growled, suspicion laced in every word. He must have risen as their self-proclaimed ruler these past few years.

He laughed, cold and unfeeling. "Jealous, Viper?"

I blanched. I had not been called that name in years. Even behind closed doors, Aya and Calliope had not dared utter it.

He laughed again.

My blood boiled. "You bastard. Stealing one of my kingdoms wasn't enough for you?"

"I didn't steal your kingdom. I *saved* you," he growled.

My lips pulled upward into a scowl. "From what? A happy marriage?"

"You still don't know, do you?" he said softly, almost pitying. I felt his surprise splash across my ring finger.

"What?" I demanded, digging my blades in deeper. One more touch of pressure and I would draw blood. I salivated at the thought of it. Ophidia purred.

Sapphire eyes met mine, and he said steadily, "Doric Venrylst is an Allurant. He's been controlling your decisions."

The blood drained from my face. This wasn't possible. I had been *aware* of every decision I made, every thought, these last few years. "Why should I believe you?"

"Because" —his gaze fell on the dagger at his chest, then back to my face, his expression turning wary— "I'm a Protector. I've spent the last few days unraveling Lord Venrylst's hold."

That wasn't possible. I took in his scales, allowing the realization to sink in. The headaches I'd been having, the look on Doric's face when I'd openly defied him at the last meeting. The prince was not *a* Protector. He was *my* Protector.

"You're the Ophidian's Protector." My knife did not leave its resting place at the prince's throat, even as my brows drew together.

He attempted a nod, only bringing his skin closer to my blade.

"You allowed Doric to sink his magic into my mind."

His eyes blazed at the accusation. "After the war, there were no more meetings in the Pit, no more regularly scheduled cleansings. I tried to get to you, but I had to protect our own too. It took me *years* to find a way into the palace."

"If you had told me who you were—"

"Doric would have found out." The finality with which he spoke stung.

My mind was stronger than that. But it hadn't been. I'd had no idea what was being done to me. I frowned, shaking my head. I needed to process all this. My eyes roved the ground around us, searching for something to say. They landed on the ornate hilt of a sword.

"Are you going to say the council made these?" I looked at him incredulously as I dropped the knife pinning his neck and picked up the sword. My other dagger remained firmly against his chest.

It was made of fine steel, the hilt featuring a coiled serpent, poised to strike. They were the same blades I had seen in Malnova. Was Doric Venrylst arrogant enough to imitate the Ophidians?

Caryk studied the blade, eyes falling to the blood both caked onto and still dripping from it. "I wonder if they even know how deep it cuts to see a serpent-hilted blade kill a mage," he murmured, his eyes far away.

That's when I felt it. The stabbing pain slicing across my ring finger. The pain that I hadn't noticed because it so closely mirrored the grief that was racking my body, my anger the only thing to keep it at bay.

"You captured my second and third. You captured *me*," I whispered fiercely, rocking back on my heels. My dagger hung in my hand, forgotten.

"I needed to get you back, and I had to do it quickly. There was no other way," he rumbled, pressing a hand to his forehead and gripping his hair. As he closed his eyes, I noticed the red underline to his slitted pupils. Then the smudges on his cheeks from the rivers that had cascaded down them. They mirrored mine.

"You're not a rebel." I couldn't believe it. Caryk was one of us. He was one of *my* people. I remembered the agony I felt when he tortured me. Like a part of my mind was being shredded. He had nearly killed me trying to extract Doric from my mind. My swollen eyes burned.

What the prince had said about the council was true. About Doric. About me. I had been their puppet in every sense of the word.

Doric had wanted me to remain behind in Egryt. He had told me time and again that a queen's job was to sit upon her throne and *rule*. And I had believed him.

You didn't have a choice. I hadn't changed at all.

My mind went to every decision I had made since taking the throne. Coronation Day, staying away from the Ophidians, the decision to marry the Etruscan prince. The memories flashed before me. Was there a single decision that had been my own? A single instance that I had acted of my own free will?

A vein pulsed in my neck as darkness thrashed within me. I had sworn oaths while forsaking those I made to the Ophidians. I was no queen, certainly not one worthy of the title "Viper."

The darkness took form, smoky tendrils curling around me. I was no one. Or worse, I was a fraud. I had absolutely no idea who I was. All this time, I thought I was controlling the monster that raged within me; I was keeping *her* concealed. But it wasn't me. It was Lord Venrylst, working his magic into my mind and keeping the Viper at bay.

But the Prince of Etrusca had freed me. I smirked. What a fool.

My council had just burned the mages I swore to protect, my wards, to the ground.

My gift whipped around me. It tumbled as my thoughts evolved, flowing, like the chaos raging within.

There was one piece, one thing, that I would not let myself think. One betrayal that was so unspeakable I could not form the thought. It was not possible—there had to be another way that the court found the mages. But there was only one other person who knew they remained in the city.

When Katzima came out of hiding to save me, she signed her death warrant. She knew that I would never betray her, and she trusted the man who pulled me out of a cell. I had trusted him when he said that he loved me; I knew in my soul that he had meant it. *Traitor.*

The mist was black as I felt my world crumble. I rose into a crouch, glaring.

I had no interest in containing my gift. The more I thought of the traitor, the more it grew. It fed on my despair, my anguish, my fury. It rotated in a swirling vortex, expanding to encompass the entire Mage Quarter. It grew into the city, whipping up the alleys and between the streets. I could feel each lifeform it ensnared.

Half a thought and they would all be dead. Their lives were meaningless. I was no hero of Naqad. I was the Viper. I was ruthless, and I did not care who I left in my wake.

Two orbs pierced the mist before me. There was a warmth on my neck and the scratch of calloused hands. A brush of fingertips on my cheek. My face was being held tightly in place. The floating orbs held me in a trance. They were the brightest blue, with a splash of white lightning running through them. A tiny fissure of black opened up right in their center. They were the most fascinating things I had ever seen.

"Tamariya." The voice was strained, but gentle. "Save your wrath for those who have earned it." Eyes. The perfect blue orbs were eyes, and they spoke to me now. That voice. Unfamiliar at first, I had only heard it drip with ire. My full name on his tongue called to me. I allowed the mist to ebb so I could see his face.

The Etruscan prince. The man who had captured and tortured me. A powerful Ophidian. My rival in every sense. Caryk Cazaar. I inhaled sharply. As I exhaled, I collapsed my power, focusing it onto the man before me. His body was briefly covered by a dark mass that constricted around him. It entered his chest, disappearing in a swirl. He collapsed.

His body hit the ground with a thud that rocked the earth and reverberated through me. With the use of my gift, my head felt clearer. The prince was a powerful Protector; my magic should not be able to touch him. The Black Gift killed by snuffing out the minds of my victims. It was, by all means, mind magic. I fell to my knees.

I reached out a hand, hesitant.

The prince was an Ophidian. Worse, he had assumed control of the Ophidians and was ruling in my place. But what if he was the only ally I had left? I prayed that Aya and Cali had not been in the Mage Quarter.

Tentatively, I placed my hands on the prince's shoulder and rolled him over. He groaned, pressing his palms into his temples. "You're alive," I breathed. An unexpected relief rushed through me.

"You'll have to try harder than that to kill me, love." He smirked, flexing his ring finger where my emotions betrayed me.

I glared. "Pity I didn't succeed."

His smirk deepened; the Etruscan prince did not believe my act.

But the act was all I had. If he had been unraveling the lord's mind control, that meant I was most myself when I was around him. My loathing for the prince was genuine, then. I clung to my distaste like a lifeline.

He grimaced, pushing up from the ground. "We need to get back." The prince was no fool. He understood the cool fear that likely gripped his finger. I felt as if I was seeing the prince clearly for the first time.

I rose to my feet and offered him a hand up. It was the least I could do after concentrating the full force of the Gift of Ophidia on him.

Looking around Katzima's yard one last time, I committed the razed earth to memory. I would get my revenge, and when I did, this memory would fuel my rage.

My gift was restless as we walked through the desolate Quarter, flames still flickering on piles of wood. Ash crackled as we walked past.

"Do you really need to keep your mist swirling about? It may surprise you to know that despite my Ophidian form, I cannot see in complete obscurity," Caryk said dryly.

"I can't think with it curled up inside of me. It feels like a part of me is being stifled," I retorted. I wasn't sure what compelled me, but I added, "It's like something within me broke free when Katzima died, and I can't shove it back inside."

"Probably your murderous passenger," he grumbled.

My eyes flashed. "Excuse me?" Caryk could not know who I carried with me. No one knew, apart from Aya and Calliope, what had really been done to me the day I drank that viper's blood.

He rolled his shoulders, taking his time. "You weren't exactly known for being merciful," he said carefully.

I scoffed. "I'm the Viper. We don't show mercy."

He trained his eyes on the road. The fire cast his jaw in sharp relief. "While I was unraveling... what he did to you," he ventured, "I got to see you, the real you. Without any of the world's expectations. Yes, you're the Viper. But you're so much more than that, Tamariya."

I rolled my eyes. "You saw me under Doric's influence," I insisted. "I'm no different than I was the day he put me under his spell. It would serve you to remember that." I nodded pointedly at the presumptuous prince.

"If you insist." He acquiesced. A dash of some unknown emotion played across my finger.

I cleared my throat, changing the subject. "Were they truly being kept at the inn?"

He glanced at me sideways. "You won't find them without me, you know that right?"

I blinked up at him expectantly.

He sighed. "Yes. But they're well-guarded."

I exhaled. "More like were."

His face darkened. "What happened at the inn?"

"Who else was at the inn?" I asked cautiously. I knew the answer already, but I needed to hear him say it.

"I would have thought it obvious: the Ophidians." He had halted his walk to search my gaze for answers, eyes clouding in confusion.

"The Ophidians follow me; I'm their queen." I dismissed the thought, sounding almost bored. My tone didn't match the war raging inside me. "Why would they be under your command?" My heart raced as I awaited his answer. I had known it, but to hear him claim my kingdom as his own was different.

"When was the last time you were truly a leader to them?" the prince challenged. "You shrank into such a pitiful ruler that the Ophidians hardly recognized you." He did not wear his usual smirk. The earnestness with which he spoke was almost worse.

"And stealing my crown was the answer?" The swirling mist paused. I waited with deadly calm for the prince to admit his attempt to steal *both* of my thrones.

"I do not want your blood crown." His eyes were ablaze as his jaw flexed.

I laughed coldly. "As if I would believe that. You wore it so well my own people attacked me." The mist resumed motion, bouncing around the prince, excited to have prey to toy with.

"It was the only way to save the mages."

"That worked out well," I commented.

"As if I need reminding!" he shouted, eyes ablaze. Pain shot through my hand, and I crumpled. It wasn't Caryk's fault the mages were gone. It was mine.

He took a deliberate step toward me. "As if for one moment I wanted control over those child-stealing monsters."

"You're one of them."

"Not by any choice of my own."

My brow creased. "I watched your induction. You seemed willing enough." The memory was distant, but I would never forget the first changing I'd witnessed. He had been scared, sure, but he was no captive.

The prince said nothing. Conflict boiled down the bond, but he remained silent.

"So now that you have me back, will you leave us?" I asked, suddenly nervous.

"I can't," Caryk said through his teeth. "I kind of hitched my wagon to yours, remember?" He wiggled his hand in front of me, as if either of us could ever forget.

I would not feel sorry for the prince. He knew the consequences when he offered his hand to me. If the prince was miserable enough, perhaps we could appeal to his father and avoid starting a war.

"Besides, being an Ophidian isn't something you can change your mind about."

I wanted to know more. I ached to ask why he had become one of us in the first place, but something told me he wouldn't answer.

"Will you at least tell me what I'm walking into with the Ophidians? I killed nearly half of them; they won't be pleased." This seemed safer territory.

The bastard had the audacity to smirk. "It's hard to understand an Allurant's power unless you've seen it. The Ophidians feel abandoned. They will view the part you played in the mages' downfall mercilessly. Not to mention the dozens of our own you killed. Not pleased is an understatement." Bright blue jewels glittered down at me. The manic fire within reminded me of my own.

A chill ran down my spine. While I was playing court games, he was weaseling his way into the Ophidic Court, turning my people against me. The very people I had sacrificed everything for. The people who I had agreed to marry the Etruscan prince for.

No. You didn't agree to marry the prince, Doric did. I paled. It was hard to remember what was real. My head was beginning to ache.

The prince smirked, sensing my discomfort. Gods, I needed to kill someone. I looked around for any lingering crown soldiers. There wasn't a living soul in sight besides the one before me, who was frustratingly difficult to kill.

Later, then. If I knew one thing for certain, it was that Caryk Cazaar and I were not finished.

TWENTY-FOUR

I hadn't faced this many Ophidians at once since I led them screeching into battle. The past three years, I'd been a docile and compliant leader, quietly observing from the wings and making dull, peaceful proclamations when called upon. I'd become so weak that the council had all but declared war on the mages behind my back. The Viper was no longer feared.

But my memories were returning. I remembered the queen I used to be. I had pushed her down, deeper and deeper, until I could almost convince myself that she was gone. Or I supposed that Doric had pushed her down. I swore under my breath.

She could be free now. All I had to do was recall the feel of my daggers slicing through flesh or the squeeze of my gift draining someone's life. She was free. There was no one around to restrain her.

I was the Viper, Queen of Assassins, Wielder of the Gift of Ophidia, and the Queen of Naqad. I was a tornado of death, and I would not yield to any man. I was done being a pathetic pacifist.

I unleashed the dark mist, allowing it to spread across the yard, oozing ahead of us. I wanted the assassins in the inn to know who it was that returned to them. The air would be thick with fear by the time we crossed the threshold.

The prince glared at me sideways, knowing full well what I was up to. He drew his fingers across his silver rings, cracking his knuckles slowly. The Viper did not care about the opinion of a presumptuous Protector. I smiled at him, eyes glistening like deep pools of toxic emerald.

The door opened before we could reach the knob.

"Protector, Viper." We were greeted with deep bows and two jet-black heads. One with long, flowing hair, pulled into a thick, messy ponytail and the other with thick but close-cropped hair. The Zemyslah twins.

"You may rise," I articulated, trying not to grit my teeth at the slight of being named second.

They raised their heads, glancing at the prince. My power snaked around us, flicking back and forth. Two pairs of eyes slid back to me, one a somber brown, the other a glittering pale sage.

It was Ives who spoke first, his wise, walnut eyes guarded. "Survivors?"

Caryk shook his head, closing his eyes briefly.

"We would have been there to help were we not caring for our wounded and burying our own dead," Rohesia seethed, glaring at me with cactus-needle eyes. "Don't think we didn't notice who slithered through here earlier tonight."

The mist thickened. "And whose idea was it to bait me here?" My own eyes flashed a poisonous green.

"How were we to know if our queen remained underneath those extravagant gowns and glittering jewels? We've been living in hiding, waiting for you to return to us for *three years*. Are you honestly surprised that our loyalty falters?"

"Sister," Ives rumbled. Her dark-brown skin didn't deepen with her twin's warning. Rohesia had always been outspoken, but it appeared that my absence had emboldened her.

"You witnessed me swear the Ophidic oath," I growled, eyes flashing. "I would die before I betrayed this order. And I was willing to let my second and third die for it too."

Rohesia blocked the door, pale-green eyes glowing like moons, as she said, "You've made it clear whose side you're on. You are not welcome among the Ophidians, Viper."

My gift coiled around her and constricted ever so slightly. I watched her face slacken, and she began to gasp for air. It was a miracle that I could restrain myself from killing her, but I managed. I had no interest in adding to the pile of Ophidian bodies I was responsible for this evening. The Viper was no fool.

For good measure, I entwined my gift around Ives as well. He noticed his sister first, and the little surprise he allowed himself to show turned to horror as he registered his own peril. Their skin began to turn to dark ash.

I took a step toward them. "You betrayed this order when you took me, then Aya Jesper and Calliope Torino, hostage. I am the Viper, Wielder of the Gift of Ophidia, Queen of Naqad *and* Ophidians alike. How dare you question *my* loyalty after all you have done. What Doric Venrylst did to me for *years* was beyond my control. Yet only one of you attempted to save your *queen*." I paused, letting them digest my words. "You have committed treason, and for that you should pay the price."

Ives' eyes rolled with murky turmoil. Rohesia's gaze only glowed brighter, her fury unquenchable. They needed to understand that the Viper Queen had returned, and she would not tolerate insubordination. The Ophidians had run unchecked for too long.

"Enough blood has been spilt this evening, by my hands and the council's scheming." I released the coils that were slowly draining their lives. I prayed the threat was enough. It was the closest I would come to an apology. Warmth spread slowly back into their faces, and I pushed past them into the inn.

I did my best to ignore the blood splatter on the walls of the hall and the stench of death that hung low over the entire inn. Guilt threatened to seep through the obsidian wall I had built in my heart. I repaired the crack. Now was not the time for feelings of regret. If my people saw a weak queen, I would lose them to Caryk Cazaar forever.

"It was foolish, you know," I said tiredly to the prince as he walked beside me into the hall.

"What?" He looked at me, mouth twisted, disgust showing deep in his eyes as he surveyed the mess I had made mere hours ago. Another crack in my dark fortress.

Caryk had looked at me with anger and hatred, loathing and disrespect, but never like this. He had known all this time that I wasn't myself. But the slaughter here, that had been all me. It was my first act of defiance against Lord Venrylst in years. Did the prince already regret freeing the Viper?

Ophidians were cruel, but even amongst them, I stood out. I would sit alone in this darkness. I set my jaw, praying my turmoil did not show in my eyes.

The prince ran a finger over the pale scar on his knuckle. He opened his mouth to say something, but I stopped him. I did not need to be consoled. I was the Viper, and Vipers did not feel. I was not human or Ophidian. I was something *other*.

"It was foolish to think that you could earn my compliance by threatening me." I articulated each word, a snarl poised on my lips.

"I succeeded in drawing you out," he purred.

I laughed. "You still don't get it, do you? Have you never heard the story of Ophidia?"

His expression turned quizzical.

I scoffed. "She was not some random person gifted by the gods with the power to hold life in her hands. She was already a queen, a fierce defender of her people. The mages used to have an army, and she stood at its helm. Their enemies learned the army's weaknesses and decimated nearly her entire force. Ophidia was born a mage, so she had a small gift of strength and speed, but nothing remarkable. She leveraged that gift by putting every ounce of her being into training, honing her body into a weapon unmatched by any other. But even her heightened skill in battle could not make up for an entire army.

"So, on the night when, what we now know as Galeston, was surrounded, she flung up a desperate prayer to the gods that they help her, and the mere dozens of her forces remaining, to protect this city and her people inside it. The gods answered her prayers and bestowed on her the power to fell hundreds of troops at once: the Gift of Ophidia.

"The gift then passed down to her offspring and theirs, but only once the ruling Viper was deceased to ensure that the gift never fell into the wrong hands. You see, to become the Viper is not just to inherit a gift, it is to inherit the legacy that Ophidia left behind, a legacy of determination, perseverance, and loyalty. How do you think the Ophidians test such a thing? How do you think they weed out weakness before the ruling Viper passes?" My mouth twisted in a cruel line. "I have been stabbed, threatened, skinned, broken, and bruised in every way imaginable since I was child. I assure you,

Protector," I spat with contempt, "there is nothing that you can do to me that hasn't already been done."

For once, the prince was silent.

"You drew me to this inn and expected me to act with anything but vengeance." I let my words hang in the air, pressing down on him. The blood of these Ophidians was on the prince's hands, not mine.

Rohesia and Ives were silent behind us as well. Perhaps they all needed a reminder of who exactly I was to them.

I walked into the sitting room facing the back wall of windows where I had begun the slaughter of the disloyal Ophidians. My guilt was lukewarm. I scanned the room.

There, sitting in the overstuffed faded leather chairs, chatting quietly with an older blonde woman, were my second and third. Aya's eyes were sharp as she processed what the older woman was saying, but deep bruises lined her almond-shaped sockets, traveling across her cheekbone on one side. I looked down, and her hands were bandaged too. The mist in the room shifted, thickening. With an Ophidian's quick healing, even hours old wounds should not have shown.

I looked to Aya's side where Calliope sat, her thick blonde braid messy and tangled, her arm sitting at an odd angle by her side. She bore scratches on her face that were barely healing. If Aya's demeanor was quietly calculated, Calliope's eyes were thunderstorms of rage, her jaw set with hostility as she glared at the other blonde. I had forgotten how much they had changed in the human world.

I smirked. I supposed I was in no position to pass judgment. My smirk quickly faded as I recalled why Calliope reacted so strongly around the Ophidians. I had never seen it before, but now that I knew what we'd done to her, her behavior made a lot more sense. I scanned the room with a critical eye, wondering how many of my cabal were here by choice.

Relief battled rage inside me as the mist ebbed and thickened, a visual display of my turmoil. They were clearly not treated with the discretion that the prince had promised, but at least their spirits appeared unbroken.

Aya noticed me first, seeing the mist coiling around the room. She turned her gaze from her lover, her obsidian eyes glittering briefly with a thousand questions before returning to her signature expression of polite interest. I almost cracked a smile. Aya would sooner burn alive than let anyone read what she was thinking. She nudged Calliope, and my third looked at me at last, a grim smile on her face as she saw that I was not visibly crippled.

I slid over to them, each step calculated. I had proven my point when I held Rohesia and Ives with my gift. There were several other Ophidians sitting in the room and leaning against the walls. All looked tired, and several had eyes rimmed red. Grief that I had caused. These people knew my strength; now I needed to win back their trust.

"Welcome home," I said softly. "I see you were treated with the utmost respect." I let my words hang in the air. I did not need to point out what we all saw.

"Home?" Calliope laughed coolly, looking around the room at the hostile faces turned to me.

"Home," I echoed. "For now, while we plot our revenge." I turned to face the room. "Today we saw a glimpse of Hel. Tomorrow, we work to ensure that it does not spread." The assassins leaning against the walls stirred, glancing at where Caryk stood next to Rohesia and Ives. "We have wronged each other, and the creed of our order has suffered because of it. I did not burn our people to the ground, nor did you. Let us remember who did. This assault shall not go unavenged."

The Ophidians looked angrily at the prince. "You bring this traitor back into our midst?" someone demanded from the shadows.

Bastard. What had he done in a matter of months to earn this devotion from my soldiers? Was it months? No, I had been absent for years. Guilt pierced my gut, battling with the anger.

The Etruscan prince smiled tightly. "Our Viper was trapped in a web she could not escape. She did not break her oaths."

My stomach roiled at the proclamation of my weakness, quelled only by the knowledge that the prince wasn't demanding my abdication with the rest.

"As if slaughtering her own army did not constitute breaking an oath," another indignant, grief-stricken voice called out.

"Who turned on who first?" I ventured. "Do not blame me for making you lie in the nest you made yourselves."

Caryk glared at me, but he ran his hand through his hair and straightened his expression. "She's right," he said. "Our division has already caused us to implode. We need the Ophidians to be united if we are to survive. This isn't about revenge or pointing blades, this is about the survival of magic in our world. Do not scorn the Queen of Naqad for her second title, for we will need both her, and the Viper's power, if we are to win this war."

I nearly stumbled. The prince had all but issued a proclamation of loyalty to me. My mind spun, trying to make sense of his words. Meanwhile, the room was silent. I kept my mist low, waiting to see what the Ophidians would decide.

It was Rohesia who stepped forward. "No queen of mine turns on her own people," she said, looking between me and her prince. "You are not my queen, but that does not change the fact that you are still the Viper. I will not follow you, but I will work with you."

The assassins around the room nodded their agreement. Something deep within me stung at her brutal words. Somehow, I would remind them why they followed me into battle against Hel itself. But for now, this would have to be enough.

My shoulders sagged; I prayed to the gods that no one noticed. Mercifully, the prince motioned for me, Aya, and Calliope to follow him. We traveled back through the bloodstained hallway and up to the second floor. The stench was stronger up here, and several of the doors hung open unnaturally. Shame crept up my neck, but Aya caught my eye and shook her head almost imperceptibly. Now was not the time.

"There is a shortage of clean rooms at the moment," Caryk murmured. "We moved Aya and Calliope into this room once we ascertained that they were not under Doric Venrylst's influence." He opened a door on the left.

I creased my brow in confusion, sending Caryk a sharp look, pointedly glancing at the many bruises that plagued my friends.

"Despite my efforts to free you, you must understand how your behavior looked. I could not be sure of your motives. Any of you." He faced my friends now, meeting their eyes. "I make no apologies for defending our kind."

Aya nodded; she had accepted the ways of the Ophidians long ago. Brutality and cruelty. That was the code we lived by. Calliope narrowed her eyes, fury stored just below the surface, but held her tongue. With a promise to debrief tomorrow, they shuffled into their room. I wanted nothing more than to follow them, but I imagined that the prince had other plans.

He faced me, trepidation on his face. A knot twisted in my stomach. I had never seen the prince this way. "Allow me to explain."

My eyes narrowed, but I remained silent.

"I think it's a good idea for us to share a room," he said slowly.

"Absolutely not." Anger bubbled within me at the absurdity of the request. Not to mention the impropriety. Not that I particularly cared about the latter, but I was a *queen* for the gods' sake.

The prince arched a brow. "Hear me out."

I glared at him but kept my mouth shut.

He raised his hands in surrender, silver rings glistening. "We need the Ophidians to be united. Our obvious disdain for each other will make that difficult." His hands flexed as he spoke.

"You're fucked in the head if you think that you've earned any kindness from me," I hissed.

He frowned, opened his mouth to say something, and then closed it. His hands traveled down to rest at his waist. He sighed. "We are engaged, remember?"

"For the time being," I grit out between my teeth.

His reptilian eyes flashed. "An alliance with me is as advantageous as it ever was. More so, perhaps, now that I control your serpent army."

"So, you seek to control the Serpent's Crown as well?" I challenged.

A muscle in his jaw twitched. "You're impossible."

Fire sparked within me. "I have just been informed that not a single decision I have made for *years* has been my own. Forgive me for questioning your usefulness as a consort."

"Usefulness?" he spat. "Let's not forget who freed you. I can cease *using* my powers to protect you at any time."

My blood went cold as I stilled. I took a slow and deliberate step toward the prince. I felt my eyes constrict, transforming to glowing green slits. "Is that a threat?" I said in a low, quiet voice.

The Etruscan prince paled. A cool splash of emotion hit my finger.

A serpentine smile spread across my face. The prince was afraid.

He recovered quickly, scowling. "Threat or not, you want me on your side in this war."

I rolled my eyes. "The war ended years ago, Prince."

"Did it?" he challenged quietly. "The burning Mage Quarter was only the beginning. You know it as well as I."

I grimaced. He was right. I had known Lord Venrylst my entire life. The man did not do anything without thinking three steps ahead. He had been this way in the war; he would be no different in this vendetta against the mages. But why? What had turned him against the class of people he belonged to?

Reluctantly, I released the tendrils on my budding anger. "You really think sharing a room will bring the Ophidians together?" I arched a dubious brow.

He shrugged. "People talk. Even serpent killers. Let them."

"And when one of those serpent killers asks, you'll tell them you're fucking me?" I shot back, narrowing my eyes. I would not be used as some pawn for Caryk to assert his control.

He held up his hands again. "We share a room, that's all. Tell them we were out of clean rooms. Tell them it's a peace offering— I don't care."

My eyes remained slitted. My mind turned, wondering if the prince was right. "You want them to think we're secret lovers," I said flatly.

"Not so secret when you're making eyes at me all day long, is it?" A sparkle returned to the prince's eyes as he wiggled his eyebrows at me.

"Lies." I looked at him incredulously. "You're after both my thrones. Whatever may have begun between us is through."

His face remained impassive, but I felt a small spark ignite down the bond. "They took one look at my scales and hardly asked another question. I've been the highest-ranking Ophidian here since we convened to protect their breeding grounds," he said carefully, hand reaching up to smooth his short beard. A bitter note dashed down the bond.

My core began to heat again as I felt the anger surface. My eyes flashed. *Breeding grounds?*

He turned, and I followed him to his quarters. *Our* quarters, I supposed.

A small wave of relief washed over me as we walked. *You can end this betrothal.* The rush that followed the thought brought a small smile to my face. One way or another, I would find a way to free myself of this wretched betrothal bond.

The rooms were on the top floor, with a sweeping view of the forest below and a massive four poster bed, separate sitting area, and even a small powder room. I noted the bed and rolled my eyes again.

The prince noticed my gaze and smirked, placing his hands in his pockets.

"The last time we slept near one another I woke up handcuffed to a wall. It would be rather inconvenient for your head were the situation to repeat itself," I said, eyes flashing.

His blue eyes darkened, deep as the ocean. "Usually women give the opposite request, love."

"Expect to lose a finger if you so much as snore in my direction."

He reached up and ran his hand through his hair, rings flashing in the dim light. I had underestimated the Prince of Etrusca.

I would not make that mistake again.

TWENTY-FIVE

I lay awake, staring up at the ceiling. The prince snored lightly next to me, radiating false innocence in his slumber. I would have thought it funny had my thoughts not been turning restlessly.

If I put my anger aside, guilt threatened to consume me. My gift was leashed and stowed away, so whenever I concentrated too hard, my head grew foggy. It was like being back under Doric's control all over again.

Except this time the voice in my head belonged to *her*. I had let the Viper out today, and once she was released, she needed to fulfill her purpose before she could be contained again. She needed a kill.

I glanced at Caryk next to me, still snoring softly. I shook my head and chucked the covers aside, stepping into my boots.

I threw on a coat and walked through the inn, letting my legs carry me to the woods that framed our hideout. I searched the trees for any sign of movement. Straining my eyes, I could barely make out the dark shape of a bush just a few feet in front of me. Every so often, a firefly briefly illuminated the patterned bark of a tree, or a cricket chirped, but there were no sounds from anything larger than a rabbit. I was alone. Truly alone. There were no small breaths from watching eyes in the trees or snapping twigs from following feet. It felt like it had been a lifetime since I could look out into a forest and see and hear nothing but what made its home within.

I shifted, freeing her at last. As my eyes transformed, I could see the forest floor well. I grimaced, and sharp fangs rubbed against my lips. For the first time in years, I reached a hand up and felt the slick scales that adorned my face. The skin there was harder, resistant to any blade. My scales were such a deep shade of green they were almost black, the mark of a queen. I brought my hands down. I had been anything but a leader to these people.

Breathing deeply, I let go of my gift. It coated the forest floor, straining for any sign of life, anything to grasp on to, anything to distract myself from what I knew was coming. The memories of who I had been, had really *been*, cascaded around me.

My palms started shaking as cold crept into my chest, right into the obsidian wall where my heart should have been. I had murdered and killed and tortured so many.

It was like waking up from a long dream. The memories had been there when Doric was controlling me, but they were hazy. Only a few had ever been sharp. Even then, it wasn't until the prince had entered my life that I had begun to remember more.

How had I been so *stupid*? Doric had been able to convince me that I was a saint so easily. Maybe that was why. It *was* easier. It was easier to be a naive lady, someone to be adored, a prized mare for the richest prince. My mouth soured.

I remembered my frustration in the recent council meetings and how Doric had seemed outraged that I dared to have an opinion. I tried to think back to before I had met the prince. The memories didn't come. What had happened on coronation day after the crown had been placed on my head?

A few memories came to me, but it felt like they had happened to someone else. A flowery queen sat on a throne, beaming at her loyal subjects. I sank to my knees. My hands came to my face, cradling my head.

But the war, and before the war, I remembered as if it had been yesterday. *She* had been magnificent. *I* had been magnificent.

Every kill I had made as the Viper rushed through me. Their bones snapped under my fist, sword, foot, and even against my own body. The crunch reverberated in my bones, and my hands faltered. Tears escaped my eyes, pain reflected in his, as I twisted my knife into his leg. Surprise in hers, as I snuffed out her life entirely.

I was gasping for air now, my gift thick around me, cocooning me. I would never be free of them; the guilt would eat at me until the day I was finally free of this world. I was not the demure damsel that Doric had tried to paint me as, nor was I the righteous warrior I masqueraded as before the Ophidians.

I was a monster, bred for exactly one purpose. Death. I brought death to all who met me. The legends were wrong; Ophidia was not given a gift. It was a curse, the Curse of Ophidia. And I would carry it with me until it consumed me.

My gift savored my distress, using it to grow into the forest. I felt the life in the foliage around me, glowing embers in my mind's eye. With half a thought, all the trees and shrubs in my grasp were dead. A small weight lifted off me, the brief satisfaction of a long-awaited kill. I reached out and smothered another tree. I was lighter and darker at the same time. The darkness inside me grew with each tree that I felled, each plant that I snuffed out. It was nothing compared to taking a human life, but my gift danced in a swirling wind around my body. My mind turned back to the lives I had taken today, but it played back the slaughter in a different light this time. I was exhilarated.

A crunch behind me that was different from the bones snapping in my mind jolted me back to the moment. Someone was here, their initial approach masked by my haunting memories. I yanked myself back to my body, ready to spring on whoever dared interrupt me. My mist reached out, yearning to make a real kill this time. It felt nothing. I could not sense the life approaching me.

I shifted my stance, ready to strike out with the knives, grateful that I'd had the sense to strap them to my thighs before leaving.

"Come to take vengeance on the trees?" a drawling voice asked. I narrowed my eyes and directed the force of my gift at him. I couldn't kill him, but maybe I could knock him unconscious again.

I was not successful.

"Leave, before my grip slips on one of these knives," I grit out.

"Did it occur to you that more than one person could have insomnia at a time?" he said mildly. I couldn't see the prince through the mist, but I could imagine him examining a glistening ring.

My lip curled back, baring my fangs, but I allowed the black fog to thin enough to study his face. I opened my mouth to say something accusatory, but the haunted look I beheld made me close it. It was hard to tell in the moonlight, but his eyes looked sunken.

He gave me a grim smile. "Did you know there used to be moon moss in these woods?" he said sadly, eyes wandering to the trees surrounding us. "Before the war, these woods were filled with it. It must have died when the magic left the city."

My eyes turned the trees too, remembering the enchanting beauty of the glowing moss. Katzima had used the moss for her healing poultices. Like so much of the magic in Galeston, the flora must have been tied to the mages as well. "I know," I whispered. "I spent most of my childhood in Galeston."

"You started your training here?"

I shrugged. "Kind of. Really, it started the day I was born. My mother was never one to coddle."

The prince's eyes were endless pools, starlight reflected in their depths. "She was a formidable Viper," he said somberly.

The sour taste returned to my mouth. *Her mind had been shredded.* I still wasn't convinced that the prince didn't somehow have something to do with it.

"Why agree to this truce?" I asked, changing the subject.

"Is it so unbelievable that I want to prevent more death?" he rasped.

"Because you are responsible for the lives lost today?"

He flinched. "As are you." His voice was pained.

"We are not the... same."

"I think we have more in common than you think we do," he said softly.

The prince had no idea how *easy* today had been for me. It was so easy that I barely even realized what I was doing until I had slaughtered half of my own army. When I forgot to even question why there were so many "rebel" Ophidians. To question why the prince searched so ardently for the mages. Caryk thought he could see the being lurking just beneath the surface, but the look on his face when he saw what I had done to the inn gave him away. He had no idea what it meant to be the Viper.

The anguish I felt coming from the betrothal bond was further proof.

He had moved closer to me. The moonlight threw his jaw into sharp contrast as he stared intently down at me, searching for something.

His deep eyes were unreadable as I stood before him, cold and sneering, giving him a glimpse of my true self. He knew what I was;

it was time to stop pretending like he saw me as anything other than the soulless monster I was bred to be. Although I suppose he had known from the moment we met that I was no damsel.

"I could help you, you know."

"You know nothing of what I am," I hissed.

Waves crashed in his eyes as he said quietly, "Tell me, who truly controls the Black Gift?" I had not noticed his use of its more sinister title before, but now it made me hesitate.

"Why undo Doric's control at all? I'd be far easier to usurp with Ophidia buried in my subconscious."

The frown lines around his mouth deepened. Even in the dark, his blue eyes glowed as they held mine. "I knew what Doric was planning," he whispered. "He's powerful, and his political influence is an army unto itself." He ran his hands through his hair. "If I told you what he was doing, he would inevitably find out—his magic was so deeply entwined with your mind. But I needed you. I can't beat him on my own."

I scowled. "You're afraid of an old man?"

He snorted. "Perhaps he guarded you from seeing it, but Doric Venrylst is hiding more than just that he's an Allurant. I hear whispers..."

"Whispers? Of what?"

He shook his head. "I can't explain it, but there's something uncanny about him. Mark my words."

I had the sense Caryk wasn't being entirely truthful, even now.

The prince gave me one last long look before he turned and left, leaving me alone in the woods to contemplate his cryptic warning.

I wasn't sure how long I stood there, staring after him and hearing his words echo in my mind. I did not need Caryk's judgments to heal my soul, or however he thought he could help the twisted queen who abandoned her people.

The echoes of his words faded, and I was left with nothing but my own thoughts. I sank against the cold bark of a tree, feeling cool earth through my coat as my ass hit the ground. I pulled my knees into my chest.

The prince's grief had reminded me of my own. The feeling on my ring finger lingered. I closed my eyes, letting the sensation wash over me. Behind my lashes, I saw her. The woman who coached me through the worst parts of my life. The friend who I had just been reunited with.

Her raven hair floated around a kind face, chocolatey eyes twinkling like the night sky. Katzima. She was dead. My chest ached as I replayed the memory of the woman who had raised me take her last breath. My head fell to my knees.

My gift was a black ball around me as emotion cascaded through me. What would I do without the witch? She was good and kind. Everything the Ophidians weren't, everything that I was not. And she was gone.

Gone because I was too weak to resist Lord Venrylst. Gone because I had trusted the men who mentored my father. Gone because I had trusted... I could not think his name.

A sob bubbled up through my throat. My eyes burned. I breathed in a shaky breath. As I exhaled, my body shook with grief.

Once the tears began to flow, I was unable to reel them in. I let everything that I had done, and almost done today, crash into me, racking my body with a blunt force I could not contain any longer. If the prince were to return now, I wouldn't be able to pull it together.

But he wouldn't. He was after my crown, maybe he already had it, and I was just too scared to admit it. I sat there for what felt like hours, letting my devastation flood me.

When I lifted my head once more, my anguish began to subside. Slowly, the ache in my heart fell away. There was one person responsible for my pain. One person who I had trusted above anyone else.

Marcus. Ice crept up from the earth and into my body as I finally thought his name. It reached my heart, hardening it completely. I closed my eyes against the pain.

I had been betrayed. Marcus had met Katzima, had seen the mages, had understood how peaceful they were. And still he had chosen the council. He had chosen to trust Doric Venrylst over me, the woman he had claimed to love.

My eyes flashed open. My tears and pain were pathetic. They would not serve me now. There was only one thing that could satisfy me.

Vengeance. A cold smile spread across my face.

I would savor every moment I spent extracting it.

My gift swirled around me in a torrent, threatening to topple the entire forest. It flowed, thick and strong. I pushed it harder, faster.

I would take the entire city with me. There was no Etruscan prince here to stop me this time.

My smile grew. I nudged another burst of power forward, pushing my gift further. I gasped as a piercing pain split my head. I had pushed too far. My well of magic was at its limit. My power slipped from me, evaporating as if it was nothing.

I fell sideways. Cold dirt scraped my cheek.

And then I felt nothing at all.

TWENTY-SIX

I awoke with my cheek pressed to the cool earth. I sat up, peeling damp leaves from my face. The shrubs around me were devoid of life. I lifted my gaze further to a shriveled log just past my feet. Its branches appeared brittle; the leaves had already decayed into piles of dust. The fallen tree had been inches from crushing my legs.

My cheeks burned at the memory of what I had done to the forest. Caryk was right. I had let my gift control me, both last night in the woods and when I discovered Katzima's body. A pang struck my chest with the thought of my mentor. The feeling only deepened as I took in the entirety of the forest.

I could clearly see the inn now. Nothing but barren decay sat between me and the Ophidians I pretended to lead.

I dropped back to the earth, casting my gaze skyward, resisting the urge to groan, to scream, to throw a tantrum. But I was no child. I could no longer blame my actions on the compulsions of others. I had done this. Me. Ry. Tamariya Amunet, Queen of Naqad, wearer of the Serpent's Crown, Viper Queen of Ophidians.

I exhaled. I didn't feel like any of those things. I had been so easily influenced, manipulated, and controlled. Even now, I could sense the Prince of Etrusca's hold over me. It sent a chill down my spine. I clenched my jaw. This would not happen to me again.

Drawing my palms under me, I heaved myself up from the ashy earth and into a sitting position. I would not be manipulated. The prince would hold no sway over me. Our betrothal would end the moment I relieved him of his head—if I could ever win the Ophidians back. There were some cruelties even they could not forgive.

I allowed myself a grunt as I pulled my knees under me and came to a full stand in the center of this desert of my own making. My nose wrinkled, and I winced at the irony of it all.

Sucking in one final, long breath, I squared my shoulders. On the exhale, I placed one foot steadily in front of the other, parting the desert, returning to the inn.

At the foot of the staircase, I paused. I wasn't particularly interested in admitting to the prince that I had spent the night on the floor, and I wasn't sure I had any clothes in our room anyways. I knocked on the door of Aya and Cali's room, hoping they would be awake.

Calliope opened the door, looking pissed.

"Good morning to you, too," I mumbled.

Aya smirked from behind the tall warrior.

"I thought you were one of those idiots, come to summon us like cattle," Calliope bit out.

I frowned. "You once commanded those idiots, you know. You still do," I pointed out as I sauntered past her into the room. I would never again question her hatred for them, but she needed a reminder of her power over the Ophidians.

She scowled, crinkling the healing wound that stretched across her brow. My eyes flashed. Those wounds should be bright scars by now. Guilt racked my frame. They had been tortured because of me. No, because of what Doric had done to me.

"We will remind them of who we are," I whispered, intending the words to come out much clearer than they had.

Calliope stepped toward me, wrapping me in a hug. I bristled.

"We missed you," she said into my hair. Tears threatened to well up, and I stifled the urge to break out of the hug. Cali released me. I stood in shock for a moment, overwhelmed by her affection.

I met both women's gazes. Aya's obsidians sparkled with a million unsaid words, while Cali's shone with a kindness I had never seen. My chest tightened.

"I'm sorry that I couldn't stop..." I trailed off as I looked at their faces and the obvious markings of what they had been through.

"It is our way," Aya said, eyes flinty. For a moment, I could see beneath the hardness there to a puddling guilt. I turned to Calliope and the same emotions reflected in her hazy eyes.

Neither woman had known what Doric had done to me.

Guilt pierced my chest at their pity. They didn't know the full truth. I swallowed, the saliva getting stuck in my throat. "There are some memories that are... cloudier... than others. Those are the ones where I think Doric influenced me the most. My decision to marry Caryk, taking the Serpent's Crown, but not slaughtering the Ophidians." I met their gazes steadily as I spoke. "That was all me. The prince had undone most of Doric's compulsion by that point. I slaughtered our people of my own volition," I admitted, my voice trembling on the last words as water began to cloud my vision.

"We are all monsters in a way," Cali whispered, eyes cast downward.

My jaw slackened as I looked at the warrior clearly for what seemed like the first time in years. Calliope had been on this earth much longer than Aya or me. Like Aya had said, she had been surrounded by atrocities her whole life, but never lost the ability to call a horror what it was.

I smiled, and a single tear traced down my cheek.

Cali lifted her gaze. A tumultuous storm brewed within her eyes. "I knew," she breathed.

It was as if lightning had struck my body. I froze, mouth agape, blood draining from my face.

Rain began to pool in the cloudiness of her eyes. "It was at the coronation; there was something in the way Lord Venrylst looked at you when the crown was placed on your head... you were miserable, I could see it. But then... he whispered something, and you smiled, and it was *radiant*. I thought he had said something to cheer you up. I thought you were *happy*. I had not seen you happy since the day you drank the Viper's blood."

My thoughts raced while my body stood frozen, unable to react.

Aya, however, was not frozen. "You *what*?" she said, seething, hands balled into fists at her sides, eyes like blazing coals. "You never breathed a word of this to me."

Calliope met her lover's fiery gaze as she pulled in a rattling breath. "I thought you were better off leaving the murdering and vengeance behind. I had no idea what the council was planning, or I wouldn't have stood for it." Her eyes were glued to Aya's, pleading as tears trailed down her face.

"You allowed them to control her *thoughts*!" Aya screeched, hands flying up, dark hair bobbing with the movement. Tears thick with betrayal formed in her eyes now.

Calliope fell to her knees, hands clasped before her. "Please, believe me. I did not know what Doric planned."

I frowned, my first movement since the blonde warrior began her confession.

"There was no other choice." Her chest deflated slowly as she attempted to control her breathing. "We were living in a new world. Neither of you would have *survived* cooped up in the palace. I thought he was giving you a small mercy, calming your tempers. I swear to you I did not know more." Her gray eyes were wide, switching from her lover to her queen, imploring us to believe her.

Aya's face appeared to flicker, shifting from one form of herself into the next. First shadows drew across her face, then she was cast in brightness as her hair began to lengthen and shorten in a chaotic cycle.

My second had lost control.

Calliope's confession was surprising, yes. But she had never hidden her desire for us to be civil. The warrior had preached and preached her morals for over a decade. Why should she bat an eye if she suspected someone was influencing us in a way she never could?

My frown deepened. Perhaps it had something to do with exhausting my gift the night before, but I did not feel the familiar caress of rage building within me.

Aya whirled her head to face me. "Do something!" she shouted, tears streaking down her face.

I inhaled deeply. I could not believe what I was about to do. "Calliope is not to blame for Doric's wrongdoing," I said evenly. "We behaved exactly as she asked us to." I wasn't sure I believed my own words, but what else could I do? I'd spilt enough blood already, and we needed all the allies we could get if we were to defeat Doric.

My feet carried me across the room, pacing. "What I really need to know is, are you with us now?" I let the question hang in the air between us. Cali was no traitor; she was exactly as she had always been: insufferably moral. She would do everything in her power to take down the man responsible for destroying the mages.

My second looked at me, jaw hanging open. "What the *fuck*?" she hissed.

I met her obsidian gaze with a hard emerald one of my own. "*Think*, Aya. What could we have done? Banished Doric? Taken him head on? As soon as he got a whiff of what we were planning, he'd have stopped us in our tracks. Based on what Caryk's told me, he's powerful, even among Allurants. The knowledge would have driven us to madness. Do not let your personal feelings get in the way."

Her eyes bugged. "My PERSONAL feelings? What about you, *Tamariya*? You slaughtered half of the Ophidians because of your *feelings*."

I halted my pacing. She was right. I was entirely ruled by my emotions, so who was I to talk? I inhaled deeply, dropping my hips to a seat on the bed. "But that's the point, isn't it?" I whispered.

Aya glared. But Cali turned her gaze to me again, nodding sagely.

"Cali is the only one among us not ruled by her emotions. She chose to protect us, as is her job," I said, sitting up straighter.

The warrior's eyes widened, whether at the unexpected compliment or my use of her nickname, I was not sure.

Aya's eyes were mere slashes across her face.

I looked at her steadily, letting my resolve show. Aya stared back, her expression softening slightly.

"You knew what she was," I whispered to my friend, as gently as I could. Aya of all people knew Calliope to her core. She would forgive her partner.

Calliope swallowed and looked to her. "And I know exactly what both of you are. I love you despite our differences. We balance each other," she said, her eyes wide and pleading.

Aya grimaced, nodding almost imperceptibly. It wouldn't be the end of their conversation, but I suspected it was the most they wanted to air in front of me.

Aya turned to me, scanning my body as she took in the thin nightgown I wore under my heavy coat, paired with ash-caked boots. Her brow creased.

I grimaced. "Neither of you have any clothes here, do you?" I asked wearily. My shoulders sagged. It seemed Aya had at least begun to accept the warrior's actions.

"You didn't sleep outside in that, did you?" Cali demanded.

I attempted a weak smile. "I didn't mean to."

She rolled her eyes. "It's a miracle you didn't freeze to death," she mumbled with halfhearted indignation. Neither woman pressed me on the details of my evening. I'm sure they'd seen the forest this morning and guessed.

Aya walked over to a far corner of the room. "As luck would have it, they stole our luggage when they took us. They were looking for something; I nicked our bags back when they had grown bored of them," Aya said coyly.

I raised an eyebrow. "What could they possibly have been looking for?" I shook my head as Aya gestured to the bags sitting on the ground beside the bed.

I noted their cozy quarters for the first time and groaned.

"What?" Aya looked at me sharply as she held up a pair of wool socks.

"I think Caryk is playing some kind of power move with the sleeping accommodations. We're sharing a bed. He seems to think that it will unite the Ophidians. I think he just wants an excuse to piss me off." I pushed off the bed, walked over to where Aya knelt, and unbuckled my own saddlebags.

"Prick." Cali glared at a pair of riding pants.

Aya laughed, sliding her socks on. It sounded empty, but I appreciated her effort at normalcy. "Unfortunately, he's probably right. Serpent shifters are not immune to gossip."

I stuck my tongue out at her before turning back to the meager selection of shirts I had in my luggage. "As if I would ever share a bed with him *that way*."

I peeked over at Cali's suitcase. Aya's frame was far too slender for us to share clothes, not to mention the several inches of height I had on her, but Cali and I could sometimes share. We were of similar height, but the decades she had spent commanding armies and wielding every weapon known to man had given her arms a strength that mine lacked. Luckily, she wore her pants loose; they could usually accommodate my well-muscled thighs.

"Got any black tops?" I asked, eyebrows raised innocently.

"Fuck off," she said, shoving me away from her suitcase playfully. It felt strange, given our blowout, but I leaned into it.

"You don't think the prince could be trying to win you over?" Aya looked up at me, brow furrowed.

I snorted and threw a white shirt to Cali. "Here, trade me for this." I glanced at Aya. "You would forgive someone for kidnapping you and your best friends?"

Aya pulled on her pants, sighing. "I would have done the exact same thing, were the roles reversed. And you know you would have, too. You two are cut from the same cloth." She had her hands on her hips now, looking rather imposing for a lithe woman in a nightshirt and leather pants. She had a point, too.

But I was a monster. I would have let my best friends burn.

I threw Cali's shirt over my head, liking the snug fit of the black hide. I pulled on matching black pants. "I'll get my revenge on the prince soon," I said, jaw set.

Aya rolled her eyes. "People change their minds," she mumbled, almost too quiet for me to hear.

I glared at her as I laced up my boots.

Cali pulled on her weapons belt over the baggy tunic I had given her. "She's right, but that doesn't mean we have to like it," Cali said, the set of her lips making it clear what she thought of the Etruscan prince.

Good, at least one of us had sense.

"We should discuss who betrayed the mages' position to the council," Aya said, pulling on a billowing, red tunic dress that contained folds to hide an absurd number of weapons. Even surrounded by those who feared her, her style would be unmatched.

The ice that had formed within me as I slept on the cool earth cracked. "He's a dead man," I hissed.

"He loved you," Aya whispered.

"Did he? What really is love, but a weapon to be used against you?" I demanded. My fangs slid out as a growl erupted from my throat.

"He *rescued* you. He had no way of knowing who Katzima was or that she would even come for you." Aya shot back.

"What if it was Doric's influence?" Calliope cut in.

I scowled. "Then, he is a weak man."

Aya arched a brow. "Only as weak as you."

I growled, buckling my weapons belt into place. In truth, I hadn't considered the possibility of Doric's influence on Marcus.

Aya's eyes narrowed. Cali was still, glancing between us uneasily. Aya must have seen the desperation in my expression because she relaxed her posture a bit and gave a small nod saying, "It's possible. No one knows the full extent of Lord Venrylst's power."

Possible. I clung to the word with the fluttery hands of hope, melting the ice around my heart in a futile effort.

"Perhaps we should focus on the present. The Ophidians could be meeting any minute without us. We must all be on our guard," Cali pointed out in a clipped tone.

Aya's eyes were glittering as she smirked. "I thought we would at least know what was going on since you're sleeping with the Etruscan."

I cringed. "Do me a favor and never phrase it like that again. I'll go find him and make sure they didn't start without us."

Rolling my eyes, I left the room and walked back to the one I shared with the prince. Part of me hoped he had already left, and I wouldn't have to face him alone in our quarters. I opened the door and stepped inside.

I scanned the room slowly. There he was, lounging on the bed, bare chested and arms stretched behind his head. A lazy grin spread across his face when he noticed me.

"You never came back to bed last night, love," he drawled, sapphire eyes sparkling.

"I'm sure you missed my company deeply," I purred, sauntering into the room, exhaustion from the morning fading away.

His eyes glowed as they took in the tight pants and shirt I had borrowed from Cali. "I fear a different rumor will spread if you start spending the night in another's room."

I smirked, taking in the chest muscles visible above the sheets. "The only company I had last night was the desolate forest."

His playful eyes went flat. "You never left the forest." It wasn't a question.

I shrugged, confused by his change of tone. Rising swiftly from the bed, he prowled toward me. "You were wearing a thin nightgown when I left you." He glowered down at me.

"So?" I challenged, distracted as I took in his bare chest, ending in a deep V where his pajamas rested on his hips.

"It's nearly winter—are you trying to get yourself killed?" His chest heaved as he stood over me, forcing me to look up at him.

"I can handle myself," I grit out, annoyed. Did he really think he could intimidate me? *He* was the half-naked one. I took a step forward, landing my foot between his legs, forcing him to back up.

He didn't budge, so my leather shirt now rested against his bare chest.

His eyes flashed. "You could have frozen to death last night."

"What does it matter to you anyway?" I snapped.

A muscle in his jaw twitched. "What does it *matter*?" he said through his teeth. "What *matters* is that Lord Venrylst is still out there hunting us."

When I opened my mouth to object, he grabbed my chin and silenced me with a furious look. "You are their queen whether they like you right now or not. I did what I had to do to protect them when you wouldn't, but I'm not foolish enough to believe that someone without the Black Gift could ever rule here for long. Don't you *dare* ask me what it matters when all I've done the past three years is fight for *our* people's lives." He released my chin, but his heavy breathing hit my cheeks as he glared at me.

Prick. "You think I don't know?" I seethed. "I was born for one purpose; it's not something you forget." I was not backing down an inch. I leaned into him. "I asked what it matters to *you*." I smirked. "And I got my answer. You still think you're going to weasel your way into power as my betrothed."

"It would certainly solve your loyalty problem, wouldn't it?" He wiggled his eyebrows, eyes sparkling.

I laughed. "And be the sword at the side of the beloved king? Yours to deploy at will? A queen in name alone? I think not." My chest heaved against his at the insult.

"Or perhaps you've deluded yourself into thinking that your beloved traitor will come running back to you once you kill Doric."

I nearly staggered back at his words. They flowed down my back to pool in my gut. A twisted smile formed on my lips. "Those who betray me can consider themselves already dead."

The bastard laughed in my face. "When will you realize, love? I see you for exactly what you are." He rubbed his right ring finger over the pale scar on his left. "You would no sooner kill that lying traitor than you would harm your second or third."

The liquid in my stomach hardened, and my twisted smirk turned feral. "You have no idea what I am capable of, *prince*." I wasn't sure it was possible for our bodies to get much nearer, but still I inhaled deeply, pressing even closer, convinced he would stumble back.

The prince held his ground, eyes like the depths of the ocean. "There are those who would do almost anything for love."

"Is that why you became an Ophidian?" I challenged. I had to know what drove the prince to join an order he so clearly hated.

His jaw clenched. "Not exactly."

"Then, why?" I demanded, chest heaving against his. I would not go into battle with someone whose intentions I could not trust.

His hands fisted at his sides, clenching and unclenching. They splayed wide for a moment, and a sigh escaped his lips.

"Call it a family tradition, set forth by my grandfather. The curse of our power." The disgust in his gaze hit me as if he'd slapped me.

I had never thought that anyone else's gift would come with a curse. The prince had once made a comment about second sons not being able to choose their fate. I wondered if he hadn't been referencing our marriage, but instead joining the order. For the first time since meeting the Prince of Etrusca, I understood him.

Lightning blue eyes gazed down at me. Their scrutiny traveled down my nose to my lips and hovered there before sliding down to where the leather over my breasts pressed against his bare chest.

When he looked in my eyes again, I beheld a night sky. He dipped his head down, coming closer and closer to my face. My eyes were saucers, transfixed. Right as his lips were about to brush against mine, I snapped my lips shut, glaring. Bringing my hands up between us, I shoved him back.

He caught himself easily. Taking his time, his eyes traveled up my body. A grin spread across his face. There was a wild look in his eyes as he stepped around me to whisper in my ear, "I win." He walked around the bed and grabbed his shirt from the dresser.

"The Ophidians are meeting in about ten minutes to talk strategy. I assume you and your *cabal* would like to join us." He threw the words casually over his shoulder.

I grit my teeth, fighting the urge to hurl a knife at his back. I doubted that it would win me many points with the Ophidians, but gods, the prince drove me to madness.

TWENTY-SEVEN

A day later, I crouched hidden with Aya and Calliope at my side as we surveyed the guards outside of Galeston's keep.

"Gods, I hope they show up," I whispered, more to myself than to my comrades.

"They'll be here," Cali said firmly. I looked at my third. Red still rimmed her eyes from yesterday's events. She and Aya had been civil as we met with the other Ophidians, but there was a palpable coldness between the two women that set me on edge. I doubted either one slept well last night.

"Rohesia swore it as well. She hates you, but she hates the council more," Aya said reassuringly, squinting against the brisk early winter wind.

Calliope gave her a surprised look and opened her mouth, likely to comment on *why* Aya had been getting so cozy with the Ophidian's scout.

Aya glared at her.

Cali shut her mouth before she could speak.

I released a breath. I did not dare get in the middle. I had done my duty as their leader yesterday; this was between them now.

Aya spun her dark bob back to me. "There's nothing more to do but move forward. Either they show, or they don't. We will be prepared. The Naqadian throne is yours as long as you still breathe; we will let no one forget this."

I nodded, mouth in a tight line as I stood.

"One thing first," Aya whispered.

I turned back to her to see her pulling a long object from her pack. Handling the parcel carefully, she undid the string that bound it.

The cloth fell away to reveal a shining steel sword. The hilt resembled a coiled serpent.

My eyes widened. "Where did you...?"

Aya smiled coyly. "I went back after you arrived. Use it to enact your revenge." Her gaze darkened as she spoke, promising death to all who had participated in this sick joke.

I nodded slowly. Tears threatened my eyes. For the first time in years, I could *feel* the bond between us. What it really meant that I fought for and defended the Ophidians.

I cleared my throat. "The last mage this blade kills will be Doric Venrylst," I swore.

Aya's eyes shone. "There's our queen," she whispered.

Cali nodded. If I wasn't mistaken, her eyes were cloudy as well.

We walked toward the castle in a well-rehearsed formation. I relaxed, feeling at home with my cabal, and the full power of my gift settled around me. Vengeance blazed in my gaze.

We were dressed for battle. While Cali wore her usual guard's uniform, Aya and I barely passed as ladies by the open skirts we wore over tight fitting pants. I did not care. This was the uniform of serpents, and that is what we were. My deep-purple dress crisscrossed at the top, in perfect position for the protective metal chains I wore around my bodice. Down my arms rested thick leather sleeves so green they were almost black. My knives were strapped to every inch of me, both visible and concealed.

As we reached the gates, the guards motioned for us to stop.

"No one is to enter the castle, ma'am."

I stared at the two guards, waiting for them to register who stood before them. I cocked an eyebrow.

"Even you, Majesty," one of them added after a long pause. A bead of sweat fell down the man's forehead.

A sickly, sweet smile caressed my face. "What's your name, sir?" I asked the sweaty one.

"Emilio, Your Majesty." He shifted uneasily.

"Emilio, who leads the Royal Guard?" I batted my eyes at him.

He cleared his throat. "Lord Brom, the Strong." He offered a weak smile.

My own deepened. Aya smirked next to me, knowing what would happen next. "And who does Brom answer to?" I inquired.

He gulped. "I can't let you in, ma'am. They'll have my head for it." He placed his staff against the ground and widened his stance, as if he could stop the three of us. His partner nodded eagerly, mirroring his actions.

Fools.

My smile dropped. "What a shame." And with half a thought, my power snaked up around their necks and twisted. They fell to the gravel.

We walked easily through the doors to the keep and were met with several more soldiers blocking the way. The corner of my mouth twitched. *We're expected.*

Another thought, and the soldiers hit the ground. We walked through the once grand entrance, over cracked marble floors and past dying vines. The flowing rivers throughout the keep were empty, the marble stained red. I smirked at the visual of the mages' last act of defiance. I should have realized it before.

There were several members of the Royal Guard lining the pathway to the council chamber. My gift purred with each life I devoured.

I was positively radiant by the time we stood outside the council chamber. Two guards blocked our path.

"Stand aside," I said tiredly.

They did not budge. I shrugged. They fell to the ground, and I pushed open the door to the council chambers.

I smiled broadly at the members amassed before me. They were seated with the utmost civility, as if they had not engineered the massacre of hundreds mere days ago.

I beamed. "Lovely to see you all could make it."

Doric was the first to stand, glaring as his hands palpated against the wooden table. Terrin remained seated, cautiously watching Lord Venrylst. I didn't dare scan the room to see if Marcus sat in their midst. The Viper Queen did not lower herself to care about something so human as a betrayal. I feared she would disappear altogether if I met his golden eyes.

"What do you want?" Lord Venrylst spat.

I cocked my head to the side, allowing my gaze to travel lazily up his body. "Interesting."

He only continued to glare.

I smirked. *I'm in his head.*

Aya stirred beside me, a look of feigned interest on her face. "Your Majesty, what is so interesting?"

A feral grin spread across my face. My gift purred, billowing around the floorboards, to the council table, snaking through the guards positioned around the walls.

"I'm glad you asked, *handmaiden*." I threw her mock title in their faces as they beheld the lithe woman coiled beside me. Knives draped my second's frame, complementing the wicked grin on her face. "It's rather *interesting* that my own guards were ordered to keep me from the castle. It's *interesting* that Lord Venrylst, my chief advisor, greets me with such hostility. But the most interesting of all is this council's decision to commit genocide in complete disregard for their monarch's direct orders." My eyes glowed as I finally swept my gaze around the room.

Not one of them looked surprised. My heart sank. They were all in on the decision. My hope that Doric had staged a coup fizzled out. A different kind of hope fluttered as I scanned the faces of my council members. No Marcus. I pushed those thoughts aside. They did not belong here.

I raised my eyebrows, returning my gaze to Doric. "How might you defend your actions?"

"Your Majesty, the mages attacked our keep. We had no choice but to retaliate." His words were so smooth I almost believed them. I could practically *feel* his magic trying to work its way back into my mind. I prayed that my Protector had kept his word and was hiding nearby.

But I had been there when the city burned. The castle was miles from any carnage.

I smiled sweetly. The guards along the wall fell. Council members turned, some gasped. "I'll ask once more. Give me one good reason not to kill every last one of you."

"Viper," Brom Balenek muttered as he beheld the piles of bodies near the wall.

"Took you long enough." I sighed, examining a fingernail.

"We are not the ones who committed treason," Doric said calmly. He'd known. He had planned this exact moment to out me. *Good thing the lord was predictable.*

I mirrored his nonchalance. "The mages were a peaceful people who sacrificed their way of life to fight in a war that was not theirs. It was in the best interest of Naqad to leave them alone." I flicked a speck of dirt from my bodice. "The Ophidians I lead, however, are not peaceful. Now you have no one to blame but yourselves for the vengeance you brought upon yourself." My eyes flashed, revealing my rage at last.

Lord Venrylst spat at the mention of our species. "You lead ruthless assassins and murderers. You would have come for us eventually."

"We wouldn't have," I said mildly. "But that doesn't really matter now, does it?" The corner of my mouth raised in a crooked grin. I *had* been planning to take the human realms for the Ophidians as soon as I was crowned, but I would never admit it, not here.

Doric laughed. "And we finally hear how you truly speak of them. You consider yourself one of the people who've pillaged our cities and destroyed our lands. Do you honestly believe the council will allow you to keep your crown after this confession?"

"I wasn't aware that was the council's decision to make," I purred, my eyes glittering emeralds. "I asked you to give me a reason not to kill you, and all you've supplied me with is empty threats and accusations of crimes against Naqadians that were committed by you."

I watched as my words reverberated around the room. The assembled lords began to stir. It was clear they did not know that Doric was behind the cities burning, installing leaders like Gerome, starving our people. I fought the smug smile that threatened to take over my face. I could not wait to inform them.

Doric snarled. "You dare."

I smirked, pulling the council's manufactured weaponry halfway from its sheath. "Look familiar?" I asked in a low voice.

A flash of uncertainty crossed the pompous lord's eyes.

"You made swords to look like the head of the serpent and used them as an excuse to kill thousands of mages," I spat. "Gerome, the famine, all the uprisings, it was all you. You cannot claim one and not the other. Your ridiculous weaponry gives you away."

A gasp slipped out from the one of the council members. Lord Venrylst opened his mouth.

I held up a hand to silence him. The less he spoke the less he could infuse his magic into the rest of the council. I prayed that Caryk was strong enough to protect them all. "Anyone else want to vouch for your lives? Going once..." I scanned the room, a cat playing with its food.

"We didn't know," a soft voice said from the corner. My heart stopped. The monster within me paused. The death raging in my eyes met calm amber pools. My bravado shattered. It was all I could do to keep my face arranged in a smirk. "The mages were the ones fueling the Ophidians, allowing them to exist." His voice was like warm honey, begging me to forgive him.

Terrin was nodding gravely. "They had to be dealt with," he rasped.

"Because it's true," Doric spat.

The amber eyes in the corner looked uncertain. Terrin's hazel ones echoed the doubt.

I recovered my smirk. "One way to find out." With half a thought, my gift snaked up Lord Venrylst's body. Another thought, and I twisted it. He remained standing. I squeezed. Still, he stood, face free of strain. I pulled, searching for the bright spot of life. Nothing. I'd felt this before.

My eyes narrowed. "You've found yourself a Protector." I searched the faces of the council behind me, looking for any sign that one of them was using magic.

"And you just tried to kill me," Doric seethed. "Seize her!"

Despite their words just moments before, the council members burst into action, flinging themselves at our trio.

"If you insist," I drawled, drawing my twin blades.

Three dark forms dropped from the rafters. Caryk lifted his head, bright eyes glowing against tan skin. His scales were out, dark inky wells that mirrored mine. Ives and Rohesia were twin shadows behind him, scales several shades brighter than the prince's. Dark metal glinted at their sides. Their slitted pupils promised death. My heart soared to see them standing with me, prepared to fight behind their leader. I fought to hide my relief.

With a wicked grin, I shifted. Scales covered my arms, accenting my face in perfect armor. I kept the smile, allowing my pointed canines to show.

Brom was the first to reach us. He swung his sword in a wide arc at Caryk. My heart pounded as the prince parried with his own massive broadsword. Their brutal dance around the room began.

The door behind us burst open. Cali pulled me to the side as an enormous boar rushed past us—one of Terrin's creatures. Calliope and I locked eyes, and I nodded at her gratefully.

The boar stopped just before the table and pivoted. Tusks the size of a man's thigh hurtled toward me. I sheathed my blades and jogged to meet it. Right as it was about to skewer me, I leapt, grabbing hold of the horns. With a grunt, I flipped my body into the air and landed on the creature's back.

I thrust my hands into its long tufts of fur, gripping tightly. The boar now veered in the direction of the council members. My gaze met Terrin's briefly, and the wild grin on his face was not entirely human.

Without warning, the boar turned sharply back to face the Ophidians. As it charged, I leaned my chest forward until a knife hilt brushed against the back of my hand. Carefully, I released one hand from the boar's fur. My palm closed around the dagger. The boar bucked, and I lost my balance, falling to the right side.

As I fell, I thrust my dagger into its neck, dragging the knife with me. My left hand gripped its fur tightly, and I heaved both my feet to one side. With a final grunt, I propelled myself off the beast. A guttural sound tore from its throat as my dagger exited its flesh. I landed on my back, rolling to my feet just in time to see the boar fall to the ground, just shy of where Aya stood dueling a councilman.

She did not spare the boar a glance. The councilman, however, staggered, gaze drawn to the fallen animal. Aya chastised his negligence with a slash of her knife down his arm.

I turned to face the battle, reaching my mist out, sensing for lifeforms. Perhaps someone would get lucky and kill their Protector. But I felt no warning pull from any of the bodies rushing me. I took a deep breath as I drew my long knives once more, focusing on the space around me.

A stir disrupted the air to my left as a blade sliced near my face. I twisted just in time, and the sharp edge ricocheted off the scales framing my cheekbone. I retaliated with a swift strike. They parried. As I went in with a knife, I glanced at their face. The young lord's features were unfamiliar. Had the council been adding more members? The pommel of his sword collided with my gut, and I exhaled.

Throwing myself at him, I sprang into the offensive, pushing my musings to the side and focusing only on slashing and cutting, blocking and ducking. I stopped worrying about who I was attacking but rather just trying to penetrate the circle. If I could get to Doric, this would be over. My dagger plunged into flesh, and I withdrew it, moving on to the next flailing sword.

I blocked this one easily, but a shield hit me in my ribs before I could bring my blade down to block. Gritting my teeth, I forced my body to unbuckle and swing my blades, but this sword was far heavier than my daggers, my opponent stronger. They parried both my blades with the shield. I felt their sword whistle through the air, straight for my exposed side.

Grunting, I launched myself into the assailant, throwing my weight onto the shield. They stumbled back long enough for me to twist the pommel of my blade to whack their hand with a crunch. The sword fell to the ground. I attacked their shield mercilessly, spinning and ducking too quickly for the heavy shield to keep up. They stumbled again. Enough that I could knock the shield from their grip with a swift elbow. I swung back around with my blade to finish the job.

"NO!" a deep voice boomed.

A ring sounded as my blade collided with a heavy broadsword. Someone had saved my defenseless opponent.

"Tamariya," the voice grit out.

I felt like a blind woman as I tried to force my vision to see their face. It would be another one of Lord Venrylst's tricks. I spun to face my new opponent to knock the sword from his grip. He was ready for me.

"Gods, Tamariya," he wheezed. The anger. I knew that voice. My full name on his lips resonated within me. My eyes focused, and I was face-to-face with a blue strike of lightning. I took a step back. It was the prince, eyes aglow.

"What the fuck, Caryk?" I spat. "I could have killed you."

He narrowed his eyes. "That remains to be seen."

Cocky bastard.

"Did you even see who you were trying to kill?" the prince challenged.

I looked over his shoulder at the man lying on the ground, relieved of his shield and sword. Deep pools of red shone on dark skin, and eyes like cracked amber glass looked past me. The blood drained from my face. My heart nearly stopped. I sagged, and Caryk caught me. I stumbled over to Marcus, kneeling next to him.

"Oh my gods, Marcus. I'm sorry," I breathed. Was I? Had Marcus been under Doric's control, just as I had? Or had he given up my family willingly? My gift roiled and snapped inside me. Long smoky tendrils stretched out and coiled around his neck.

Traitor.

Marcus' eyes widened, and he scrambled back. I gasped too and tried to call them back in. I couldn't focus. *Kill, kill* was all my mind would say. I was blinking too much. Black mist clouded my vision. The mist solidified into a glass wall between my consciousness and the council chamber.

A growl sounded beside me, and there was a hand on my chin and another on my shoulder. "No you don't." Caryk was forcing me to look at him. His face was blurry. My head was rolling.

"What's happening to her?" Marcus said, breathless.

"It's the Gift. Ophidia is taking over." Was I imagining it or did the prince sound desperate? A sharp pain pricked my ring finger. "Come on, Tamariya, fight this. Fight *her.*"

Cieri, he was pissed at me. I tried to break the glass to tell him what an annoying ass he was. Ophidia laughed at my pounding fists. She pushed me further away.

"Do something."

"What do you want me to do?" A snarl.

"Anything, she's slipping away."

I couldn't see them anymore. I had no idea who spoke.

"Damnit, Tamariya, look at me." A growl.

"Oh, fuck it." An exhale.

Warmth seeped into my lips. My subconscious pressed against the glass. His hands were laced in my hair. Fists pounded on the glass. A hand pressed into my back, pulling me into a hard chest. Cracks formed. My hand grazed his chest as my lips moved against his. He let out an involuntary growl, and the glass shattered.

I moved my lips against his, savoring the desperation I tasted there. His hands tightened in my hair. I could feel every inch of his body on mine. Every muscle in his arms. The sculpted planes of his back. Sharp metal from his armor. I could hear the clash of swords around me, but I was lost in a different way. His mouth was fire on mine, burning throughout my entire body. The betrothal bond on my finger burned right along with me.

"Ehem." Someone cleared their throat next to us.

I opened my eyes to tell Caryk to fuck off, but gasped. *Marcus* had cleared his throat. Slowly, I turned my head back to the man whose arms I was still gripping. Dancing blue flames met my horrified gaze. He smiled lazily at me. "Hello, My Queen. Glad to have you back." Prince Caryk Cazaar's eyes blazed back at me.

The spell was broken, and I became aware of the battle surging around us. I remembered what I was here to do. I pushed Caryk away, which was harder than expected as our limbs were firmly entangled. I managed to stand and held up a hand as both men made to open their mouths. Caryk wore a devilish grin. Marcus looked like he wanted to punch Caryk in the throat.

"I'm back. We need to kill Doric." I prayed they couldn't see the flush I felt in my cheeks. I would murder Caryk for this later. Or not. He had brought me back, unorthodox as it was. Maybe I would give him a pass.

The men stared at each other.

Marcus' fists twitched toward his sword.

Caryk's mirth faded, and a muscle flexed in his jaw.

I stepped between them. "Seriously?"

They shifted their focus back to me. Caryk shook his head. Marcus blinked.

"Get. To. Doric." I enunciated each word, looking at them both in turn.

I stepped forward without waiting for them to respond—let them continue their pissing contest. I launched myself back into the fray, spinning my blade. Maybe if I killed someone it would get rid of the lingering heat coursing through my veins.

I was slicing my way to the center of the room when the ground began to shake. Turning, I found Rohesia grinning wickedly as the floor cracked and roots sprang up. Her roots wrapped around council members' ankles, pulling them into the ground. They clambered to cut the vines before the earth swallowed them. I used the distraction to dash across the room. Dirt flew at the council members, in their faces and eyes, down their throats. Strangled noises pierced the hall. I smiled. They wanted a reason to fear magic; we would give them one.

I thrust my blade into flesh. A body fell. I looked up. The pathway before me was clear, and standing a few feet away, there he was. Lord Doric Venrylst, smug as ever. I sheathed my knives, instead pulling the blade I had reserved just for the mage killer from my belt. Its serpentine hilt was justice's blade in my hands.

Doric smiled. His teeth were yellow. How had I not noticed before? "Thank you for revealing yourself so publicly. You've made this a lot easier for me."

I took a deliberate step forward, shrugging. "Hard to tell anyone with your head on the other side of the room."

He smirked. "Your grand plan is to kill every last one of us? You'll have a rebellion on your hands within a fortnight."

"I already do, thanks to you." Another step.

"Child, you have yet to learn what true rebellion is." Doric looked down his nose, ever the condescending mentor.

"Is that a threat?" My voice was innocent as I arched a brow and slid a finger down my blade.

"A promise, dear. You need us to quell the rebellion." Was that a hint of desperation I detected? The sniveling lord took a half step back.

I laughed. "The same one that you started? I wonder what the rest of the council will think when they are no longer under your *influence.*"

Doric's eyes flashed.

"I gave you a chance to provide me with a reason to keep you alive, and you declined my offer," I said simply.

Doric frowned. "I was your father's most trusted advisor for good reason, Tamariya."

I scoffed. "It seems you afforded my father a level of deference that you have not given me."

"I will when you prove you are more than a child playing at a man's game," he hissed.

My hand twitched toward my throwing knives. His blood would paint a beautiful mural on these marble floors. But I pulled it back. That was not how he was to die.

"Insults aren't the way to my heart, Doric," I chastised.

"Do you even have one? The 'people' that you fight so desperately to protect have preyed on Naqadians for centuries." He put his hands in his pockets, as if we were discussing the day's events over tea. "The Ophidians are soulless monsters, bred to kill." I opened my mouth, but he continued. "This kingdom needs peace, not a killing machine at its helm."

"The Ophidians delivered that peace to Naqad under my leadership." I wasn't sure why I was allowing this debate to go on. One flick of my wrist and he'd be dead.

"You rule a band of murderers and outcasts who kidnapped your own court. You are holding on to both kingdoms by a *thread*."

"And you? You're starving your own people! For what?" I spat back.

"Do you honestly believe that you could rule Naqad? The only choices you've made for this kingdom have ended in bloodshed."

I grit my teeth together. But he was right. I'd beheaded Gerome on sight. I'd fought in the war. I came into this very room with blood on my hands. It was what I did well.

"You can't treat Naqad like the festering snake pit you slithered out of. Naqadians deserve better than that." His eyes glowed like orbs as he uttered the words I already knew. The words that I agonized over. I didn't know the first thing about ruling in peace. I was a warrior, a trained assassin. I was bred to kill, not lead. "Take the Ophidians back to their pits and leave Naqad alone. Our armies won't pursue you. Let Naqad flourish."

His words were compelling, even with Caryk's magic protecting me. It would be easy to give up my throne. Doric would stop trying to destabilize my reign, and the people would be well fed again. If I ruled Naqad, the monster stirring within would inevitably consume me, and the Naqadians would pay the price.

With the Ophidians, I didn't need to pretend to be someone I wasn't. Caryk had them wrapped around his finger, but that was nothing that a well-timed assassination couldn't fix. Doric was right, killing was the only way I knew to hold onto a crown. No one follows a monster willingly. I would never command the respect of the Naqadians. But Doric did. Somehow this sniveling, conniving man had managed to get an entire kingdom in the palm of his hand.

Swords clashed around us, dirt flew through the air, and the castle itself was shaking. Rohesia's vines had penetrated the walls. Terrin's animals were doing their best to tear them to shreds. Ives was by Rohesia's side, heading off anyone who dared interrupt her.

Caryk and Marcus stood back-to-back fighting a pack of Terrin's wolves, each the size of a man, thick fangs protruding from their mouths. Terrin wore a pained expression as he watched the beasts he controlled claw toward his own spy.

Doric smiled at me, but it wasn't a cruel smile. It was almost kind, understanding. Like he knew exactly what I had been struggling with for the past three years. Maybe Doric and I were not all that different. Or the lord had spent too much time messing with my head.

I loosened my grip on my long knife. The castle was crumbling. Was I willing to destroy everyone inside for my vengeance? What about the damage that the collapse would cause to the city?

"Is this what Katzima would want?" Doric asked gently.

"You knew Katzima?" Blood rushed to my head.

"Did you think you were the only one she taught?"

My hand flexed around the serpentine blade. "Yet you killed her anyway."

"The witch was dangerous." His pale blue eyes glowed.

"She was an old woman. A Healer."

Doric seethed, eyes flashing. "Responsible for creating monsters like the Viper."

My skin burned. He would see exactly what kind of monster the Viper was. I coiled my gift around his neck, squeezing the magical protection. If I had knocked Caryk on his back with my grief, my rage could shatter this shield. I gathered my strength around me, pooling it in a thick black cloud. It coiled. And struck. Over and over, like an asp. Doric staggered back, but the magic held. I gathered my gift.

"No wonder she agreed to help us quell your gift. Your *gift* pulses with your emotions, as if we needed more proof that you are not fit to rule." His lip curled in a sneer.

"Liar!" I struck again. His nose began to bleed. All I could see was black mist. My gift roared around me, and I thrust its full power at him. He fell, and I smiled, eyes gleaming. "She would never help you."

Doric groaned, pushing himself onto his elbows. "Why do you think the Black Gift returned the moment she died?"

"No," I whispered. The blood drained from my face.

Doric rose, smirking. "The spell that kept you in check, kept you from becoming the Viper, was of your precious mentor's making."

Fury raged within me. It could not be true. I would not accept it. Reaching down, I drew a knife from my belt, temporarily sheathing my sword. I flung the knife through the air. The blade turned end over end.

Doric slid sideways, my blade merely skimming the sleeve of his tunic.

Quick as an asp, I released another blade.

He dodged again. I cocked my head to the side. Good reflexes for a man nearing his sixth decade of life. A man who hadn't seen battle for decades.

I sprang into motion, launching blade after blade, emptying my weapons belt of all but my twin long knives and the serpentine blade. I would save it until the moment was right. Doric scrambled back, dodging each blade. His tunic was nearly shredded, but there was no evidence of blood. The cursed liar would pay for this.

I stalked toward him, balancing a knife on my palm. My power coiled around me too.

"Your mother was emotional too," Doric sneered. "It made her easy to kill."

TWENTY-EIGHT

I dropped my knife. The ground lurched. I couldn't seem to keep my feet under me. Katzima, my mother. Was any part of my life untouched by this man?

"She liked to flaunt the Black Gift too, but that didn't do her much good in the end."

My hands collided with cool stone. Katzima had said it was someone close to them. Someone in their inner circle. My mother's mind had been shredded. The Etruscan prince had nothing to do with it. That meant I was face-to-face with an Allurant who could shred minds at will. Doric Venrylst killed my mother.

Katzima had been helping him. Did she truly not know he had killed my mother? Had she helped him with that as well? She had believed me so past redemption that she used magic to keep me from shifting, from using my magic.

She had known what Doric was doing to me. And did nothing to save me. Because she knew the Viper Queen was a monster that I could not control. The only person I had ever truly trusted didn't believe that I could handle my power. I tried to breathe, but the air wouldn't come fast enough. She was right, I didn't know the first thing about commanding this torrent of rage.

My eyes met Doric's, deep loathing etched across his face. He knew what I had been denying for years. He drew his blade from its sheath. I didn't move to stop him. I deserved this. I couldn't be the court's puppet anymore. And I couldn't be the Viper either. Katzima must have known that I couldn't handle it. That was why she stifled my magic, to protect me from Ophidia.

My purpose had been served. When Doric called off his rebellion, the Naqadians would heal. I was never supposed to survive. Metal whirred through the air. I exhaled, closing my eyes, waiting for the blade to drop.

Steel rang. Moisture dripped on my face. I opened my eyes. I was met by the hurricane raging in the Prince of Etrusca's eyes. He grit his teeth as beads of sweat fell from his forehead.

"The monster is supposed to be slayed in the end," I whispered.

"Then, go kill it," he growled, arms trembling against the weight of Doric's blade.

I shook my head. I had destroyed enough.

"She knew what you were capable of."

My brow furrowed. Katzima? She molded me into a weapon and then decided that I had to be kept in a cage. She knew the destruction I would cause.

"She believed in you. Bred for evil but turned to good." Caryk recounted the words that Katzima had uttered on her deathbed. The sword wobbled as he held off the older man.

The raven necklace. It still pressed against my throat. I hadn't had the courage to bury it yet. I reached up and touched it.

Doric didn't get to commit genocide and call himself a savior.

Could her message have been about me? I had been bred to kill. But maybe...

"Tamariya," Caryk grunted.

His sword gave.

I rolled.

Doric's blade clanged against the stone where my heart had been. The prince lurched back, dragging his broadsword with him.

I jumped to my feet, scouring the floor for my knives. The glimmer of black metal caught my eye, and I drew my gaze up to see the owner of the hands that grasped my weapons. Amber eyes gazed at me somberly. I stared at Marcus. He looked to the knives caked in blood he held in his hands, crease on his brow, and his pained gaze met mine. Doubt clouded his face as he looked at Doric.

"Marcus, please," I begged. "Let me end this."

He looked at me again, and I saw every moment we had spent together. A brush of our hands passing in the hall, a stolen kiss in the garden, a strong arm wrapped around my waist. His eyes, like pools of whiskey, were the same ones I had stared into as he told me he loved me and promised me a life together. Did he see the same in mine now? After all I had done, after I had almost killed him tonight?

His expression morphed into hard resolve. I braced myself. He turned a blade over in his hand. And then the weapon was turning end over end in an arc toward me. I caught it handily, and my heart warmed.

I faced Doric, who was up on his feet, recovered from colliding with the ground. I drew the serpentine blade from my belt at last, a weapon in each hand. He spat. I was vaguely aware of Brom charging at us and Caryk intercepting his blade. The fighting continued to surge around us as Doric and I circled each other. I smiled, showing my elongated canines.

Doric staggered back a step, and I took the opening, lunging to thrust the knife into his abdomen. He dodged, striking out with his longer sword. He was too fast. No human should be able to match my speed. I spun out of his reach. He stabbed and thrust his blade, keeping me too far away to strike, then slashed at my left side, and I had no choice but to block with the knife. The shock reverberated through my hand. My smaller weapon couldn't take the brunt of his full strength. *Something isn't right.*

The knife clattered to the stone. I hissed as pain seared through my abdomen. I didn't dare look down to see the bloody gash his sword had left, right between my scaly armor. I darted in and slashed with the serpentine sword, dancing around Doric. His heavy blade couldn't keep up, and I landed a slice on his rib cage. Black blood spilt from the wound. I spun, but he struck my back with the hilt, and I lurched forward. The serpent's sword dropped to the chipped marble.

"What are you?" I hissed.

My hands hit the stone floor. *Not this time.* I shot back up, twisting to dodge his onslaught. I ducked as his blade passed over where my head had been.

He laughed, a blood curdling sound. "You haven't figured it out yet?"

"Some kind of *demon*," I spat.

He smiled, a wild look in his eyes. And that's when I noticed it. The yellowing to his teeth. The black blood oozing out of him. The uncanny speed for a man of his age. Doric Venrylst *was* a demon.

His horrible laugh continued. "I'm not so powerless as a lowly demon. I'm the god of Hel's chosen. You see, *I* summoned the helmai. Anu fuels my power—you cannot defeat me."

No. It wasn't possible. But we had never found the summoner. We had never understood why someone would summon Hel's armies to Naqad.

Another sword came racing for my head. Instinctively, I reached a weaponless arm upward to block it. A ring sounded as the metal skated off my forearm. *The scales.*

I smiled. I wasn't used to my Ophidian form. Doric stood, momentarily stunned. Apparently, neither was he.

My grin deepened, and I lunged at him, the manic gleam back in my eye. He swung, and I parried with my scaly arms.

Breathing deeply, I felt what it truly meant to be an Ophidian. To be more than human. To rule the world. It was intoxicating.

The lord continued his futile attempts to harm me. It did not matter that he was Anu's chosen. I was the Viper Queen. I was not merely Ophidia's chosen. I *was* Ophidia. I was a *god*. A loud cackle escaped my lips as I parried another blow. Then I released my hold keeping Ophidia at bay.

I had to end this before she grew too powerful. If she took over completely, I would not be strong enough to shove her down again. But I needed her to win this battle.

I was toying with him now, baring my fangs. If only I could get close enough to bite him, however uncivilized it would be, this could be over.

As I ducked beneath another attack, I cast my gaze around the floor for a weapon. All I needed was a blade and his life would be forfeit. There was no steel within reach. I grunted in frustration. My grip on reality was loosening by the second. *I had to end this.*

Caryk was still locked in battle with Brom, and Marcus was nowhere to be seen. *Cieri,* I prayed he was still alive. Or not. There wasn't time to sort out my feelings on the matter as Doric swung again. I lifted an arm to block, and he threw his entire weight onto me. He was heavy, and my arm trembled with the effort of keeping him at bay. At the last second, I withdrew the arm and dodged the swing.

His body flew past me; he had been counting on me to meet his blow.

Doric was overextended.

This was my chance.

"Tamariya!" I turned to the shout — a massive broadsword looped through the air. I jumped. My hand fastened around the heavy hilt. Both hands gripped it as I brought the blade to the ground in a sweeping motion. My muscles flexed and strained, and I was fueled not by revenge, but by need. A need to be more. To do more. A need to prove to myself that I was not the monster I feared.

The broadsword hit flesh, giving way as the blade tore through Doric Venrylst's neck. The council leader's head fell at Brom Balenek's feet, who was hoisting a blade high, seconds from plunging it into the Prince of Etrusca's chest.

Caryk, who lay without his broadsword. The sword that I now held.

My heart raced. With the prince dead, I would rule the Ophidians unchallenged. My phony betrothal would be at an end. I would be free.

My stomach fluttered with anticipation.

Time moved slowly as I watched the sword glide through the air.

I smiled. At last, I would be free of the prince who had plotted against me for years. The assassin who had captured and tortured me. The Ophidian who had looked at me with disgust when he saw what I had done to our own kind.

The man that had seen me for exactly what I was.

I was going to kill the prince anyways, so what did it matter if Brom did it for me?

My chest ached. *Caryk.* The man who had freed me from the deepest trenches of my consciousness.

As Brom's broadsword hurtled toward him, the prince's head turned.

Piercing blue eyes met mine, penetrating through to my soul. They did not beg me to save him. Instead, the prince gazed at me with understanding and acceptance.

"CARYK!" The word erupted from my lips as I sprang forward, dropping the blade. I did not recall gathering my magic, but it pooled behind me, propelling me as I leapt toward the massive warrior.

I had no clue why my body moved, but I had to reach the prince. Brom's blade neared Caryk, whose eyes had flown wide in disbelief.

My body collided with solid brick. The warrior grunted. Then my magic hit him. Black clouds charged his frame as Brom collapsed to the stone, my body atop his.

He groaned. My magic had not killed him. I exhaled. Then I pinned him to the ground with my knee.

"You're free, Brom. Doric is dead," I said, shaking his shoulders.

A clouded look came over his face. His hazel eyes cleared. "My Queen," he breathed. Relief coursed through me.

I clambered over him, brushing myself off. The fighting had stopped. Terrin was walking in my direction, the rest of the council behind him. Caryk was pulling himself up, a strange expression on his face.

Aya reached me first, Calliope trailing just behind her, holding a serpent-hilted sword.

She offered the blade to me. "Perhaps not the poetic ending you craved, but he is dead nonetheless," the warrior remarked.

I accepted the blade, nodding my gratitude.

My second stared at me with resolve in her deep obsidian eyes. Wordlessly, she pulled something glittering from her pack.

"You really did bring the Serpent's Crown to Galeston," I said fervently. "They just couldn't find it."

She scoffed, handing me the crown of glittering amethysts set in dark steel. "Of course they couldn't find it." In the waning sunlight filtering through the sparse windows of the chamber, it was easier to imagine the coiled serpent slithering off the headpiece.

I accepted the crown with a crooked smile.

Terrin reached me next. He staggered back a step as I turned to the assembling crowd and raised the crown to my head. "Doric had us under his control, Your Majesty," he said. "He was the one who starved the Naqadians and made Gerome into a monster. He destroyed Malnova and the other cities. He had us all under his compulsion. I swear Tamariya, we didn't have a choice." Terrin trembled as he spoke, wisps of gray hair falling into his face.

Something within me twisted to see the old man begging for his life.

"Doric sought to destroy any magic he could not control," I said somberly. "In his madness, he would have destroyed the entire kingdom." I leveled a look at each of the remaining council members, daring them to disagree. A god of Hel had been funneling his power to Doric. That power had allowed him to sink his claws into every member of the council. Something within me sagged with relief. They had not all been in on it.

I imagined that I struck quite the image, standing with my back to the windows, my fighting leathers torn, Doric Venrylst's poisoned blood staining the hard fabric. I wore my scales proudly. The council knew what I was. I had flaunted it before them and used it against them in battle. There was no reason for me to hide it now.

But I had been an absent leader for years. I swallowed.

I was their queen. By blood and by right. I prayed the mirage before them would be convincing enough.

"You saved us from Doric's compulsion. You saved Naqad," Brom said with a bow.

The rest of the council nodded their agreement. The others began to drop to their knees. I should have killed them all. Whether aware of it or not, they had betrayed me. Against everything I had fought for, I had allowed the Prince of Etrusca to live. I was no better than them.

I would be paying for that mistake until the day he died. And it would be at my hand, when I chose. I had given him a chance to try his hand as well, for we could not both live. I did not need to be questioning the loyalty of my entire council while watching my back for an assassination attempt. They could all be dead within seconds, and I wouldn't need to play this cursed game anymore.

I reached for my power; smoke began to fill the room.

"You cannot rule two kingdoms without them." Lips brushed against my ear, the words loud enough for only me to hear.

My hard emerald stare met Caryk's sapphire gaze. We stood there, faces nearly touching, for what felt like forever. My ring finger throbbed with an emotion I could not name. The crown on my head seemed to pulse.

At last, I broke away and turned to the council brusquely.

"Then, I look forward to our partnership. We have a kingdom to rebuild," I snapped. I did not know what compelled me to trust the prince's judgment.

It would surely be my doom.

TWENTY-NINE

I turned to leave the destroyed hall, but Caryk grabbed my arm. He leaned down, speaking in my ear once more. "You know that one of them is a Protector."

I nodded, turning to meet his eyes. *Someone had acted of their own free will.* The words passed between us unspoken.

"It would have been easier to kill them all," he murmured, blue eyes glittering.

"You were right though. I need them if I'm going to rule both kingdoms."

He smirked. "I know." His voice was filled with mirth.

I rolled my eyes at the prince. He was insufferable as ever.

"Ry." Marcus stood in front of us, jaw tight, glaring at where Caryk's mouth nearly brushed my ear. I arched a brow, meeting his honey eyes. His gaze transformed until I was staring into eyes that were like shattered glass.

"Can we talk?" he asked with a pointed look at Caryk. "Alone?"

I nodded. Before I could step forward, Caryk's hand snaked around my wrist.

He turned me, shielding his mouth from Marcus' view. "Remember what I said," he whispered, his eyes fierce as they held mine captive. I swallowed, staring into the intoxicating abyss before me. I jerked my chin and stepped back.

Marcus was watching us, his entire body rigid. I squared my shoulders and faced him, gesturing to a room off the side of the council chamber. Marcus closed the door behind us. He sighed, his back to me. "The prince is... intense around you."

I rolled my eyes. "When isn't Caryk intense? I don't think he's relaxed since he left his mother's belly." I fought to hide my annoyance. I didn't have time for Marcus' petty jealousy. I was exhausted.

Marcus turned, unamused. "No, he's different, protective."

"He's a Protector," I said flatly.

"I don't like it."

My eyes blazed. "*I* don't like how the one person I thought I could trust betrayed me." I crossed my arms.

He had the decency to look guilty.

"And where were you tonight? That *intense Protector* saved me more than once, but I barely saw you lift a sword."

"Ry, I—"

"How could you, Marcus? After all your grand promises, how could you sell the mages out?"

"I didn't know what they were going to do to them."

"You saw me with Katzima. You knew that town was sacred." My voice was a deadly calm.

"You lied to me about who you were. I've known you my whole life!" He threw his hands in the air.

"They were my family, Marcus."

"And I wanted to be yours."

I flinched. "Wanted to?" I said quietly, embarrassed to admit how much the words stung, despite my fury.

He sighed. "I don't know, Ry. Finding out that the woman you love is the queen of the most brutal assassins ever created is tough to take in." Marcus looked at me, something dark brewing in his eyes, an emotion I had not seen from him before.

I recoiled, drawing my hand up to my crown. "You've fought by my side before. You knew exactly what I was capable of," I hissed, glaring.

"You can kill someone with half a thought." He ran a hand through his tight curls, causing some of them to spring loose from the tightly wound bun at the back of his neck. Barely even touched from the fighting.

I bared my teeth. "How is that any different from sticking a sword through a heart?"

"You lead an *army* of trained killers."

"You led an army of trained killers to my family's doorstep," I spat back.

"I didn't know, okay? I didn't know what Doric was going to do. He said he wanted to protect them! He said he needed to know their location so he could follow *your* orders," he said, pacing around the tiny room.

"Were you compelled?" I asked quietly. My gut twisted, dreading the answer.

He threw his hands up. "I don't know that either! I didn't even know that Doric *could* compel people until moments ago. Yet another thing you kept from me!"

I winced. "I didn't know. He got to me as well. Caryk was the one to free me," I whispered.

"Why didn't he think to look in my mind too, huh? Or the rest of the council for that matter!" The hurt in his eyes was raw.

"Caryk had only been in Egryt for a matter of *days*. He's one man, not an army," I retorted. I couldn't believe I was defending the Etruscan.

He stepped toward me, cupping his palm on my cheek. "Ry," he said softly. "I would do anything for you, you know that right? Everything I've done has been for you. But I can't help you if you don't tell me what's going on." His gaze was like warm honey.

He was right. How could I ask for unquestioning trust from him if I couldn't give him the same? I sighed. Doric was dead. We didn't need to debate what Doric had compelled Marcus to do versus simply convinced him. I was tired. So tired of fighting. Of fighting the council, fighting the Ophidians, and fighting Marcus.

I leaned into his hand, closing my eyes. His arm circled around my waist, and Marcus was pulling me into him. I collapsed into his chest, breathing in his warm, musky scent. He stroked my hair, and I was home. I smiled, relaxing for the first time in weeks.

Two hypnotic blue orbs pierced my perfect oasis, and Caryk's words echoed in my mind. My eyes flew open.

The crown felt suddenly heavy on my head where Marcus' words reverberated. He had done what he thought was best for Naqad. He had given up my family in my name, thinking that was what was best for me. Marcus had decided on his own what I needed. He had not bothered to consult me.

I raised a hand to his face. His eyes were full of love and admiration. He would move mountains for us to be together.

And there it was. The truth. I inhaled sharply. They must have promised him something, something big for him to disobey my direct orders.

My eyes widened.

They had promised him *me*. A marriage to me, blessed by the council. And he had taken the deal. I could see it, there in his eyes.

Ice grew in my veins. My heart froze over. Marcus loved me so much he would burn my world so he could have me.

I smiled at him. My hero, my love, the man who had committed genocide to be by my side.

My other hand caressed the cool hilt of the serpentine blade.

My smile stayed frozen as I gazed lovingly into his eyes, and my hand on his face pulled his lips down to meet my own.

The sound of our lips clashing disguised the swish of metal as I pulled the blade from its sheath.

"I love you, Marcus," I whispered against his lips.

I hoisted the beautiful weapon.

He pulled back to gaze at me, his eyes warm and kind.

"And I love you, Ry." His lips brushed mine again.

I plunged the sword down.

Something hard gripped my arm, halting its movement.

I broke the kiss, snarling.

Marcus' eyes flew open. Confusion clouded his gaze. Slowly, he turned his head to where my arm hung suspended mid strike, frozen in place by the strong hands of none other than the Etruscan prince.

Marcus' mouth gaped.

"Ry?" Fear clouded his vision for the first time since he beheld me.

Distantly, I realized the same emotion had been stabbing my own finger. Some deep, barely conscious part of me wondered at it.

A twisted snarl spread across my face. My eyes blazed with poison.

"You destroyed everything. My home, my people, Katzima. You met them and saw their kindness and still you sold them out to Hel's chosen, for *what*?" I writhed in the Etruscan's arms, my eyes glazing over as I slashed my blade through the air.

The traitor before me did not speak.

"Say it." The hiss upon my lips was not entirely my own.

"For love," Marcus whispered.

A laugh sprang from my throat, cold and unfeeling. "Love, the greatest poison of all," I spat. I thrust an elbow at Caryk, but his grip was unyielding. My eyes were glazing over.

A great hiss left my lips. "One day you, too, shall feel the pain of my people. You will wish that you had died on this day, and only then shall I end it. I shall have vengeance."

It was not Tamariya Amunet, Savior of Naqad, who spoke, but Ophidia, the Viper Queen herself.

AUTHOR'S NOTE

Thank you so much for reading *The Curse of Ophidia*. I hope you enjoyed Tamariya's story as much as I enjoyed writing it. It truly means the world to me that you would spend your spare time reading the words I've written. It has been a privilege to build the world of Palegos and an even greater one to have you read about it. I have two more books planned for our Viper Queen and I would be thrilled if you came back for the second.

If you enjoyed this book, I would be incredibly grateful if you'd consider leaving a review on Amazon or Goodreads. I cannot overstate how important reviews are for authors! I'd love to keep in touch, so please scan the QR code below for my most up to date social media and newsletter links. I can't wait to share information about sequels, cover reveals, and other exciting news with you!

ACKNOWLEDGEMENTS

Thank you for taking a chance on a new book from a brand new author. From the bottom of my heart, I am honored.

Claire, my lovely alpha reader, who read this story in its infancy when it was really just a collection of sometimes nonsensical scenes. Thank you for your endless patience and encouragement that helped make this dream a reality.

Betsey, thank you for the beta reading, but also for believing in me and offering encouragement and support at every turn. You're the best sister I could ask for.

To my wonderful beta readers Becca, Jannelle, Loren, and Christine, thank you for helping shape this story into all that it could be.

The fantastic team at Stardust Book Services, thank you Hayley for strengthening this story, world, and its characters, Norman for a truly stunning book cover, and Nastasia for making me a better writer with your fabulous editing.

All of my friends and family, thank you for your kind words and support and for not laughing when I told you I wanted to publish a book.

If you've found this book from social media, thank you for interacting with my content. It means the world to me that you're here.

And finally, to Dan, thank you for being my biggest cheerleader when I need to believe, toughest coach when I need a push forward, and most patient partner when I come to you with crazy ideas. I could not have made this happen without your endless support. I love you.

ABOUT THE AUTHOR

Victoria is a fantasy romance author from Cincinnati, Ohio. She's been dreaming about other worlds since she forced her entire seventh grade Creative Writing class to listen to her weekly love triangle update, twisted to meet that week's prompt. *The Curse of Ophidia* is her first book in what she hopes will be a long career in writing. When she's not writing, Victoria can be found hanging out with her partner and corgi, going brewery hopping, or doing yoga.